for Dena

The quotes at the beginning of each chapter are all taken from Jean-Jacques Rousseau's novel *Julie*, originally published in 1761. The translations are mine.

PART I

Munich, Late Winter 1806

1.

Shall I show you things as they are or as it's convenient for you to see them?

The bells rang one o'clock, the end of parade—a time when soldiers are at liberty, disappointed that there's been no news to break their boredom. He walked up a lane that promised to take him back toward the Marienplatz, occupied mostly by Marianne's absence.

Look for me tonight, that's what she said; tonight—a time as distant as the horizon of a graying, wind-blown steppe.

His footfalls echoed and disappeared against windows made from sheets of plate glass. The street was much better drained than those in Brest-Litovsk or Kracόw, the gutters swept clean. But here and there, patches of dark ice touched the cobblestones, and he shortened his stride to avoid a fall.

Down the narrow passage, a closed post chaise swayed toward him, and to avoid being run over, he pressed back into a watchmaker's door-way. Within the scattered echo of the hooves, the chains, and the snap of the postilion's whip, the bells of the cathedral rang the quarter-hour. He stepped out once the way was clear, looking over his shoulder at the receding chaise, curious about its haste.

"Oof!" The wind left his lungs, bringing back all the pain that had been absent during the past month. As he bent over struggling to catch his breath, two figures pressed close to his right flank; to his left, a pair of foreshortened shadows loomed across a building's wooden façade.

"*Mon Dieu!*" a voice said. "We didn't see you there."

He straightened and squinted; he'd collided with a French cavalry officer, a captain—if he understood their insignia—accompanied by a *chef d'escadron*, an older man who walked with a cane. "Please excuse me," he said. "I wasn't paying attention."

"The fault was mine, sir," the Captain said. "You appeared out of nowhere. Are you certain you're not injured?"

"You're Russian, aren't you," the Chef d'Escadron said.

The man's challenging tone was rude. He took a step back, and the others stepped back too, as if the three of them had begun the figures of a dance.

Whatever was happening was happening too fast. The merchant's clothes he wore made him feel naked, and he glanced around, searching for a line of retreat, a cache of arms. But at this hour past midday, the street was empty and silent except for a trundling wagon hauling firewood and a more distant flock of sheep. He turned back to face these soldiers, enemies from the past, recognizing that they both wore the blue and silver uniforms of the Tenth Hussars—Valsin's regiment.

"You have a fine mustache, monsieur. Were you in the war?" the Chef d'Escadron continued, easing his weight onto the cane.

His left hand flew to his upper lip; they'd picked him out right away. Although his temple locks were gathered along with the rest of his hair and clubbed back, a mustache like an eagle's wings spread above his mouth—a mark as clear as any brightly colored insignia.

"Yes, Pavlograd Hussars, I'm a premier major," he replied. "It's the equivalent rank to your chef d'escadron. We are, I believe, of the same rank."

The older officer inclined his head. "Ah, I thought you looked like a cavalryman. You fought in the great battle north of Vienna?"

"Yes."

"Austerlitz," the Captain said. "That's what the newspapers are calling it. Crépin," he said to his companion, "let's buy this gentleman a drink. What do you say?" he asked, turning back. "We're all Hussars, after all."

"I regret that I'm already late for an appointment," he said, pulling at his watch chain. "A lady. I thank you though."

"No," the Captain said. "Please, one drink, and we'll all feel the better for it. I beg you. Surely the lady will wait."

"Oh yes, by all means. The war is over." The older officer put a hand on his forearm, leaning close enough that, as the man spoke, there was a slight, not unpleasant, odor of garlic. "Chef D'Escadron Pierre Crépin, Tenth Hussars, this is Capitaine Antoine Merseult."

The two Frenchmen seemed genuinely concerned that he would refuse. The most likely explanation was that they were anxious to demonstrate that they were gentlemen, not conquerors, swollen with arrogant pride. *Besides, Munich teems with Bonaparte's army; this encounter is nothing but coincidence.*

"Very well. One drink. I'm Ruzhensky, Premier Major Alexi Ruzhensky."

"Ruzhensky, you said?" the older man asked, giving the name an unusual pronunciation. "Let's go—there's a place close by. Watch out for the ice there."

The Marienplatz was just ahead; they drew him into it and then down the next side street to the left and on until they reached a coffeehouse. The interior, painted dark green, had wooden candleholders suspended from the high ceiling by blackened chains. Several stoves gave off heat, their iron chimneys making a maze of pipe as they twisted and turned aloft, and light from the street filtered in through colored glass panes framing the door.

They settled around three sides of a square table and ordered brandy. The Frenchmen were friendly enough and eager to discuss the political situation in Europe in neutral terms; they made no wild boasts about their Emperor, no exhortations toward Jacobinism or democracy. Like him, they were middle-aged soldiers in the middle ranks of the army, accustomed to giving commands and being commanded.

No doubt, he thought, *Valsin himself stares at them in the same way, awaiting orders or merely fascinated by the sheen of Merseult's cropped but elegant hair.*

"The Emperor Napoleon only desires peace," Merseult was saying, "for all of Europe. Imagine, a Europe without borders, open to unobstructed commerce and travel. In time, we could all enjoy a single currency!"

Crèpin snorted and winked. "Come now, that would put soldiers out of a job."

"Soldiers will always have things to do—even in times of peace. Don't you agree, Ruzhensky?" Merseult signaled for more brandy. "So, a Russian officer in Munich. By the way, if you don't mind me asking, what brings you here?"

"Merseult," Crèpin interrupted, "I'm sure the premier major will tell us in his own time. Unless it's none of our business." He looked at Ruzhensky and raised his brows.

"No, no, that's quite all right. It's my family—my father, business dealings in Austria. The war has…disturbed accounts. I'm here to straighten things out."

"Ah," Merseult said, "then you must understand ciphers."

"War disturbs everything," Crèpin said, making a clucking sound with his tongue. "We soldiers blunder forward, never looking back to see what we've left behind."

"You were wounded at the great battle, I take it?" Ruzhensky asked, extending his chin toward Crèpin's injured leg.

"Austerlitz," Merseult said.

"No, I didn't have that honor. I was shot in the hip a few days before, at a place called Wischau."

His hand gripped the glass hard enough he expected it to crack and give way.

Wischau—Mischa died at Wischau.

From one moment to the next, Mischa and Valsin had each moved closer, both of them—the dead and the unknown living—crowding around the table, reaching out to hear, to bear witness to what was being said and would be done.

"I've heard about the skirmish at Wischau," he said at last. "Your Emperor was drawing us into a trap there, wasn't he?"

"I suppose that was the grand strategy," Merseult said, nodding. "But we light cavalrymen weren't told anything; we just followed orders."

"That's right," Crèpin said with a laugh. "No one asked our opinion." He paused and sipped loudly at the brandy. "The thing I remember about Wischau—besides being shot—was the single combat, Lieutenant Valsin's single combat."

A silence, not at all empty, occupied him. His feet pushed against the floor, the muscles around his knees tense and hard, as if he were gripping a saddle instead of a chair. Outside, on the street, a horse whinnied, and then, like bubbles breaking loose from the bottom of a red-hot iron cauldron, the sound of gunfire began to pour through the windows of the coffeehouse. The shutters opened, the walls dissolved, and—his senses worn and beginning to fray—he was once again astride his mare Pyerits, leading a charge over a snow-covered field. Above her tossing mane, riders in green surged forward—French cavalry, shouting, shaking their swords. He pressed down against the stirrups and heard a wild cry.

A different awareness scurried across his brow, pinning him between the past and the present. He was dreaming the dream, the one that tortured him most early mornings—at least a section of it, like an installment of a story serialized in a newspaper. How could that be—was he asleep?

An instant later, back within the dream, the horses of both nations made way for each other by some animal agreement, and scores of men came together, stabbing, scrambling, sealing the joint with their blood.

"—Valsin's single combat."

He looked up, blinking, forcing himself to notice real things: the orange hue of the serving woman's hair, the sweet-sour residue of the brandy in his mouth, the tremor in his hands. Only a faint odor of gunpowder and horse remained, and the pounding of his heart began to slow.

"Were you familiar with that yourself, Premier Major?"

The Frenchmen regarded him with solicitous, inclined heads, as if they'd become aware of the gravity of his wounds, and he straightened and frowned. The duel had been discussed throughout the army, so he reasoned he could admit knowledge of it. "Yes," he said, alert for any loosening of his voice. "Of course. The single combat." He balanced on the front of the chair, crossing his arms over his chest, squeezing each hand against a bicep to quell their trembling.

"Listen," Crèpin continued, "it was most unfortunate. Your cadet was too young; no one likes to see that sort of thing happen. Valsin felt terrible—I can assure you of that. He wouldn't deliver the coup de grace; he could not. Your man—there's no doubt he had courage. Valsin begged him to retire. At the end, he knocked him out of the saddle." Crèpin shrugged. "You know—to put an end to it. What choice did he have?"

Now his hands were not only shaking, his palms were moist, and he wiped them on his sleeves and swallowed spit. The story was coming out, unraveling like a cut hem.

"Yes, it was regrettable," Merseult said. "The incident haunts Valsin. He told me so just the other day. To have to kill someone whose courage you admire, who obviously isn't a worthy opponent; it's a heavy burden." The Frenchmen each took a drink.

"Please excuse me," he said, the words coming harsh and staccato. "But did you say—not a worthy opponent?" His shoulders had become like stone.

"Yes, that's right," Merseult said after taking time to wipe his mouth with a handkerchief. "Valsin was shaken by it. Does that surprise you?" A touch of steel had entered the Frenchman's voice, a slender warning.

I understand. This is no chance encounter, no victor's magnanimous gesture. These men know who I am; that accounts for their telling me what I'm not prepared to hear. Like a pair of gamblers, they're playing me, building—not to a fleecing— but a denunciation. They'll close ranks around Valsin, and I'll be checked.

He had been exposed; someone—no doubt the Austrian police official he'd bribed to learn of Valsin's whereabouts—had sent word to be on guard against a Russian gentleman. These two had spotted him on the street and known right away who he was. Despite his civilian clothes, his identity was as clear as if a sign printed with his name had been hung on his back. He had to think, to calm himself. His hands were now still, and he laid them flat on the table. For defense, his only recourse was a walking stick and his wits. He must do something unexpected, something to forestall the inevitable violence until he was prepared.

"Gentlemen," he began, choosing his words as he would soldiers for an important mission. "It's just that…this story you tell of the duel…it's… different from the one I've heard—the one that we on our side believed. If I seem surprised, that's the reason."

"What have you heard, monsieur?"

He drained the glass. "I've heard that he…that is…we—we were told that your officer—what did you call him, Valsin?—that he behaved in an arrogant fashion…and…that he…he boasted of the killing and abused the Russian officers as they tried to retrieve their comrade's body."

Crèpin and Merseult looked at each other with widened eyes. "I assure you, that wasn't the case, and I was there," Merseult said, sitting forward in his chair. "I rode out as Valsin's second. When one of your countrymen asked for it, he did announce his name—too loudly, I suppose, but Pierre, would you describe Valsin as arrogant?"

"Not all the time."

"He spit on the ground—in contempt. That's what I heard."

"No." Merseult leaned forward, his eyes glittering. "I'll tell you what really happened: Your infantry—several battalions' worth—was preparing for assault, drums rolling, flags flying. We were behind a stone wall, ready to snipe at them. All of a sudden, two riders galloped out in front of the column, between the two armies. The drums stopped; we could hear your officers roaring. One of the horsemen advanced twenty paces and spoke. 'Messieurs,' he said, 'I challenge any of you French gentlemen! Come and fight me, for the honor of both our Tsars!' It was well said, we all agreed. Valsin was the most junior officer among us; Pierre ordered him to respond—you did, Pierre, don't you remember? Valsin was reluctant, not that he lacked courage, but to duel like that in front of all of us—well, it was a hero's job. He asked if I would second him, and I said yes.

"We advanced, and he called something to me that, at the time, I didn't understand. 'If something happens,' he said, 'take care of her.' 'Take care of whom?' I said, but he'd already spurred ahead, and his reply was lost in a rush of wind.

"The two champions charged, striking at one another as they passed. But as your countryman struggled to turn his horse, I could see that he was unskilled. Valsin saw it too—he told me later. For several minutes, they hacked and stabbed with their weapons, searching for flesh but finding only steel and air. Finally, Valsin got inside your man's guard and laid a saber against his throat. 'You're my prisoner,' he called. 'Stop.'

"But no. With his gauntlet, your man grabbed Valsin's saber and pushed it away. He made a lunge for Valsin's chest, dead-on, but Valsin parried and followed through, getting his point into the man's side.

"Valsin told me. He said: 'Right away I knew it was over. I'd killed him. I called on him again to stop, but he urged his horse forward in a charge. And I pulled toward the flank and knocked him to the ground with the flat of my sword.'" The Captain paused to drain his cup.

"But really, Premier Major Ruzhensky," Crèpin said. "We don't wish to dispute this with you—you can be sure. Let's just agree it was an unfortunate affair."

The Frenchman stared at him with narrowed eyes, as if he were judging the effect of his words, and he felt even more certain they knew him, that this was all an elaborate piece of theater staged, if not to unmask, at least to deceive. His thumb and finger found the ring—Natasha's ring—suspended around his neck by a chain and hanging in the center of his chest. Small and hard, a sapphire, the stone set in silver, elegant, as she had been. Because it hung next to his skin, the metal was buffed smooth and always warm.

"Yes, of course," he began and stopped, squeezing the ring until his voice gathered strength. "As you say."

"No, no, let me finish," Merseult said, signaling to the proprietor for more brandy. Then he turned back, squeezing his eyes shut and opening them, revealing a distant focus, a lens of a power that Ruzhensky himself had regarded the world through—the sort of lens used by those who've witnessed mortal events, births and deaths, and must learn to remember them as blurred and indistinct, so that ordinary life can be viewed without distortion.

"Please. I feel it's important that I tell you this," Merseult continued. "Perhaps I have a need for confession, eh? There's a little more. I rode up to find Valsin retching on the frozen grass—as you are a soldier, Major, I'm sure you can understand that part of a duel. I told him to get a souvenir of the combat. After all, that's the custom, isn't it? Your man was lying on the ground, curled on his side; his headgear had come off, and his life's blood emptied out onto the snow. Valsin knelt down to cut off the sword knot. 'I could not, he said later,' take my eyes from the Russian's face. 'He was too young; I felt I'd killed myself.'

"By that time, a party of your fellows had ridden out to retrieve their comrade. They began cursing us, and I drew my pistols, thinking there'd be a fight. One of them called, 'Who are you, sir? Tell us your name so that we will not forget you.' And Valsin rose and—you're correct, he did spit, not in contempt but to clear his throat—and he said, 'Valsin, Louis Valsin.' Now, tell me, what else could he have done? What else?"

The Captain let the question hang, fixing it with his gaze. The other Frenchman, Crèpin, had become absorbed in a study of his brandy glass.

He shifted to one side of the chair, then the other, rolling the bones in his hips, trying to regain purchase, a fresh point of balance. The Frenchmen's words had riddled him, run him through again. Perhaps they hadn't recognized him, but they knew he was Russian; it could be that they were exaggerating Valsin's innocence out of loyalty, to present a killing done with little honor in a better light. Yet the faraway look of Merseult's eyes, the gravel in the depths of his voice, rang with truth. Even the other officer's obvious discomfort only added to the story's force.

If it were true, he thought, shaking his head.

"Gentlemen," he began, "Valsin, is he—"

"Major," the Captain said, "we're all such pawns, pawns of fate. Don't you agree? Valsin responded as best he could, but your comrades perceive it in a different way than he intended. From that—well, wars begin over such things." He shook his head. "Puppets…that's what…"

He stared hard, unblinking, aware of all the times he'd felt the pull of strings against his own limbs. "What did you say?"

"That we're all puppets, controlled by others whom we can't see. Fate."

"Philosophy, I don't understand it. Do you, Major?" Crèpin asked.

"No. But—"

"So," Crèpin said, picking up his gloves and standing. "I think Capitaine Merseult and I must excuse ourselves—other duties, and I believe you mentioned a rendezvous. It's been a pleasure to meet you—may I say, despite the sad tale we've had to share. I hope we meet again, to speak of happier things."

"Yes. Munich isn't such a big city," Merseult said, also getting to his feet. "We'll watch for you. Adieu."

2.

I am like those unfortunates whose torments are only interrupted to make them more noticeable.

The hearth was silent and uncared for and the room racked with cold. He stretched his neck and shoulders, thinking he should rise, smoke a pipe, change his clothing. Since he'd left the coffeehouse—after paying the bill—and returned, he'd only been a weight in the armchair, a weight scribing four points ever more deeply into the worn, wool rug.

Where is Marianne? She should have stayed here as I ordered. I've spent an hour in a chair, an hour, a futile hour wasted. It means nothing; the Frenchmen's stories mean nothing. By happenstance, I came close to Valsin—too close—but didn't actually see him. The past, memory, it's a plague of sentiment, an affliction requiring quarantine.

He shook his head and cast about the room, desperate for something he couldn't name. On the seat of the other chair by the hearth lay the book he'd been reading while recovering in the hospital at Vienna—*Julie* by the

Frenchman, Rousseau. But he couldn't read a book now; his concentration was like a rabbit darting around a garden maze, careening off walls.

For the hundredth time, the encounter with the French officers returned, this time not as memory but as if it had been written on pages read backward in a book—a book written in a foreign language, thrown hard, across a room—leaving him populated with unfamiliar words, lacking a dictionary to translate them.

On the day it described, the day of Mischa's death, it had been midafternoon when he'd ventured out of his tent. For once, the ceaseless, irregular rhythms of the camp had not irritated him, and he'd sat on a stool of canvas and wood and lit a pipe.

"Premier Major."

I looked up, squeezing my eyes to slits. Against a sky filled with creamy shells of cloud, two figures began speaking in French, but I was only able to catch certain phrases: "the armies stopped to watch," "a big, rough-looking fellow," mounted on "a magnificent bay charger," who "spit on the ground in contempt." Finally I recognized that they were two of Prince Bagration's aides. I rose.

"Your brother died bravely, Premier Major Ruzhensky, with great honor. He wished to fight the French and was successful; he'd only want you to feel pride."

The wind threatened to carry away the youth's tall plumes. Both young men blinked again and again, their faces compressed by what—pity? Of course, they expected me to react, to say something, but I was smothered by the clouds, suffocated by the wind. If I did attempt to speak, I was sure no sound would be released.

"Mikhail Davidovich waited for an opportunity, Premier Major. For single combat. He was sent to deliver a dispatch and saw the French officers across the meadow. Lieutenant Chernigev acted as his second; I hope you won't blame him."

"Chernigev—no."

"Prince Bagration sends his regrets. He said to tell you he would see you later. He thought that…with your permission, the body might be embalmed so you could send it—ah, send him—home. Please forgive me for being abrupt, Premier Major."

His chin nodded. "A good idea, young man. My father would appreciate it, by all means."

"Would you like to see him, Premier Major?"

"Leave me alone now," he said in Russian. Over the shoulders of the two officers, others were beginning to stare, looking away when he met their gaze.

The whole camp must know, and they're curious; they want to see my face, to see grief. Is that what I'm feeling? I feel soiled, covered in noxious sores; my heart actually burns—is that grief?

He'd retreated to his tent, and as he tried to secure the flaps, the ties had resisted his fingers.

In Munich, the chill had grown intolerable. Across the room, the traveler's toiletry box lay on the table amid layers of shadow. An object of ingenious design, a small, oval mirror, was fixed behind the lid, and by an internal mechanism, its drawers opened on the horizontal and vertical axes, ready to receive an array of brushes and razors. However, at that moment, all it contained was his father's letter of instruction.

Every day since receiving the letter—climbing out of a fever at the hospital in Vienna to find it on his pillow—he'd read it, sometimes more than once. It had piled naphtha and gunpowder around his bed, warming him in those short, dark December days after the battle.

The repetition of reading itself had become important, as if the paper were not just a letter of instruction but a religious tract, a hermeneutic, holding not only the secret of all that had happened but a prophecy of what was to come. Between the lines, it conveyed its truth: he was a soldier. For all his adult life, he'd been commanded by the Tsar, a monarch whose instructions were to be obeyed without reservation. If, during one week, the Austrians were fraternal allies and then in the next treacherous foes, so be it; it wasn't for him to question orders. Duty must be done.

But the letter demanded an even more primal duty. His father—a general himself—had taken over from the other generals, those men who occupied the heights and peered through their telescopes at the awful acts they set in motion. Despite a son's fatigue, his many wounds, he was ordered to rouse himself and become his father's instrument of revenge.

"This murderer, this Valsin—finish what you've begun."

His father was an arsonist, a madman bent on a single act of destruction. His own feelings had been obscured, like embers choked for air by a thick coat of ash. And they remained obscured, so that his father's demands, crowding and suffocating him just as they always had, were all he had to go on.

He lurched from the chair and put on a heavy robe. The cathedral bells rang the hour; he counted them and called out, "Yevgeny!—a fire, quickly." His servant, who spent his own time behind a screen of wood and fabric, emerged, and soon the kindling crackled and the room began to gather warmth.

At the window, he stretched his fingertips, trying to span the filigrees of frost knitted by winter. A shape was there, larger than his hand.

Moment by moment, like a slow drip of mercury into a stone jar, he felt an increasing weight. He looked over his right shoulder, then to the left. No, he thought, jamming both hands into the deep pockets of the robe. The story the Frenchmen told was like an official bulletin explaining real events in such a way as to make them appear more favorable to only one of two sides.

It's clear what really happened; I have no need for someone else's opinion. Except—except it can't be ignored. The Frenchmen stared backward into the depths of their own eyes; they looked inward, deep in the cups of memory—a familiar intoxication. By the rules of reminiscence, they might exaggerate but never lie.

He faced the room.

The fire's already gone out; is there tea?

"Yevgeny."

Where is the man?

He flung open the wings of the toiletry box. The lower drawer rattled, and he nearly tore the knob off before remembering the key. When he withdrew it from his waistcoat pocket, his shaking hand sent it flying across the room. Finally, after retrieving it on hands and knees and opening the small lock, he took out his father's letter. The frost on the window was another layer of shadow observing him, waiting, and the letter wavered in his grasp. He set it down, still folded, and turned away to face the door.

3.

By the way, tell me: does our sailor smoke, curse, drink brandy? Does he carry a big saber?

On the other side of the wall, in the corridor, she heard a cavalryman's tread, jingling metal. The door in the next room opened, and then a belt pulled through a buckle made a whirring rasp, a saber laid across the table, a solid, fond clunk.

"Valsin?" she called, putting down the book.

"Who else?"

He entered their bedchamber grinning and sat on the edge of the bed to take off his boots. In the half-light from the single tallow candle she had burning, he grimaced and pulled, with his chin tucked into his throat. The strip of fabric he used to tie his hair back came loose, allowing a fall of shining black reeds to sprawl over his ears and shoulders. The first boot yielded, and against the far wall, a shadow reached again.

The synchrony distracted her. Often occupied in blending dreams with sensation, she was an artist who covered many canvases set upon an inner easel. A number were of her husband, dead four years. Those images—a smile seen in an instant, a particular look of concentration—had begun to break up. But this one, she thought—regarding Valsin, not his shadow—was fresh and alive and certainly far from complete.

"Sorry to be away so long," he said. "After our drills, I went out for a drink with some officers from the Ninth."

He unhooked his braces and stood to splash water from the basin onto his face and neck. When he sat again on the edge of the bed, she ran her palms down his back, making him shiver and grunt. Her hands slid further, over the top of his uniform pants and onto his hips; she felt the roughness of the bunched cloth, remembering how the uniform she'd worn had seethed against her skin. How did men bear it all the time?

"Listen," he said. "Crèpin was prepared to fight a duel over you. With an officer of the infantry. Even with his bad leg!"

"What did he say? What happened?" She grabbed his shoulders and tried to pull him backward.

"Stop!" he said, laughing. "The usual. The other fellow said you were a camp follower we'd all falsely elevated. I wish I'd been there; I would have called him out. I still may."

"A loose woman," she said, letting go. Many things pleased her about their life in Munich, but Valsin's fellow officers did not. Except for Merseult, they were coarse and brutal men who stared and made comments about her under their breath, comments that would provoke Valsin to violence should he ever hear. How the men frightened her with their murderous pride.

"Everyone's in love with you," he continued. "That's the truth; they're maddened with jealousy. Camp follower—no, you inspire heroes. It's rumored that even the Emperor Napoleon has heard your name. Boasts are made to the officers of other regiments, the story told to anyone who'll listen. And I have to sit like an idiot and hear it again and again."

She understood how it shamed him and put her arms around his shoulders and laid her cheek against his back.

He took off his pants and, smelling of smoke and wine, got into bed. By the light of the candle, a flush spread over his nose and cheeks, spilling over his chin to his neck. The sight of the many scars on his pale skin still upset her because they reminded her of his fragility, as if he might suddenly open and spill his insides out onto the floor. Old wounds—ten years' worth—were a map of his combats. In minute detail, she'd learned the history behind each one, tracing the whitened edges with a solemn finger as he told the tales. The most recent—the one he'd received at Austerlitz—remained pink and puckered.

He rolled on his side to face her. "Now tell me, are you happy?"

Happy? The question—one that no one else had ever asked—itself made her happy, and she kissed him, engaging his tongue. His hand began a long, slow journey from her shoulder to below her hip, pulling up and under her chemise; an urgent, hot bolt poked against her bare thigh.

His face was a palm's breadth away—too close to see. "Ah, don't stop!"

The bed becomes narrower, and then, it's a new bed, no longer narrow but close, enfolding us in the envelope of the sheets, full of double breath and motion.

Like a boat full of letters, crowded in a sack, silent letters waiting to be opened, a boat waiting for release. The seals are broken; hips press. The sheets have become manacles; an enchaining tongue penetrates my mouth, a thirsty, hard hand drinks the offering of moisture held between my thighs. To be staked, held fast.

Vertigo makes the bed float higher. Moorings are dropped; a sail is hoisted around a firm, upright mast, and—dancing up and down among the waves—the boat scuds away into the night. A happy voyage.

4.

I believe, I hope, that a heart that had seemed to me to merit my attachment will not deny the generosity I expect from it.

In the morning, she struggled with a crust of kisses, twisting her cheeks and squeezing her eyes to break through. Something in sleep had frightened her; her heart made a drumbeat against her ribs. She tried to remember, but there was nothing but a play of images across a sunlit room, unconnected, dissolving as soon as she recalled them.

On particular days that arrived with no rhythm or regularity, just after waking, she'd imagine Valsin gone. For a moment, before the pattern of the sheets shifted, she'd see how only the memory of him would impress the mattress, making a concave image like one-half of a whole wax mold. With her eyes still closed, she reached out with her palm, but the bed was full of him.

She dressed and stared at the mirror. Stretched by the glass, her pale face didn't hold her attention; her gaze slid to the crinkled silver paper at the edges, where a section of the wooden frame had broken off.

Back in the mirror, she saw movement, the reflection of a sleeping man rolling over.

After the battle, at the hospital in Brünn, the wounded had been attended not only by nuns but also by the women of the city who'd come dressed in simple clothes to nurse the shattered soldiers. They'd whispered about her, clucking their tongues in disapproval as she kept watch by his bed. She'd stared them down, shooing them away, sure she'd won all rights to tend him. Chef Dalhousie—Valsin's sergeant—had bought her a dress of cream-colored linen with a pattern of orange flowers and a pale violet sash encircling the fashionably high waist, a lady's dress that she wore as a uniform of femininity. Her face had been scrubbed clean, the soot and tallow on the upper lip gone, only a touch of borrowed rouge against each cheek. She wore neither headgear nor bonnet; her hair was parted in the middle and caught behind with a comb.

He'd woken; she'd reached over, but his gunshot collarbone had restrained them from embracing. She'd had to settle for the pressure of his hand and voice.

"Before the battle, I touched you," he said. "Do you remember? For luck."

"It didn't work very well."

"I'm alive, aren't I? Thanks to you."

"Hush, you'll tire yourself."

"No, I have to tell you everything. Before the moment passes. At the battle, when you led me to safety, I forgot for a moment where I was, who you were. I remembered when I was a child, how the peasant women would tell stories about mariners wrecked on Normandy's iron-bound coast, how just when they saw death and stopped looking, a woman would appear among them—in that place where no women dwelt—shining with the phosphorescence of the sea. Do you understand?"

She understood she was an anchor to him and that he was grateful.

In Munich, she put fresh wood on the hearth in the other room and stabbed at the fire with an iron poker; the ashes exhaled green and blue sparks into the gray morning light. Only a small fire was needed; their snug, third-floor rooms above The White Hound trapped the building's heat like the clay walls of an oven. In the chimney, the wind howled and banged, and she reveled in the extravagant luxury of warmth, wanting to preserve it for as long as possible. To make these moments last until comfort as well as love were themselves transformed, like sparks disappearing into a dark, empty space. She wiped soot from her hands and returned to the smaller chamber.

He sat up and gave a great yawn. "I was waiting," he said. "Pretending to be asleep so you'd build the fire."

"You're on duty today?"

"An hour or so, for parade. Otherwise, I'm yours to command. Let's go to the coffeehouse."

✳ ✳ ✳

On the late-morning street, a sift of snow fell through the air like damp, cold flour, and she pulled the collar of her fur coat tight beneath her chin. It was a beautiful coat, with well-stitched seams and soft lining. The sleeves were short for her long arms, but there wasn't any extra material to alter them. She pushed the fur cap back above her brow.

He bought it all for me—the coat, the hat; he buys me whatever I want.

Down the street, an older couple approached, peering, no doubt, with disapproval at a French officer with a woman, an officer's lady: a whore. She moved to Valsin's side and took his arm, trying to think of something she could say to make him laugh. "So, am I like a Russian today?"

"Yes, my beautiful Russian."

They drew nearer, and the couple's faces tightened into frowns. Valsin understood; he pulled her closer and winked, and the man drew himself up and set his jaw. The woman's eyes snapped away to one side. Valsin burst into laughter, a laughter she was glad to imitate.

It's nothing. These old people on the street; they scowl to protect themselves from the intrusion of youth, which they imagine as only happiness.

In the coffeehouse, they ordered bread and coffee, and Valsin began to study a newspaper, asking her to translate some of the German. Later he put it down and was quiet. He said, "I still don't understand why the Russian officer tried to kill me, singling me out that way. I remember how he came forward, shouting, and his face—it was empty. Like a child's toy, a doll of straw."

"You've said this before, and I don't understand. You were all trying to kill each other, weren't you? What made him different?"

"He knew me, I think."

Memory clamored—the screaming, the blood, the faces distorted by fury, then the sight of the horseman in the strange uniform aiming his pistol. She swallowed and closed her eyes, shuddering at the sensation of the sword piercing flesh, the horrifying resistance as it was pulled free.

"But that's not possible."

5.

*I must confess a suspicion that was conceived in shame and humiliation.
You know better than I how to love.*

Clogs clattered up the stairs, and he put his father's letter back in the box and
nodded at Yevgeny, who stepped forward to open the door. The pale twilight
reduced his servant's profile to a play of bleached bone and crimson ink.
Yevgeny, silent and steady. Many things had changed but not Yevgeny.

Before the old man could move aside, a fur muff and two blue eyes
pushed him away and rushed across the room. "Alyosha—my God it's cold,"
Marianne said in French—not the same French he spoke but one close
enough to allow them to communicate in words. She rose on her toes to
kiss him on the mouth. Woodsmoke clung to her hair and skin; under his
fingertips, her cheeks were burning. "And dark, what have you been doing?
Make him light candles."

Marianne and Yevgeny persisted in referring to one another in the third person, claiming it was too difficult to pronounce their mutually foreign names.

"Yevgeny. Candles. You shouldn't be on the streets by yourself so late."

"You're right." She hung the coat he'd bought her by the door and went to warm her hands at the fire. Silence was in her back and the angle of her head; she seemed to be watching him from the corner of her eye.

"You were out all afternoon."

"I told you I would be, sweetheart. Look, I bought this dress from a friend." She spun around and lifted her skirts to each side. "It fits pretty well; do you like it? It's red." A frown skipped across her face. "And you—you said you were also going out. Did you go to the museum?"

"No."

"The cathedral?"

"No."

"Well, will you tell me? Give me a drink—and then let's have something to eat. I bet you got lost and don't want to say. We'll get you a map, the kind you said you know how to read. Here—oh, I'll just do it myself." She went to the side table and poured two glasses of brandy. "Sit with me on the couch."

He downed the brandy all at once and sat next to her. Behind each reddened ear, her long blond hair was pinned up like a sheaf of silver grain. She turned toward him and grinned.

"So you walked around in the cold and then came back here and brooded in the dark? It's good that I arrived. I saw some of my girlfriends, and we gossiped all afternoon. They said I was very lucky to have met a kind gentleman who liked me so much. But when I said you were Russian, they had all sorts of questions: why you were here in Munich, if you were like other men."

Her speech was fast and light, and he hastened to follow the sound of her voice, abandoning fragments of men in brilliant, bloody uniforms, as if they were only a child's toys scattered by a quick, graceful hand. "And what did you say?"

"I said no; he's different. Like this." She put the glass on the floor and held her palms apart over her lap. "A bull. And he won't leave me alone. They were impressed." She gazed at him out of eyes that were as blue as the deeper part of the sea, and her mouth began to quiver with the effort of holding back laughter. "And he's very serious. I told them that about you too. I said: he likes to think important thoughts." With her palm, she covered her mouth and whooped.

He indicated Yevgeny should fill their glasses. "What was their other question—why am I here in Munich? What did you say about that?"

"That I didn't know. They said you must be very wealthy."

For a moment, the letter from his father unfurled, a length of parchment where murder was written in a tremulous hand. Then she pulled him back onto the cushions and laid her head against his shoulder.

"You're a little mad that I stayed out so long. I'm sorry; I was just having fun. Forgive me." She twisted around and put her left leg over his left, pressing close and rubbing herself against his thigh like a cat. "If you want, we could stay here," she whispered. "He could get us supper—to eat in bed. Would you like that? Ah," she said, grasping him through the fabric of his trousers. "The bull's coming."

6.

The main objection to large cities is that there, men become other than what they are.

In the morning, he rose without waking her and went into the larger of the two rooms he'd engaged, a sitting area with a generous window now shuttered against the cold.

"Yevgeny, tea."

A horse whinnied outside; men's voices began a song—a work song, no doubt, an accompaniment to mindless toil. He sat before the freshly raked hearth and let the heat of the tea warm his hands through the crockery cup.

Somewhere, perhaps very near, Valsin was smoking, drinking—the same commonplace activities he himself did for hours on end. Ever since he'd learned of the man's presence in Munich, he'd dreamed that the city would keep him nearly motionless until he was ready for their second meeting. Could that time be at hand—sooner than he'd anticipated? So quickly, too quickly.

If he were to finish this business—one way or the other—what then? The Mariupol Hussar regiment also awaited him. In precise ranks, on a parade ground hundreds of leagues to the east, did they wait in vain? His fellow officers would check their watches and glance at the angle of the sun. New recruits might not even know of Premier Major Alexi Davidovich Ruzhensky—hero of the Turkish Wars, wounded by the French; to them he would become a story.

He finished the glass of tea. Several paths led into the future, but this morning he must choose one.

After washing and shaving, he had his servant brush the copper coat several times to remove an accumulation of dust and ash. It had been years since he'd covered himself in anything but military costume, but it wouldn't do to wear a Russian Hussar's uniform in Munich, not now, after the long campaign. In Vienna, the English tailor had been quite accommodating and only too happy to furnish a gentleman with a complete wardrobe. Today, in addition to the coat, he wore a black waistcoat, black silk breeches and stockings, and a well-tied cravat. Everything fit snug; that was the latest fashion. Elegant—his costume was elegant, just like a print in one of the new fashion journals.

As Yevgeny continued his ministrations, a tousled Marianne emerged from the bedroom, covering a yawn behind the sail-like sleeve of his dressing gown. "Good morning, Alyosha," she said, blinking at the light. "You're going out—now? Take me with you. I'll get dressed and—"

"No. You may remain; I'll return in an hour or so, and—"

"But I will be too bored," she said, frowning at Yevgeny's back.

"I have some things to attend to, an errand."

"I'll make sure you don't get lost," she said. "I'll help you."

He regarded her over Yevgeny's shoulder. "No."

"But why?"

His voice, which had been measured and calm, dropped to the level he'd use to order the shooting of a captured deserter. "There's no reason to argue. Do as I say."

Yevgeny gave a last swipe with the brush and retreated behind his screen. Marianne lowered her eyes to the center of his chest and appeared to be chewing on the inside of her mouth.

It isn't worth a fight. After all, she's no Russian girl I can order around. Foreigners have different ways.

"Listen," he said. "I'll return and—"

"No, I'm not going to stay here—alone," she said. "I'll see you tonight. Unless I'm busy." She rushed back into the bedchamber and slammed the door.

He stared at the dark panel until he became aware of his fingernails digging into his palms, of the quiver of a muscle along the line of his jaw. Then, turning on his heel and accepting hat and gloves from Yevgeny, he made for the street.

✫ ✫ ✫

The first two gentlemen he addressed—inquiring about a shop that sold maps—returned blank stares and shook their heads. They must not understand French. By luck, the third person he asked nodded politely and directed him to a street across a nearby square.

All of a sudden, everywhere, French soldiers swaggered about and blocked his progress, forcing him to stop and press close against the front of a building. Songs of revolution erupted from their mouths; they beat time in the air with wine bottles and muskets. Whenever a figure in skirts appeared, their faces stretched like masks of dough. There was no discipline—any professional officer could see that. And no officers.

It was a relief when, three doors down from the entrance to the street, he entered a small, quiet space filled with cartographic and surveying equipment, as well as a generous stock of maps, both framed and unframed. He recognized a nice reproduction of Ptolemy and some original de Fers and Molls, all quite handsome. An entire wall was occupied by a selection representing the Americas; that region, he surmised, must be quite popular in Bavaria. But the only available map of Munich was antiquarian, inaccurate, and expensive. The shopkeeper had very little French, and it was a struggle to be understood; he sprinkled his speech with the only German words he knew.

"Do you have any other maps of Munich, *mein herr*?"

"You do not like this one? Very valuable, sir," the man said, nodding with a vigor that he found himself imitating until they both stood bobbing their heads.

"I'm sure it is—valuable, I mean—but it is not what I need. Something smaller, perhaps?" He put out his hands and moved the palms together as if squeezing a bladder.

"I am sorry; I cannot lower the price."

"No, *nein*, that is not what I meant. Do you have a smaller map? Smaller—less big." He gestured again, squeezing vertically instead of horizontally.

"Please excuse me, but why do you want a smaller map of the city?" The man's tone remained polite, but his eyes had become direct and probing.

"I am a visitor and would like to become familiar with her—that is— your beautiful city," he said, remembering to smile. Unlike many officers, he knew how to read maps. To him, the undulating lines, the notations made in minute script, meant something, represented real things. Marianne was correct: a map would be quite useful—to someone seeking a particular man in an unfamiliar city.

"Of course," the shopkeeper said. "Please excuse me, but you are French?"

"No."

"I see. Not so many gentlemen appreciate maps. You were in the military, perhaps?"

"I *am* in the military," he said quickly, sure that the man now believed him to be a spy but unwilling to lie about something so essential. "Mein herr."

"Ah, I am retired myself—a captain in the engineers. Your rank?"

"Premier major, a squadron commander. In the cavalry," he added, not at all of the opinion that a captain of engineers was his equal.

The man raised his eyebrows. "Since we are both military men, I could draw you a map, if you like."

A young girl served them strong coffee in small, porcelain cups, and the shopkeeper pulled out a square of paper and bottle of ink. After trimming the end of an already sharp quill, he dipped it and began sketching the outlines of neighborhoods and streets. Then—with busy scratches—he added tiny lettering. When the surface was covered, he looked at it and nodded, using a small rag to blot the ink. "Premier Major, your map."

He screwed his eyes up, in an attempt to read the miniature script. "Marvelous! You are most skillful, sir. And what do I owe you?"

"No money. It is my pleasure to assist you—a brother officer. And I have long been an admirer of your country."

"What country is that?"

"Why, Russia; you are Russian, are you not?"

He shook the shopkeeper's hand, promising to return to study the items in the shop when he had more time. "Thank you," he added. "You have been most kind." With great care—so as not to disturb the web of ink—he folded the map and left, trying to recall when he'd said he was Russian. At the corner, he turned back and—despite being unable to see anyone through the reflection of light on the window—raised his hat in farewell.

Interesting, that an officer should retire and become a shopkeeper.

Of course, he is an engineer.

Still, the man's generosity and warmth were unexpected, a rare sort of encounter.

A passing gentleman gave him directions to the central square, the Marienplatz, and he set off down Neuhauser Strasse, his sole armament a walking stick, his pace limited to the length of his stride. He'd allotted the whole morning to getting the map; now that he had it, he decided to make for Marianne's lodging. Enough time had passed he could forgive her for being so willful.

He'd met her the day after his arrival in Munich. Since Natasha's death, his encounters with women had been limited to the occasional prostitute, but the pleasure had been fleeting. Whores' limbs and mouths were slack, and he often feared he'd tumble free from their beds to fall to the ground, like a fish thrown naked and gasping onto the bank of a river. And afterward, Natasha was still dead.

But Marianne grasped him within her young arms and legs and held tight; together they made a single creature flying aboard a couch of pleasure. *How extraordinary!* he thought. He was like one of those unfortunates who lose a limb to the surgeon and report they feel it still—a phantom of a leg. But this leg of his was no phantom; he was eager to wave it around and admire it. A store of lost time had to be made up, each moment crowded with enough kisses to double its duration. He quickened his pace. Once at the Marienplatz, he'd know the way.

A new layer of snow covered the city, and its countless hearths had not yet turned the whiteness to gray. Despite the cold, the citizenry were out in force, no doubt because the market area was near. He wasn't used to seeing so many women and children and couldn't prevent himself from staring at their small, pale faces. All around, a buzz of German speech came from a multitude of voices. It was strange to hear conversations he couldn't understand, but he listened anyway, picking out the ebb and flow of questions and answers.

Across the snow, a shadow slanted, and he spun around. The shape of a woman watched him, a wraith who turned away to avoid his gaze but not before he'd caught a glimpse of wide cheekbones, dark eyes, a fall of shining, ebony hair around the edge of a bonnet.

Stop! Come back!

He struggled against a wild urge to shout. Impossible—a dead woman couldn't hear. His step faltered; he blinked three times.

Natasha. At one time, memories of her—how they'd met, the things she'd said and done—had emerged unbidden like figures from a bed of wet muck, startling him, pulling him out of whatever he was doing, sometimes even placing him in jeopardy, as if they'd been dispatched by grim furies intent on justice. Here in Bavaria, he'd hoped to escape their jurisdiction.

He blinked once more, straightened his cravat, and then turned back to his original direction. After all, that past had occurred far away; here, he had no past.

Besides Warsaw and Kraców, Munich was the first European city he'd had an opportunity to tour. He'd read all the travel guides he could lay his hands on, always anticipating being in Europe with the keenest interest. Every Russian wanted to compare modern Europe with his own country, and he was no exception.

His father was an exception, a man who didn't like cities, believing them to be the creations of evil creatures who upset Nature, beat it back, confined it in gardens and arbors. Cities outside of Russia were the worst— his father would opine—havens for criminals and prostitutes, filled with pestilence and greed.

This hatred of progress and the consequent idealization of everything rural and simple are backward ideas, ideas that keep Russia trapped in the past. Father wouldn't like Munich.

The thought amused him, and he quickened his step once again, clasping the walking stick behind his back.

Had it been only a year ago? His father had said a man shouldn't marry until he'd established himself, until he was old enough not to be dominated by a pretty face and a pleasing figure. And he'd replied he was almost forty. Their conversation had been repeated so often—almost forty, almost thirty-five, almost—like actors, they'd spoken the lines to one another over and over, as in a provincial performance in which no one wants to hear anything new.

"Well then, keep Natalya Ivanovna as your mistress," his father had said, the shoulder of his coat dappled with rice powder from his wig. "I suppose she's already pressuring you to marry, isn't she? It would be a good situation for her, making a match above her rank. Watch out, my boy, for a woman's wiles. She and her father aren't like us. When the time comes—later—you'd do well to marry someone of your own class, someone who'll add to our fortune. When you're a general, you must have a general's wife."

How he'd hated the smug face mouthing those words, a face of ignorant power. "Listen to me," he'd said. "You think you know her—you don't. She's not some serf woman, you understand? You have no idea what she and I share. She belongs to me; I don't require your permission to have her."

"I understand all about men and women. And I understand it's never good to mix rich and poor."

"She's more valuable than a hundred heiresses."

"Well, if you're sure," his father had said.

But I was not sure. A slither of excitement and fear ran from the base of my spine down through my legs, and I thought, she's trying to ensnare me into marriage; perhaps, my father is correct. Now those doubts have become a knout applied to an already bloodied back.

A score of steps ahead, the wraith walked, averting her face.

His pace was hobbled; he was wounded all over. At the intersection of the next street, he came to a halt. Assailed by a babble of foreign words, he spun to the right, then the left and behind, searching for a sign, but he recognized nothing. A small wooden church—no, he'd never been here before. With shaking hands, he withdrew the map from his pocket. It would not be easy to find his way.

7.

Who told you all the obstacles would only come from me?

The church was small, a poor, wooden cousin of the city's grand cathedrals of gold and stone. From one of the back pews, Anne-Marie listened to the sound of the prayers of a handful of hushed worshipers rising to the musty vault. To her right, a small window of colored, leaded glass held the images of a man and two women. Their angular faces looked up in rapture; their hands crossed their breasts. She could not remember the story it represented.

"Do you need anything, daughter?" a voice said, startling her so that she looked up blinking. A priest with cropped gray hair stood at her side. "Why are you here?"

Earlier—when Valsin had headed off to parade—she'd left their rooms intent on walking in a new direction. With the twin towers of the Fraüenkirche as a beacon, she'd ventured into an unfamiliar district, trusting she would blend in with the other single women—maids doing their mistresses' shopping. "I'm just resting," she said, looking away. "Father."

"You're nervous—confession?"

She'd known a different priest, Father Steiner, and an even humbler church with no windows at all. After her husband's death, that church had been one of the few places she could go unaccompanied. Father Steiner was not only a lonely man who loved to talk but also a good source of information. At first she'd endured confession, often inventing sins just for the opportunity to speak with him afterward.

It had been last autumn, before Valsin had come, when she'd sat side by side in a pew with Steiner, speaking in low tones. "Is there news, Father?"

"A little. You know the French are nearing Vienna?"

"Yes. They'll spend the winter there?"

"That's what I've heard. God has spared this part of the world the ravages of war—for now. What is it? You look troubled," Steiner had said.

"It's just that…" She'd felt a chill—as if the pew had become a block of river ice, and she no longer saw the old priest but only a vision of falling behind that past's present.

He'd patted her arm; she should remarry, fulfill her destiny as a woman—that was the way, he'd said, toward heaven.

"Daughter, did you hear me?"

She blinked again, refocusing her gaze. A priest—but unfamiliar, both nostrils of his nose covered in a river of broken capillaries flowing from watery blue eyes.

I'm in Munich; Valsin carried me away.

"I said you seem troubled; would you like confession?"

No, there was too much to confess, and besides, he'd never believe her. "No," she said, shaking her head. "Not today, no thank you." On the way out, she curtsied and crossed herself.

Her hand on the latch, she stopped, remembering her room at the farm. Despite the objections of his father, Johannes had put a lock on their door, at her request—a new bride's request, one that could not be refused. And somehow the lock had remained during widowhood, fastened on the inside, not out—as if she were more than a valuable thing to be kept in a storeroom. Her room had been a refuge, a preserve of rare privacy. Anywhere else, she was answerable to interruption and demand, her demeanor required to be arranged in a particular way, pleasing, modest—false. Each morning had been a test, an alchemist's experiment to see if dross could be turned into gold. Feet clad in wooden clogs, she'd tug at the door's dry bolt until it slid back, releasing her to the furies of the house, embodied by Johannes's father, Fröelich, who wanted to assume his son's place in her bed.

She left the church, passing outside into the fresh air. In the square, a bonfire was burning, and passers-by stretched out hands wrapped in strips of cloth for warmth.

How often she had considered killing Fröelich. The only thing that checked her was the fear of being caught, although in the time just before Valsin's arrival, she'd become less and less afraid. At dawn and again at dusk, the stables were dark; Fröelich would never have seen the knife that struck him down.

But I would have wanted him to see—to see my face.

She stopped and looked up. Above the tall, gabled houses, the domes of the Fraüenkirche were nowhere in sight; she'd lost her way. Afraid of slipping on the rutted and icy street, she lifted her skirts and stepped across slowly, entering an unfamiliar neighborhood of shops and taverns where women peered at her with closed faces. A cobbler turned his back and went inside his shop, shutting the door hard as she passed.

It was worth it—to be a little lost. Valsin never wanted to go anywhere besides the coffeehouse. The cathedral couldn't be that far away; it was because of the height of the surrounding buildings that the towers were no longer visible. She guessed at the right direction and turned down an even narrower lane.

Father Steiner had counseled her to seek friendship.

"How can I find friends here? I'm different from everyone. No one likes me."

"That isn't true. It's thought you hold yourself apart, that you believe you're better than everyone else."

He'd been right about that; the people shunned her, calling her "Fröelich's Frenchwoman." She'd tried to become one of them, standing with the other women after church, listening to them as they complained about their husbands, gossiping about those not present. The women had tolerated her, tossed her glances, suffered her brittle laughter. But once Johannes died, they'd stopped any pretense of acceptance and treated her as if she too were dead. Their gossip had been about her: she was too proud and reserved; she put herself above the others. Steiner had counseled her to pray to St. Munditia—the patron saint of lonely women.

And Valsin says St. Munditia's bones are here in Munich, in a dusty reliquary in one of the cathedrals.

A stone sailed past her head and struck a clump of dirty snow to the side of the walkway. At her back, laughter rang, and she spun around. "Ah *fraulein.*" A group of young men—boys really—stood in the middle of the street. With caps pulled over red-cheeked, shining faces, they all snickered at once, falling over themselves like destructive puppies.

For a moment, she stared at them, stunned that memory could leave her so vulnerable. Then she closed her fingers around the clasp knife in her pocket and began to walk away.

"No, pretty lady, don't leave!" Footsteps pounded behind her, and she was surrounded.

"Leave me alone!" she screamed in German. A hand tore at her dress. Another snaked under her right arm to touch her breast, and she twisted and screamed again, fumbling with the blade.

Bells jingled above her head, and different hands, small and strong, grabbed her by the shoulders. Before she could oppose them, she was pulled backward into warmth, falling onto a hard floor. Skirts brushed past her, and a figure blocked the doorway. "Go away or I'll get my husband," a woman said to those outside.

"But she's not from around here," one of the boys called. "She's a—"

"She's none of your business," the woman said, slamming the door and setting the latch. "They're not from here either," she said over her shoulder.

Anne-Marie rose, her hands trembling; she felt ashamed at not being able to control them, but the woman had stepped to a window to watch the street and had not noticed. A familiar smell of tallow candles and turpentine filled the room; workbenches were strewn with bolts of cloth, and against one wall stood a female torso made of pinewood. "You're a dressmaker," she said.

"And you're a fool to be walking around by yourself. Those boys took you for a whore. Don't you have a man to look after you?"

Tiny muscles around her eyes squeezed hard and jetted tears, and she returned to the floor, sobbing. With the tears pouring out, she was closed within; all she could manage was to heave like an animal in pain. The shop, which moments ago had been bright and familiar, disappeared, and she felt the denseness of the wooden floor beneath. Her nose ran, and she snuffled. With the back of her hand, she wiped her face and remembered a handkerchief in her sleeve. Only after using it did she look up. The woman still stood by the window, but all the fierceness she'd exhibited to the boys was gone, replaced by the shy manner in which she plucked at the front of her apron and pursed her mouth. She was full with middle age, gray-haired, and the shiny surface of a worn thimble glittered on her left forefinger.

Anne-Marie reached for her bonnet—knocked off during the violent entrance—and again got to her feet. "Thank you," she murmured and then made ready to leave.

"Don't go," the woman said, laying a hand on her arm. "Those boys may still be about. Please—are you all right?" She went to a chair by the stove and removed a bolt of dark red cloth from the seat. "Sit here, come. Your clothes are of good quality, stylish. May I look?" Anne-Marie shrugged the coat off, and the woman inspected the seams around the shoulders, nodding to herself in apparent approval.

"I don't know why I got upset just now," Anne-Marie said, sitting. "Sorry."

"You were frightened." The dressmaker sat down on a high stool by a bench and picked up a needle running with scarlet thread. "You're French, aren't you? Where do you live?"

The woman's manner, calm and reserved, soothed her, as did the dry, dusty smell of fabric. "With a soldier," she said, wiping her nose again.

"I'll make you a dress," the woman said. "A nice dress, anything you like. Won't your soldier buy you a dress?"

"He'll give me anything I want," she said, shaking her head. "Whatever I need, anything. But I don't know when I'll be back this way."

"Ah, soldiers' ladies come and go."

She got to her feet and put on her coat. "Excuse me. You're kind—I'd like to come back."

"My advice," the woman said without looking up, "don't get pregnant. If you do, he'll leave you."

When she'd been married, a certain time of month always brought disappointment. Many prayers were exhausted until she'd given up caring about the absence of a baby. With Valsin, she'd planned to take precautions, but since the battle, her flow had been so irregular that she no longer knew when to push him away. And it didn't seem necessary. No new life would grow inside her womb; it was an emptiness that only ached a little.

If, somehow, I had his child, would that keep him from going? No, this woman's right; I'd be alone.

After examining the street through the shop window, she left, and the cluster of bells rang again above her head.

She held the knife tightly—an amulet for protection, not so much from men and boys but abandonment.

8.

Appearance alone is more complicated than reality.

The shopkeeper's tiny script made the street names on the map impossible to decipher, and he became lost. After crossing a busy street—one he hadn't crossed before—he decided to walk a bit further and then hail a cab. He folded the map and advanced, swinging his stick and glancing from side to side. Many of the buildings in this district looked faded and tired, as if fresh paint and plaster had been rationed to adorn only the heart of the city. He walked along, hearing German; there were no signs of French soldiers at all.

Closer to the river, bells began ringing, and he stopped and observed people with bright, agitated faces speaking in loud voices. He wished he knew enough of the language to understand what they were saying. Suddenly a fire wagon came hurtling down the street, the horses rolling their eyes in excitement, figures in helmets and official uniforms grasping the sides, a small bell ringing over and over on the wagon itself. The driver made the team slow, and they turned down a side street, still at such a great rate of speed that the wagon nearly tipped over. He followed, smelling acrid smoke, and then saw it pouring out of a second-story window halfway down the block. The firemen grabbed axes and pikes and ran into the building.

Memory reflected another fire—a small one, unremarkable in the history of a town that burned often. It began in private, early, and ended in public, late. But at midmorning on a day two years in the past, he returned from a ride in the country to hear the bells ringing the alarm. With a squeeze of his legs, he quickened Pyerits's pace and strained forward. Three streets over from Brest-Litovsk's market square, flames crowned a whole row of houses. Men and women struggled with buckets and tubs to haul water from the river, but many others stood and wrung their hands in despair.

He jumped off the saddle and thrust the reins at the first man who met his gaze. "Mind my horse," he cried, unbuckling the sword and sliding it beneath the saddle straps. "You there, you men, make a line to haul water. Quickly now!" Soon, from the docks, many hands passed along a steady stream, across the street and onto the flames. "No, it's hopeless," he said, dismissing an inferno with a wave of his arm. "Leave it. We'll concentrate here." He started them at a house just beginning to burn. After ten minutes of hard work, the bright flames sputtered and hissed, steam rose where there had been the madness of fire. The wailing of the women drew down into sighs.

"Your Honor!" a man called in a shrill voice. "The fire! It's crossed the street—behind us."

He turned to look, and a petite figure holding up her skirts burst out of a smoking stable. "My horse! Please help me!" she shouted above the uproar. She ran forward and grabbed him by the shoulders. Out of her combs, black hair fell, and at her temple a purple pulse throbbed. "Please, my horse is trapped—there! We must get him out!"

He ran after her into a place swirling with serpentine ribbons of heat. In a stall to the right, a frantic, plunging shape whinnied and kicked through the thick haze.

"I can't get the latch open!" the woman cried in his ear. "You try."

With both hands, I took the handle and pulled—once, twice, three times; I stepped back, an ache shuddering across my shoulders, and shook my head. The fire was taking command of my senses; heat and smoke and bright flame were all I knew. The woman yelled something unintelligible and thrust a pitchfork into my hands, and I turned it around and began hammering the butt end against the latch. Again the horse kicked, the kicks like gunshots against the stall. Two streams of tears flowed over my cheeks, and in desperation, I turned the fork around again and drove the tines down into the space between the rusted latch and the stall's wooden frame. With all my weight, I hung on the handle and pulled.

A crack, and the wood splintered. The door flew open, and the huge animal bolted, sending the woman reeling back against a barrel full of grain. I moved forward to help her, but blinded by the roiling smoke, tripped over the pitchfork that had come free from the door. A burning board fell, striking me on the head and sending me to the ground. I scrambled to my feet and found the woman's hands, pulling her outside into cooler air.

For several minutes, we both stood, hanging onto one another and coughing as the men threw water on the walls and roof of the nearest house to protect it from the burning stable. I took my arm from her shoulders and drew back, wiping my face with a handkerchief from my sleeve.

Motion caught my eye—a slim white hand brushing hair away from a high cheekbone, then a glint from a ringed finger. Beneath sable eyebrows, the woman's dark eyes were red from the smoke. She took my hand as a man would. "Thank you, Premier Major!" she said in a voice gritty with fire. "I knew you'd help."

"Of course."

Her dress was pale gray with a bit of black ribbon at the bodice and waist. Despite the soot stains and the dust at the hem, she wore it with an elegant rhythm, the sheath of the dress moving an instant after she did, the fabric fluid and embracing. I was very aware of her smallness.

"You're Premier Major Ruzhensky, aren't you? The General's son? My father—Captain Antonov—served under him. I'm Natalya Ivanovna."

"Alexi Davidych." I tore my eyes away. On the side of the street where we stood, only her stable was ablaze: the house itself was no longer threatened. "Excuse me," I

said, turning back to face her. "You mentioned my father—but have we met before? You and I?"

"Oh yes—when I was a little girl—in Kiev, I used to play at your house. You were very serious."

A thin sheet of memory appeared like a sail of smoke: children running in the kitchen, giggling and peeking around corners. Their small, grimy faces had been an irritation; I had had no time for games.

"Now we're all grown up, aren't we, Premier Major?"

The ribbon at her waist had pulled the fabric close to hug her breasts. I looked up quickly to see eyes dancing with flame. All at once a tremendous crash made us both jump; the stable was collapsing, folding in on itself as each heavy timber of the roof's frame separated and fell into the ashes below. A dragon's breath of heat and danger blew out; a huge shower of sparks shot above the stooks of fire. The men hauling the water had stopped to watch, yet the sparks and embers continued to fly about and threaten the houses to either side.

"Excuse me, Natalya Ivanovna. I must go." I rushed away across the street, shouting at the men to get more water.

Later, when the fire was out, and he'd returned, she was gone.

In Munich, the firemen subdued the fire but not before it had done considerable damage. Several families stood on the street, gazing in horror as the men brought out soot-blackened remnants of furniture and clothing. Embarrassed by the tragedy, he turned away, looking for a cab.

Twenty paces to the rear, the wraith stood, searching his face through depthless, coal-black eyes, and he thought she would speak, but she cast her eyes down and turned to go. Like a swinging bell hung with coils of ebony rope, she began swaying away, and he watched her cross the street and turn down a pathway between two buildings.

The bells of a nearby church sounded the noon hour. Each stroke contained a multitude of smaller reverberations, like impressions made by stones thrown onto the surface of a still pool. He took out a handkerchief and wiped his face.

The bells stopped, and in the silence, he cocked his head to catch their echo. Without much consideration—as if he were doing the most routine thing—he entered the narrow opening where the wraith had gone.

At first, the height of the buildings on either side blocked the sunlight, and he picked his way along a path of well-worn stone. His map did not show this path; he had certainly never been here before. Above his head, he heard laughter; the warmth of the air must have caused the residents to open a window. But at ground level, he seemed to be walking through a tunnel, a connection between two different places.

The path widened and brightened, and he was on a little lane lined with two-story houses. It was where Marianne lived; he wasn't lost. A group of children played at hoops, calling to each other and laughing like miniature, enchanted adults. He marveled at the sight and sound, accustomed as he was to a rougher world of sabers and gunshots, a world where these creatures had no part. Her room was here, in the building with the green trim.

Upstairs, he struck the door three times with his stick, banging against the wooden panel like a worshipper rousing an oracle. From across the hallway, a young woman emerged and spoke in German until he turned and interrupted her with a shake of his head. "No, I don't understand," he said in Russian. "Where is Marianne?"

The girl frowned and drew back, clutching the plain white dressing gown closed about her bare throat. "No, please excuse me," he said, continuing in French. "I'm looking for Mademoiselle Marianne."

"Marianne," the girl repeated and slammed the door.

He shrugged, reassured by the silence in the room beyond. He almost smiled. Marianne was out; she'd come see him around dusk. Surely she'd forgotten the morning's anger. But just as a running rope loses slack, his fears snapped and quivered: if she wasn't in her room, then where was she?

He went outside, deciding to walk about the neighborhood. After all, he might encounter her on the street.

But what if she is at home, not alone, and not answering the door? Still angry with me. He froze in mid-stride. *My God, what if she's not alone and in bed, and*—he struggled to dispel the idea that his knocking might have silenced the beat of flailing, white limbs. Which one was her window? He peered up at the building, realizing that, to see into any second-floor room, he'd have to climb up on the roof like a thief.

He'd come back in an hour—no, thirty minutes—to see if she'd returned. The hands on his watch were motionless, and he paused, taking a second look, trying to remember if he'd wound the mechanism. Clocks made time disciplined—like a good soldier—but needed regular attention.

Then the longer hand jerked and froze like a salute, and he set off.

Down the narrow lane where he'd first found her, he passed between two buildings full of muffled cries and smells of baking bread to enter a broader avenue. In the more open area, the late-winter sun was melting the snow, leaving its surface adroop like the skin of a starving beast, consuming itself from the inside out. Ice glistened, and clear streams of water ran toward the gutters, like smaller rivers in a race to the sea. All the dirt accumulated during the long winter—hidden within the ice—was about to be sluiced away. He saw a speck of something exposed, a glimmer, and just before it could be caught by the current, scooped it up.

But whatever it was melted in his hand, and he fell back across an expanse of gray slush where the footsteps of others persisted in outline.

Long ago the two of them had raced their horses out of Brest-Litovsk. Side by side, cantering north along the River Bug, their hair streamed behind them, straining together to plait a single braid. The steel-gray river rippled and sang, in the vast forest of pine and birch the wind rustled the trees, and cicadas whined.

"I ride whenever I can," she said, reaching down to caress her horse's neck. "But my father worries about my riding alone; he's grown too old to escort me."

"I'm glad to be your escort, Natalya Ivanovna."

When she'd first appeared in my rooms—the day after I saved her horse from the fire—I was asleep. I didn't know her then; what sort of woman would come by herself to a man's rooms—a man of higher rank—and ask him to go riding? I dressed in a hurry and burst from the bedroom. There, across the threshold—pushing past a startled Yevgeny—her pale face emerged from a high-collared blouse. From under the hem of her pleated skirt, men's riding boots peeked out, the shape of a lover hiding behind the drapes.

Outside, she leaned forward, her legs squeezing her stallion's flanks, making him shoot away like a lion after prey. For a moment, I watched her go and then jumped onto my own saddle and started off, pursuing her the length of Governor's Street as the hooves of our horses scattered sparks. On into the countryside we rode at a trot, and the sun broke through the clouds, bringing a flush of warmth—a soon-to-be-forgotten memory of summer—that pierced the green and silver canopy of trees, lighting up her form with slanting light, catching against the silver ring on her left hand. Her long tresses, hanging free from a peasant's blue kerchief, were purple in the glow.

"Natalya Ivanovna, the people say you can whisper secrets into the forest."

She seemed about to reply but frowned instead and rode on a few paces. Deep grooves of paths led away in several directions, crisscrossed like tangled skeins of yarn. "I think fate placed you outside my stable, Alexi Davidych," she said in a soft burr, avoiding my eyes, turning her voice toward the trees. "My burning stable."

"It wasn't fate; it was the fire."

"You were there to help me, and I need your help."

"You do—still?"

Within his trousers, there was a stirring; between his legs, the sack of skin around his testicles shifted and stretched. He had the sensation of being erect when he was not; a fullness remained, as if a part of him remained with her, wherever she was. In his groin, a second heart beat.

A woman stepped from an arched doorway to his left, looking at him out of deep-blue eyes set wide above delicate shelves of bone. A woman, not a wraith.

"Alyosha, you found me."

9.

⁓

I spent the night listening to and performing Italian music because duets were found, and it was necessary to risk doing one of the parts.

A night, a night spent alone with her, shut into the small room with her hands and warm breath, and then, after dawn, awake, facing another separation.

In the bluish-gray light, he raised his head from the pillow and looked around the room. Marianne's possessions—her clothes, a bed with an ornate wooden headboard, a hand mirror and brush inlaid with bone—were of good quality, signs of her success. Yet a second glance showed that these things had a worn appearance, as if they'd been cast off from a wealthier person. On her face, he saw the delicate film of skin over each eye, the way a child slept within the adult. Eventually she would become worn and cast off as well, as women did who engaged in her trade for very long. He saw that too.

When they rose, she insisted on building the fire herself, breaking small sticks for kindling with her hands. He was aware of each movement she made, dreading that the next might be the last before the bells of the cathedral signaled him to depart.

What am I to do? Walk the streets? Whether it's today or tomorrow or the next, I'll find him, Valsin, and then—what? All this will end; she'll be lost. Without her, I'm left behind, with the dead.

"Here," she said, reaching up to tie his cravat. "Let me."

Her hands brushed against his neck; he could not bear it. "Marianne," he began.

"What? Hold still."

"Marianne, yesterday, I came here—before you returned. I was afraid you'd gone."

"I'm usually here till evening," she said, "I don't often have callers during the day." She looked up at him. "Except you. I can't tie this if you keep moving."

Within the half-closed armoire, her fur muff was visible; soon, when she left to walk the streets, it would enclose her hands.

"I want you to move to my rooms. We could agree on a sum—a sort of housekeeping allowance. That way I would never worry about your safety, and you would never have to worry about anything."

He'd strained toward her so that his weight wound up on his toes, and now he rocked back on his heels and swallowed. She'd become still, staring at him open-mouthed with a hand hanging onto each end of his cravat. A frown had lengthened her nose, and she gave the cravat a tug. "Never? Don't joke about such things."

"I am not joking."

"You like me that much? But there are lots of girls. What's special about me?" She paused, searching his face again, and then bent her head. "No, I know I'm not special. I'm rather plain and—"

"You're not plain at all."

She looked up at him through her lashes. "I wasn't trying to force you to say that you like me."

"I do. Very much."

"Only we just met. Of course, when a man and a woman—" Her eyes swept the unmade bed. "It's very powerful. But you're teasing." She blinked and then took both his hands in hers and squeezed them before letting go. "Thank you," she whispered and then walked slowly to the shuttered window. She clasped her hands together, making her shoulders round, and under her loosened hair, the fabric of her dressing gown stretched tight across her back.

"But I'm not teasing, either," he said. She hadn't said yes; she hadn't said no. He didn't understand how to read backs. "Marianne. Look at me."

"No, I won't, not yet. You're serious."

"Yes."

"And you want me to decide right now?" She spun around. "How can I do that? I don't even know you. You must tell me about yourself, a little anyways. My friends are right to be curious. What's brought you to Munich? Who are you?"

He rummaged in the unfamiliar pockets of his civilian trousers. Premier major in the Mariupol Hussars, his father's instrument of revenge, Natasha's lover—he was all those things, or had been, but each one of them was changing. His uniform lay hidden at the bottom of a trunk, and he wore a merchant's waistcoat and cravat. Natasha was dead, and the man his father wanted him to kill had become the subject of a new story, a sensitive hero who'd murdered Mischa by accident.

"Well?" She gave him a cross look. "Is it so hard to answer?"

He shook his head. "No, no, of course not. I'm just thinking about where to begin." He sat on the edge of the bed. "I'm Russian—that you know already. And I'm a cavalry officer on leave. A year ago, I'd planned on spending some time touring Bavaria in order to learn about German culture, but the war upset my plans. I was wounded at the battle they're calling Austerlitz, and an opportunity arose to recover here in Munich. I've decided the city offers all I need. It's filled with beautiful things." He looked at her and smirked; Valsin wasn't the only one who could be in a new story.

While he'd spoken, she'd come closer, step by step, like a child drawn by a promise of sweets. She took in sharp exhalations, encouraging him with her breath, and sat down on the other side of the bed.

"How wonderful!" she said at last, clasping her hands together again. "A wonderful opportunity. Oh yes, Munich is lovely. I haven't seen that much of it, but I've walked all around the Residenz and the English Gardens. There's a lot more, I know, the cathedral—the Frauenkirche, it's called—have you been inside?" Her face had once again become open and radiant. "You bend your neck back to look up at the roof, and it's so far away, as if giants had built it. And the mountains!"

He listened to her talk and wondered if—poor girl that she was—she was just repeating stories she'd heard others tell. Whether or not she was telling the truth, she did seem innocently glad, happy for him that he would have the pleasure of seeing all the wondrous sights—happy at his pleasure. She was generous and unselfish; she held his happiness inside herself to preserve it, to cherish it, not to make it her own.

He wanted to tell her all that, to say, "That's why you must move in with me, that's why you must love me." To lay his head on her lap and know she'd forgive him for not confessing everything right now—about vengeance and his failures.

But the wound in his side gave a sharp twinge, and he pressed it with the palm of his right hand. "I'm quite interested in Italian music as well," he said.

She frowned and shrugged her shoulders. "So you'll go to Italy? I don't understand."

"I meant I hope to hear music here in Munich."

She smiled. "I'll go with you if you like. Only, I'll need a new dress."

"Fine. It's settled then. Come, pack your things, and we'll—"

"No!" she shouted and stamped her foot; her chin bunched and trembled. "All this"—she gestured around the room—"it's all I have, and it's been hard work to get. Don't you understand?" Her palm slammed down on the bed, and her eyes raked across his. "Right now, at this moment, I hate you." She rose and took three steps but stopped, half-turning back to him. "It will pass, I'm sure. It's just that—what you're asking—you want me to trust you, trust that you won't put me out on the street when you've grown tired of me."

"You must bring it all," he said. "All of it—whatever you want. We'll find room."

"That's not what I'm talking about."

"But I'm telling you I want you with me all the time—isn't that enough? Put you out on the street, I don't understand you."

"And when," she continued in a lower voice, "will you return to Russia?"

"I have no plans to return to Russia."

"No wife awaits you there?" Her hips shifted from right to left, and her head inclined by a fraction of the distance between them so that her far eye appeared beyond the line of her nose.

"No. I loved someone very much and lost her—in Russia. You see, I know the value of a woman and would pay any price for you."

She laughed. "That's what all men say. Why?"

"Why what?"

"Why would you pay any price for me?" she said, speaking to him over her right shoulder. "Me, in particular. You hardly know me, yet you want me to live with you. How do you know what I'll cost you?"

"I haven't decided on the amount yet, perhaps...a hundred guilders?"

Her head moved from side to side.

"A hundred and fifty then—a week."

She stamped her foot again and faced him. "I'm not talking about money. Do you remember when we met? I came up behind you on the street. I was cold and I'd been watching for a while, willing you to turn around. And you did. You looked like a gentleman, and I thought if I concentrated as hard as I could that you would help me. And now it scares me that this is happening—do you see?" She moved toward him, holding her arms up so the sleeves of her dress shrugged down, and her forearms were bare. Her thighs pushed against his knees, and she turned her hands around, exposing her wrists. "I'm trembling."

Beneath the silvery down, her skin was textured, mottled like a freshly planted field. He rose, taking her right wrist and kissing it on the inside where the pulse pushed back against his lips.

"Last night," she continued, "when you were asleep, I took the candle and looked at you because I wasn't sure you were really there." Her voice sank again to a whisper, and she pressed closer. "I held it so near your face that you stirred and moaned, and I thought I'd spilled hot wax on your chin. I listened to your breathing. I wondered why you were so nice to me and who you really were."

He closed his eyes and bowed his head onto hers, straining to hear her voice.

"Maybe I wonder what you'll cost me," she murmured.

The moment lengthened, and what had been expressed in the same tender tones became a question.

"Cost you?"

"I think the things you're telling me are true," she said, speaking into his chest. "But there are other things you're not saying."

She'd spoken so softly it took him a moment to understand; he pulled away, looking at her in astonishment. "Other true things, you mean?"

"Yes. It will take me longer to find out about them."

She held him with her gaze, and he felt there was something enormous in the space she occupied that he couldn't see; each time he tried, it was as if he'd peered into the depths of the sea, trying to catch what lay beneath the rolling waves but only perceiving the beautiful play of light on the surface. He shook his head. "But my proposal; you'll move to my rooms?"

"I'm considering it. Housekeeping allowance, you said. A hundred and fifty a week. Will I have to cook and clean?" Her gaze was the same—cool and undisturbed, like a clear sheet of glass.

"Yevgeny does those things. No, you'll be my companion; I want you to be comfortable. In fact, your happiness is very important to me."

She pressed her cheek against his shoulder. "Very well. We could try it. Yes, I accept your offer."

✧ ✧ ✧

The next day, he hired a man with a cart to carry her possessions. "The young woman," he said to Yevgeny. "She's moving in."

She decided to leave the bed behind. "You already have a bed," she said. "So we don't need this one. I'll give it to the girl across the hall."

While Yevgeny withdrew behind his partition, Marianne unpacked her clothes and comb. Soon dresses and white stockings hung over the end of the bed, and by the hearth, tiny women's shoes stood in line next to men's boots. In the midst of these things, a letter arrived from his father, and he placed it on the table, facedown and unopened.

Freed from the jerking of the clock and the movement of the sun that had limited his time with her, he felt free to ask his own questions. She'd come, she replied, from a territory between Germany and France. After her father's death, she'd traveled to Munich on bad advice. Times had been hard; a man had beaten her and taken all her money. With a touching catch in her voice, she said that she didn't think she'd ever see her mother or her little sisters again.

"Poverty forced me," she said, "to rely on my native resources."

At first he didn't understand her; she'd used a rather formal term to refer to something elemental, polishing it, as if it were a precious mineral or an ore, a fragrant wood grown in her garden. Beauty, youth—like happiness—were native resources, were things of value worth guarding. He studied her; she'd had to spend some of what she owned.

"You're embarrassing me, Alyosha—staring at me like that. I'm not educated like you; I'm used to calling things by simple names, just what they really are."

"It's just that your accent—it's fine—but it takes me a moment to understand all you say. Certain words, I'm used to hearing them a different way, that's all."

"I speak very clearly, Al Oo Cha, you must listen better. Ha, I made you laugh! Is that worth a present?"

He enjoyed buying her presents. At the slightest offering—a bit of lace, a stick of sugar—her face would light up in pleasure, and she'd throw her arms around his neck and laugh in his ear until he trembled all over like a stallion. But there were still times she was absent—gone away to gossip with friends— and he suffered, gazing through the crystal of his watch. She claimed she no longer went with other men, but he couldn't be sure, and the uncertainty ate at him like a canker. He resolved to increase the amount of the sum they'd settled on for her keeping so she would never experience want.

The next day, as they lay resting in bed in the middle afternoon, he told her about the new arrangement. "Ah," she said. "I think you like me a little. But isn't there something I can do in return? To please you—something else?"

He laughed, so distracted by her warm breath that he couldn't catch the quick thoughts that ran across his brow.

Careful, she's a thief. Valsin, Mischa—she'll steal them away.

"I know," she said. "Would you like to learn to speak German? It would help you in your study, and it would make it easier for us to talk. I'm not so good with letters, but talking—I could teach you to talk."

It made good sense. A new language would challenge his mind; the practice would be a mental calisthenic. "Yes," he said. "And I think I should begin teaching you a little Russian."

He could feel her smile pressing against his neck. "A little Russian— I'd like that. In Russian, how do you say my name?"

For a moment, he considered. Marysia, maybe—no. "Your name should be the same in both languages—yours and mine. In Germany and in Russia, you are Marianne."

Later, after dusk, he awoke with her in his arms to find candles lit and Yevgeny staring down with a concerned look.

The poor fellow is used to me being the first in the saddle and the last to leave. She's so warm though, and a chill remains in the air.

10.

But maxims become less general in proportion to how well one reads hearts, and Julie's husband must conduct himself not at all like another man.

Two kings and a queen—a good hand if she could play it well. But a knock came at the door, and the game between the two of them was suspended. "Gentlemen, welcome," Valsin said, stepping back to allow their guests entry. In a wash of greatcoats, Captain Merseult advanced into the room, followed by Étienne Dalhousie. Witkowski—Valsin's servant—had already arrived. Since they'd settled into Munich, it had become a habit for them all to come together at least once a week. In this room, the aristocratic Merseult shared a pipe with Witkowski and called Dalhousie "Chef" like a comrade, being billeted together in a foreign city having eased the hierarchies of rank. Except that all the men still called Merseult "Capitaine."

Cloaks were thrown off, pipes taken out, glasses filled, a new game begun. "So, Valsin," Merseult said. "There are rumors about promotions for officers who distinguished themselves at Austerlitz."

"He distinguished himself by getting shot," Dalhousie said. "Does that count?"

"Truly, I was thinking of myself," Merseult said.

Valsin joined in the laughter, but she wondered what he was thinking. After a period of recovery from his wound, he'd described himself as simply happy to be alive. More recently, his smiles often seemed lost in the ends of his mustache. In a dull voice, he'd report the latest rumor: a lieutenant from the Ninth Hussars had been sent to the Chasseurs of the Guard—a move that meant an increase in rank and pay and a chance for further recognition, further advancement. If only he'd done more in the battle before being wounded, he'd say.

"What I want to know is—what are Le Patron's plans?"

"The Emperor, Dalhousie," Merseult interrupted. "Call him the Emperor."

"Never—not even to his face! We got rid of one tyrant."

Merseult shrugged. "He's made peace with Austria and Prussia but not England or Russia. Those kings won't stop their scheming until we force them to."

"I don't think we'll be returning to France anytime soon," Witkowski said, and all the men shook their heads in unison.

She put down the cards; she was losing again anyway.

The future, it's not a time Valsin and I can speak about, not a time I should even think about. With luck, we'll be together till spring, maybe a little longer. But beyond that, as hard as I look, all I can see is falling once again into a black ditch I can't climb out of, swallowed up.

"Anne-Marie! Share your reverie with us."

The men were staring at her with glittering eyes and moist lips, suspended, it seemed, over a joke they'd made. It was Merseult who'd called to her.

"It's nothing," she said. "Old memories."

The men returned to their game, sitting shoulder to shoulder at the table like rooks on a fence, casting glances at each other's cards. Witkowski was the only one in civilian clothes, although Valsin and Dalhousie wore their creased stable jackets open at the chest. Merseult, on the other hand, wore a clean, pressed uniform, and his hair shone with pomade.

"So," he said. "Crèpin and I met a Russian officer the other day—a cavalry officer. He's visiting Munich, as a civilian, of course. We ran into him by pure coincidence and got to talking. We told him your story, Valsin—about the duel at Wischau. He was quite interested. Do you know what he said? That the Russians thought you were a brute, a ruthless killer who murdered their innocent champion."

"They're right," Dalhousie said, placing a card.

"It appears they misunderstood some things. Valsin, you remember, after you cut off the boy's sword knot, the Russians were angry. They advanced and—"

"And you drew your pistols." Valsin hunched over the table, peering at his hand. "I remember."

"And I thought we were about to have a skirmish and didn't understand the reason. We'd followed every fine point of custom; after all, we were the ones who'd been challenged. You'd done all you could to discourage their cadet."

"He was a fool," Witkowski said.

"No," Valsin said. "Foolish maybe, but not a fool. Let's talk about something—"

"He was very brave," Merseult continued. "I believe there was a point when he knew you'd kill him, but he kept on. But listen, here's what the Russian officer told us. When the Russians asked your name, they thought you shouted—out of arrogance—and that you spit on the ground in derision instead of to clear your throat of bile."

A loud crack made her wince. Valsin had slapped the table with his palm. "No, don't get into all that," he said, and his voice broke on the second word. "It's a long time past. Whose play is it?"

In the silence, Merseult appeared to be sucking on his teeth. Finally he nodded and clasped Valsin's forearm. "You're right, we're neglecting our game."

"It's just that…certain things…I'd rather forget."

"Yes, but don't you think it's interesting? That's all I wanted to say. I told the Russian the same thing—wars begin over small misunderstandings. Two people experience something, but they take away different things, remember different things."

"People believe what they want to believe," Dalhousie said.

"I told him the truth—that you took no pleasure, that you were shaken."

Valsin began cutting the rind off a cheese with a clasp knife. "That day, at Wischau, everything was crazy."

That day, in a rolling meadow that had become a human anthill, she and Dalhousie had sat before a bonfire. To the right, a line of picketed horses marked the camp of the Tenth Hussars. The animals were restless, pulling at the tethers, their churning flanks glowing carmine in the reflection of the flames. Wood smoke curled skyward, gathering together to obscure the emerging stars.

Her disguise had become a burden, the uniform jacket too big, hanging on her thin shoulders like a weighted sack, ballooning out from the seams. The trousers revealed the curve of her hip. She felt like a performer in the theater, seen backstage before the curtain rose. "Is this the whole army?" she whispered.

"No, all night they'll be marching in," Dalhousie said. "These lads are an infantry division, twelve thousand of them." During the last hour, enormous numbers of men wrapped in brown overcoats had arrived in shuffling columns. Hunched under the weight of dappled haversacks, they leaned on their muskets, their eyes busy. The veterans were silent, holding rumors in their pockets and sleeves. The younger men stood straighter, and their mouths held many questions: "Are we where we're supposed to be?" "Can we get out our pipes?" "Who'll guide us to our bivouac?" "Where are the Russians?"

"Étienne," I had whispered. "This—" I pulled at his jacket. "It's not a good idea." After leaving the farm, Valsin had said I'd have to accompany them to the army's encampment, and I was satisfied, composing lightly sketched images of sitting in a tent while the men fought. Even after they dressed me as a man—covering me in thick cloth and smearing tallow and soot above my mouth to create a mustache—the disguise had made me feel playful. But now, dangerous creatures were all around; they were not at all like Valsin or Dalhousie, and the disguise was real, wet, and dirty.

"You want to go back to your Germans? It's too late, ma chère. I've got to get you laughing. Do you know the joke about the goat and the milkmaid? So..."

Valsin approached, leading his horse, Lily, by the bridle. He drank water from a bucket and wiped at his hands and face with a handkerchief. "Dalhousie," he said, coming up and squinting. "A merde! I can't get used to you this way."

"She's quite a sight, eh?" Dalhousie said. "Our new recruit. Witowski had her drilling with the saber earlier—she's dangerous. What did you fellows do today? The story is that—"

Valsin continued to regard me while Dalhousie spoke and then looked away, frowning. "We skirmished with the Russian infantry and then withdrew. A village called Wischau."

"Ah, but you were the bait in Le Patron's trap."

"Bait?" I asked.

"The story is that we're supposed to draw the Russians near here," Dalhousie said. "To fight. It's a big secret though; don't tell anybody. Le Patron has been all over looking at the ground. He knows what he's doing." He turned to Valsin. "Did the Ruskies follow you?"

"They moved into Wischau—when we let them. Crépin was shot in the hip as we withdrew."

"Too bad."

On the other side of the fire from where we sat, a scuffle had broken out. Dirty, unshaven men brandished bayonets, cursing each other in low, earnest tones. Valsin and Dalhousie seemed oblivious. The angriest-looking brawler was hit over the head with a musket, and the rest of them collapsed into laughter. Valsin asked if I had a new name to go with my disguise.

"No."

I looked around to see if anyone besides Dalhousie was watching and sat closer to Valsin. Earlier, I'd come upon what remained of a farmhouse after the men had torn away every scrap of wood, every single thing of value. The cellar-hole itself was broken—its edges kicked away and trodden in by scores of hob-nailed feet. All that remained of what had been the repository of an entire family's history was a pile of trash.

"Valsin, I'm afraid."

Dalhousie laughed. "She's having second thoughts. I told her it was too late."

"Is there anything to eat?" Valsin said, drawing a greatcoat around his shoulders.

I stared at him open-mouthed. To get his attention, I wanted to pick at his jacket and screech, but couldn't reveal feminine tones amid this madness. "Valsin," I whispered. "I'm frightened. Will there be a battle?"

"A big one." Dalhousie passed him a rind of cheese, and Valsin took out a clasp knife and began to slice. He nodded his head and looked at Dalhousie. "I killed a man today—a Russian cadet. A boy, really. It was a duel. Cut the knot off the hilt of his sword; I have it here."

He put the knife down and reached inside his jacket, pulling out what appeared to be a knotted, silver rope. I expected blood to be on it and drew back, but the only sign of violence was a spray of loose threads hanging off one end. "You see," he said, "when you're the victor, you're supposed to take something."

I wasn't used to soldiers and felt puzzled and upset. This man I knew to be gentle and tender was also a killer with a sharp heart.

A violin started up, and several soldiers linked arms to dance with bear-like grace. I looked back at Valsin, who was chewing. He must be two men, I thought, able to step back and forth at a pace too fast to catch.

In Munich, Merseult had begun to speak of the campaign in Italy, and Valsin was encouraging him with nods and snorts of laughter. She knew he hated hearing about such things—old war stories. His mustache was split by a grin, but his eyes were somber; she realized he was still thinking about the duel.

Just then, she had to know the limits of his strength.

He could probably push down a stone wall, kick through a stout door. That's what men are good at—destruction—he has that kind of strength. But in a storm, could he hold up a wall, keep a door fastened against enormous fists? Could he stop time?

She tried to see his portrait more clearly, widening her eyes and straining her gaze toward him, and he looked back at her and smiled, a particular kind of smile that said he knew her in a way no one else did. It surprised her, and she felt embarrassed and looked away.

✫ ✫ ✫

After the others left, she went downstairs to the cistern for water. When she returned with the sloshing bucket, he was smoking his pipe by the fire. She swept the floor and put the glasses aside for washing in the morning. Finally she sat at the table, but he remained silent and wreathed in smoke.

"What is it—the story Merseult told?"

He extended his boot into the hearth and crushed a noisy ember with the heel. "I'm going out for a while," he said, getting to his feet.

"No, stay—it's too late. What's wrong?"

He sat across from her at the table and leaned forward, rubbing the stubble on his cheeks. "Maybe they're right about me. The Russians. When I parried the boy's attack, I didn't even think, I just ran him through—under the ribs." He snapped his fingers. "Like that. I've lost track of how many men I've killed."

"Listen," she said. "What choice did you have? He wouldn't stop—that's what you said. You acted with honor." That was what men wanted—honor. "It's over now; let's go to bed."

He nodded, but swallowed and his mouth twisted to one side. "Some say that all those you kill gather around you, a pack of shades waiting for a misstep, an opportunity for revenge."

11.

I thank you for your books; but I no longer read those I understand, and it's too late to learn to read those I don't.

Marianne inserted herself into his household, carving out a distinct position by encroaching on the one occupied by Yevgeny. Once out of bed—she enjoyed sleeping late—she'd busy herself with brewing fresh tea and brushing and braiding Ruzhensky's hair, an activity he grew to anticipate with pleasure. She left shaving him to Yevgeny, and while his servant attended to this and other, humbler tasks, she'd comb her own hair and dress.

Together, they often went to the inn below their lodging to eat, and sometimes he would accompany her to a dressmaker's or cobbler's shop. But he generally was uncomfortable walking the streets in her company. When he did, he was aware of people's eyes—judging him, he was sure. An older man, well-dressed, with a cavalryman's mustache, accompanying an attractive young woman who did not appear to be his daughter. Being with her in public invited too much attention.

It became one of their few points of conflict. To spend the whole day in the rooms made him frantic with restlessness; even when the weather was bad, he liked to take a midmorning walk—alone, usually after an argument that could only be resolved by buying her a present.

But the streets fascinated him. By close observation, he tried to gauge and chart the rhythms of the restless townsfolk, following individuals for many blocks to see where they were going. He sometimes imagined others imagining him, wondering who he was.

Entire battalions of French soldiers were also abroad, but he never followed them. Yet as he walked through a series of gentle mornings and sometimes afternoons, he wondered if he might hear his—Valsin's—voice and of course, not even recognize it.

It was possible—amid all the hustle and bustle of people marching down walkways with purposeful gaits, carriages creaking and rattling, vendors hawking their wares, pails of water being emptied from side alleys, dogs barking, doors opening and shutting—it might not register. After all, he could barely hear his own boots crunching the snow.

Valsin might walk right past me and I wouldn't know—especially if I were distracted. Why, at this very moment, he could be standing behind the same wall I'm walking along, close and yet perfectly apart.

I might journey around the world, and he'd remain, waiting.

Once, far down a street, a figure paused, standing out in relief from all the others because of the way a cloud moved against the sun. But by the time he reached the spot, no one was there.

✵ ✵ ✵

Marianne's arrival had also interrupted his progress in reading *Julie*—the same book he and Natasha used to read together, sitting in her father's house in Brest-Litovsk, left alone with each other's hands and the babble of the samovar. The story of secret lovers inhabiting different worlds seemed to have been written about them.

Even before he'd met her, he'd read the Frenchman's story three times. And then, to share it with a new lover had given it new meaning, as if caresses imprinted paper as well as skin. But her death had not only brought his understanding of the book to a halt, it had also set it back to a time when the spell of words had not yet been cast. For many months after—left alone—he'd read like a printer's monkey, one of those boys who must pick out each separate letter of type, never seeing the whole. He read only to see the things her eyes had seen, touch the pages she'd touched. To clutch at, not to comprehend.

Julie had remained with him after Natasha's death, accompanying him on the fall campaign where he'd continued to read, sometimes while riding Pyerits, balancing the book atop the pommel of the saddle, ignoring the sideways glances of his troopers. At random places, he'd begun to read whole sentences, mouthing the phrases in pleasure.

However, that copy—redolent of an old love and lover—had been lost in the aftermath of the battle, along with his progress in reading it. The last time he could remember seeing its worn, leather cover was the day of Mischa's death.

At the hospital in Vienna, he'd become curious about re-reading a book he knew so well and had sent Yevgeny out to purchase a new copy. His servant returned with an edition recently published in Paris, the pages in quarto; it included all the engravings and of course, the appendix relating the story of Lord Bompston's adventures in Italy. It felt light; perhaps, he'd hoped, because all the baggage of the last year had been dropped, all the history edited out. More likely it was just that a smaller typeface had been used, creating a lesser weight of ink.

Yet, in Munich, whenever he sat down to crack its sweet-smelling spine, Marianne would begin talking—a real woman supplanting a phantom—and he'd become concerned that all his attention to her might make

Julie fade. He plotted a way to bring the three of them together. "Listen," he said to Marianne. "There's this book; it's written in French, and I was thinking of reading it aloud to you. You agree, yes?"

"A book—I don't know. What's it about?"

"A young woman named Julie and her love for two men."

"At the same time?"

"No, not exactly. She's in love with her tutor, but her father, who's a noble, forbids her to marry a commoner. Instead she marries an older man."

She looked at him from under her eyelids. "Why do you want to read it aloud? I know—to bewitch me. So go ahead."

Julie resided on the table, buried beneath two unopened letters from his father; those he pushed aside, imagining—as he grasped the book—that he could see Julie herself through the walls of paper, completing her toilette before the mirror, readying herself.

He returned to his seat by the fire and saw how Marianne had taken up her sewing. After staring at the blank cover for a few moments, he reached for the knife and held it poised. Instead of beginning at the beginning—a place where he'd several times been interrupted—he resolved to touch the edge of the pages, gently and without consideration. Wherever the point of the blade made contact, there he would slice into the interior, allowing fate to guide him to particular passages.

At this word, her needle-work fell from her hands; she turned her head, and cast on her worthy husband a look so touching, so tender, that I myself trembled. She said nothing: what could she have said to equal that look?

He touched and read again and was surprised when the cathedral clock sounded; for a half-hour, the knife had done its work, and his eyes and voice had run over the parchment, seeking favorite passages, skipping over others with impatience. *Julie* was fresh and unfamiliar, like encountering someone known years before whom the intervening years had edged out of memory. Each letter was a magnet that pulled toward some letters, pushed others away. Letters full of questions: Could the hearts of Julie and her lover understand one another? Would her lover share the tender emotion with which they were written? The answers were often suspended or sometimes withheld—even suppressed, as Monsieur Rousseau claimed.

The magnets pulled and pushed against his past as well. Perhaps, within the fresh vigor of this reading, he might discover in *Julie* answers to other questions, personal questions that troubled him, such as: was it possible for two people to understand one another, a true understanding beyond all artifice?

He looked up at Marianne. Beyond the edge of the book, she was perfectly still, listening. She'd stopped sewing, made no movements with her hands or feet, no small adjustments in her posture that might indicate her mood. "It's good," she said, smiling at the hoop on her lap. "I can't follow the French so well, but it's nice to hear your voice."

He returned to the very first letter, the first line, making a fan of the cut pages. In the light and heat of the fire, the book nestled in his hand like a captive dove.

I must flee you, Mademoiselle, I'm sure: I shouldn't have waited so long, or rather I should never have seen you.

The cathedral bells pealed the half-hour, the vibration swaying between the rooftops and the clouds. In Russia, the bells were different—they didn't swing but were fixed in their towers and struck by hammers so that the sound was a sharp crack.

Even so, Natasha lay asleep, subdued—not by death but a twilit, violet glow. Her lips were parted; finger-thick locks of hair drew across her cheek. Her arm was flung across the pillow, exposing a hemisphere of breast above the sheet, a breast that rose and fell with life.

He recognized the room—a room in Brest-Litovsk; the bed that held her was his own, and he was magically beside her. With a forefinger, he traced a line down her neck from her jaw to her collarbone and listened to her breath.

Her eyes fluttered open. "Am I so interesting?"

Before he could answer, she stretched and yawned, then sat up, a mass of dark hair falling around her shoulders. Her spine stood out as she hunched forward, clasping her knees, and with two fingertips, he climbed the hard ladder of bone.

"That's nice." She fell back into his arms, nestling against him.

"Natasha, what was wrong the other day?"

Two days past, she'd fallen into one of those fits of melancholy that seemed to paralyze her at times, a blackness that made her a different person, unreachable and frightening. In fact, this clandestine visit to his rooms appeared in large part to be an apology for that withdrawal of affection.

Instead of answering, she kicked back the sheets and rose from the bed. He watched, holding his breath as she walked naked over to the small armchair where his uniform lay. With a dancer's grace, she reached for the mentik, bringing it to her face, stroking her cheeks with the glossy fur collar. She slipped both her arms into it, pulling the sleeves up one by one to free her hands. Next she went to the other room and returned with the furred busby. She placed it on her head, and as she turned back, it covered her eyes and rested on her nose. Blinded, she laughed and reached for his trousers. On her hips, they were loose and low; the hems enveloped her feet and dragged on the floor. She tugged them up and sat down on the chair to put on the riding boots.

From the inside pocket of the mentik, she took out a short-stemmed, clay pipe, clamping it between her teeth. But the performance was not over. She frowned and removed the pipe to examine the bowl. Her little finger dipped inside and withdrew an amount of soot. At the mirror hanging on the wall she rose on tiptoe and brought her face close to the glass. With her finger, she wiped soot across both sides of her upper lip.

She turned to face me, staring as if out of a painting. I was aroused, but the arousal felt wrong; I wanted to shout at her to stop but could not. Lust made me paralyzed and swollen.

With the jacket open at her breasts, she pushed the busby back on her forehead. "From your places, charge," she said in a low voice, whispering the order that was usually bellowed.

"Who are you?" I said, feeling I might burst.

"Premier Major Ruzhensky, yours to command!"

"Alyosha, why did you stop?"

Across the width of the hearth, a woman stared at him with eyes like the sea.

"Did you fall asleep?" Marianne said. "Let's go to bed."

✠ ✠ ✠

The next night, he went through the section on St. Preux's exile to the Valois, the way he watched Julie's chateau from afar, picturing her behind the walls, engaged in simple activities. When Marianne drew thread through cloth, the needle made a slight pop in the area held taut by the hoop, and then the thread, a gentle sigh. He realized a favorite passage was coming up, one that had often comforted him, and he sped across the intervening words in anticipation.

The happy time had passed like a lightning flash; the time of disgrace has begun. Nothing will help me to know when it will end. Everything frightens and discourages me; a mortal languor seizes my soul. Without a good reason to cry, involuntary tears issue from my eyes.

His voice rang around the room, touching the fire, the face of his audience, even the page itself, but in a different way than he'd expected; it rang but did not catch. Had he misread it? He scanned the passage again. Even within himself, the words felt diminished and flat, and he became concerned that he'd spoiled something beautiful by excessive repetition.

The sounds of the sewing—the punch of the needle through the fabric, the snap made when a taut thread was bitten off—had stopped. "She's very gloomy," Marianne said.

He looked up.

Gloomy? No, she's taking it too literally; it's because she's not educated. I, on the other hand, have studied each page, each word, delving with a bright torch into the depths of their meaning.

Of course—not that he would ever admit it—but he had skipped over some of the long letters concerning the raising of children and management of estates—those omissions weren't relevant. "My dear, it's not about that, it's a story about how people transform themselves through love and—"

"Read more."

I sense, my friend, the crushing weight of absence. I cannot live without you, I sense it; it's what frightens me the most. A hundred times a day I search the places where we dwelt together and never find you there.

"You see? Isn't that beautiful?" he said, putting the book down. "Imagine the sentiment. And this is just before the first time they make love."

"He must go back to her then." She put the sewing down. "Alyosha, help me understand. She sends him away after they kiss; why is that?"

"Well, it's a test, to see if he'll obey her."

"Hmmm. And then she becomes sad and wants him back?"

"More than that, she falls ill and is near death, and it is her cousin who summons him back."

"Then they make love?"

"Yes, he and Julie do. But we're jumping ahead."

Marianne sniffed. "This man, I do not understand him. He's wasting his time being in love with someone far above him, someone he can never really possess. And she's toying with him, making him her fool. Pretending to be sick."

"No, no. Don't you see—it's beautiful and tragic because they can't be together," he said, impatient for her to understand.

"Read me more," she replied, wincing as if she'd poked herself with the needle. "Even though I think it's very gloomy. I also know how it will end—she'll marry someone else who's wealthy, and he'll be even sadder."

12.

Never abandon virtue, and never forget your Julie.

She reached across the bed but felt nothing but a region of cold between the sheets, as if a mold had been broken open and the casting removed. In an instant, she was fully awake; she parted the shutters, and her feet found the floor. Yesterday Valsin had been the duty officer, which meant he should have returned before dawn. Yet light filled the room, and he was not there.

Could war have suddenly been declared? He'd told her how, from the camps at Boulogne, they'd marched away to Austria on two hours' notice. But should such a thing happen again, he'd get word to her; he'd promised. In the other room, there was no saber and belt, only a faint smell of tobacco and leather. She dressed and went out into the corridor, hoping to find an officer who could tell her if something had happened, but no one else was present, and there were no muffled conversations to be heard behind closed doors.

On foot, she hurried downstairs and through the streets, making for the regimental stable. Her purse held the money left over from the sum Valsin had given her to buy food and wine—less than twenty francs.

How long will that last? And then?

A smiling gentleman in a frock coat blocked her path and then made way with an elaborate flourish of his hat. As she stepped past him, he murmured something she didn't catch, and she shook her head.

The rooms are paid up till the end of the month—a half bundle of firewood, two bottles of wine, a thick slice of hard cheese, and a heel of bread—that's all there is. Foolish to be caught unprepared. And if Valsin is gone, Dalhousie and Merseult will be gone as well. And Witkowski; I know no one else.

But the sight of the stable reassured her; there was no uproar of armed men dashing back and forth past lines of nervous, saddled horses. Only a single trooper exercising an officer's stallion, using the whip to force it into tight turns around an oval path in the yard. At the gate, two sentries slouched, following her with their eyes as she approached. "Where's Lieutenant Valsin?" she asked them, trying to meet their insolent stares with a stern gaze.

"Who wants to know?" one of the men asked.

"No, stop. It's her—the Lieutenant's lady, I told you," the other trooper said to his comrade. "Forgive him, mademoiselle, he's new. The Lieutenant went to his billet, I thought. To you."

In the large space within, a crowd of men in fatigue uniforms groomed a hundred horses, pitching hay, shoveling dung, and brushing glossy coats with hard brushes. The air was sweet with manure and oats and filled with voices. But when she stepped in from the entryway, all conversation stopped. Three of the soldiers put down their tools and moved toward her until a brigadier called them back. He was familiar—from the battle—and she asked him where to find Lieutenant Valsin. "The hayloft," he said. "I saw him heading that way. Go to the first floor, and you'll see a ladder."

Up the stairs, narrow side windows let in light and draughts of cold air. Around dozens of upright beams fitted with iron and gray cobwebs, there were piles of wooden crates with black lettering detailing their contents. Saddles, bridles, horseshoes and blankets. Cartridges and gunpowder. Overhead, footsteps slapped across thin flooring. A broad ladder at the back wall led up to a hole in the ceiling, and as she neared it, a column of dust and chaff floated down among the rungs, lit from above. She heard voices and began climbing.

Just under the flooring, she stopped, hanging onto the next-to-last rung. If he found out she was searching for him, what would he think? Whatever claim she had, whatever rights she'd won, it was certain she was no wife. She should leave; he was there—that was all she needed to know. Ashamed, she reached with her foot for the rung below. What if Merseult or one of the others saw her? They'd make him miserable with teasing.

"It's ruined, all wet," a man spoke from above. "Someone will pay." The voice was familiar—was it Merseult's? "It's lucky we discovered it. Listen, we'll get a detail up here to clean the whole place out and then dry it with sand."

It *was* Merseult; he must be referring to the hay; it was wet, spoiled.

"Get a fire going," another man said.

"A good thing we discovered it, and the way we discovered it was quite pleasant," Merseult's voice continued. There was a giggle, and a woman said something she couldn't make out, and then Merseult spoke again. "No, mademoiselle, we'll escort you ladies out first—through the back way. The Lieutenant will show you. But you'd better get dressed."

She drove with her feet, pushing her head and shoulders into the loft. In the angle of light from an unshuttered lantern, Valsin squatted on the ground, sniffing at a handful of straw; Merseult stood at his shoulder in front of a wall of hay. He wore no pants, and the tails of his chemise hung over his lean, white flanks. Valsin—wearing shirt and trousers—was the more dressed, the only sign of disarray the droop of his braces toward the floor.

They did not see her, nor did the two women whose clothes were strewn over several bales of hay. The light from the single lantern was yellow, and it made their nakedness red, made deep shadows below the mounds of their hips and the clefts between their legs. Their tousled hair was full of straw; the one closest to Valsin had even redder marks on her buttocks and back, as if her flesh had been pressed down against the hard floor, kneaded like dough.

The loft was hot and close with an odor of fermentation.

What is it like, to be taken in such a rough place?

Below her, footsteps sounded, and she scurried the rest of the way up, pulling at her skirts.

"Who's there?" Merseult said, turning and covering his nakedness with his hands. Without a word, the women began gathering their clothes.

Valsin stood up. "Mon Dieu," he said. "Where did you come from?"

"I was worried," she said, not looking at him. "When you didn't return."

"Listen, it's not what you think," Merseult said, reaching for his trousers. "My fault, you mustn't think that Valsin was—get dressed," he hissed at the women. "Get dressed and go downstairs. I was up here with these two ladies and called for him to come when I saw the hay was spoiled."

In a quiet voice, she spoke to Valsin. "I thought there was war, and you'd left, that you'd try to get word to me later. Would you have done that?"

"Who's she—his wife?" one of the women said.

"*Ma chère*, it's the truth," Valsin said. "You're upset. It's hot; I had my jacket off. I was just going to leave when the Capitaine sent for me. Let me finish, and we'll walk home."

She didn't listen to whatever else he said; she studied the women, trying to fix their images in her mind. They pulled on their clothes and picked at the straw in each other's hair, all the while darting glances at her. At a time now past, they had been prettier. On the floor beside Merseult's feet, two bottles of wine were open and empty. The women took two steps forward, eyeing her and then looking away. She realized they were waiting for her to step aside to allow them access to the ladder.

A pitchfork lay on the ground, its rusted tines half-buried in a heap of dirty straw, and she stretched out her arms with a casualness she did not feel, as if to show that the heat had affected her as well, made her innocent and harmless like a drowsy bee lulled by the keepers' smoke. Merseult gave a strangled cry and lunged for the fork, but she reached it before he could and spun it around in her hands.

The two women did not scream and hide behind the men the way many women would have done, women who were wives and could count on being protected. They backed away until one of them was able to reach one of the wine bottles, which she smashed against the floor to form a weapon of jagged glass. Merseult moved toward her with his hands outspread, but the woman brandished the bottle at him.

"Get out of the way," she cried and joined arms with her companion to advance on Anne-Marie.

Two steps closer, three, the floorboards thudded like a drum. She watched the bottle, saw how it trembled in the woman's grip. When it was thrust at her face, she put her weight forward to the left and slashed at the nearest leg with the fork. The woman screamed and fell, dropping the bottle to clutch at a knee bright with sudden blood.

Merseult took the bottle, watching the pitchfork. Valsin remained in the shadows, but she could make out the movement of his eyes. He emerged on slow, deliberate steps, right up to her, all the time staring into her face. "Give it to me," he said, grasping the fork, so they both held it.

"I wanted you to see how angry I am," she whispered, looking up at him and pushing the shaft close to his chest. "I wanted to show you with this, you understand?" She pushed harder.

☆ ☆ ☆

Afterward, walking down the street, she lagged behind him until he took her arm above the elbow, forcing her to walk alongside. "What—am I your prisoner?" she asked.

He glanced at her. "I think I am yours. You won't suffer me to stray, that's clear."

"If I'd come a half hour earlier or not come at all?"

"But you did. Let's get some wine."

At such an early hour, only a handful of workmen occupied the tavern they entered; an old man sat by himself, speaking into an empty beaker of brandy. She and Valsin were alone but not alone, and the unfamiliar surroundings were a distraction—a much better one than she would have found in the privacy of their rooms. There, without relief, she'd have been forced to listen to his stories.

"It did happen as I said; Merseult called me up to see the hay. He was drunk. What does that mean?" he asked, responding to her shrug. "You believe me?"

"Is it important that I do?"

"Yes."

She hesitated. To say she believed him would be to cede something, to give him another advantage when he already had many. "About most things, I believe you. This—I'm not sure. It's unfair of you to press me on it. So soon."

He nodded and raised his glass to her. "Believe that I love only you." He drank. "I'd be crazy not to. My God, the way you handled that pitchfork, like a street fighter. Where did you learn to do that? Merseult's face—it was...superb." He looked off to the left, shaking his head. Then his face turned dark. "You—"

"No, I—go ahead."

"What?"

"It's nothing." She knew why they were tripping over each other's words—not only a pitchfork but a saber flashed between them. "It's just that, when I thought you'd gone—"

"How could you ever think that?"

"Listen to me. Because you're all I have. No—don't misunderstand. I mean—besides you—I have nothing. Do you realize, when I woke and found you gone, I thought that you'd been called away on campaign, and that I had the rooms paid till the end of the month and twenty francs left over. Twenty francs between that and climbing into a hayloft with strange men."

"I would never leave so suddenly and—"

"I want to believe you. But—"

"Here," he said, taking his purse from his waistcoat and setting it in front of her. "Take it, take all of it, and when I have more, I'll give you that too. I won't always be in the army."

She didn't believe him, and while he went on—saying that someday, they'd go to America the way she wanted—she thought about taking money for love.

It cheapens love, that's what everyone says, but what if, instead of taking away its value, money reduces all love to different quantities of the same thing, a thing measured greater or smaller by the fee one receives? Is that the way whores think? No, they're past imagining love.

"Are you listening to me?" Valsin said. "You have that half asleep look you get sometimes."

Had she sold herself to escape oblivion? That was what concerned her—that she was like the women in the hayloft or that he thought of her that way. Bartered herself into love, was more like it.

She looked at him; he wasn't perfect, but her life was infinitely better than it had been six months ago. But when she'd saved him, when—out of a maelstrom of desperation—she'd killed the Russian officer at the battle, everything had shifted. If there'd never been an Austerlitz, or if she'd just waited in the tents while the men fought, she might have been able to let him go. But the killing had changed the terms, linked her to him with bonds stronger than those of marriage. She reached over to touch his cheek.

"What?" he said. "You forgive me?"

"Tell me more," she said. "About anything. Just don't stop talking."

13.

Tell me, my dear friend, in what language or jargon is the narration in your latest letter? By chance, might it not be anything but an instance of wit?

A knock sounded at the door, and he heard Yevgeny's part in a conversation of single words, then a clink of coins. Another letter had arrived, and with a rightward jerk of his head, he indicated it should be placed in the pile on the table. It was not necessary to examine it to know it was from his father; no one else knew where he was.

After a moment, he took it up. Like the others, the original inscription had been written in Russian and then translated to French in a feminine hand—his stepmother's. The weight of a single page. It was an old habit to slit the seal and unfold the paper, a habit that had been suspended.

23rd April

Alyosha,

I don't understand why I haven't heard from you. The War Ministry tells me you are still officially on leave in Munich and that other letters are getting through from there to Russia.

Have you located the man and killed him? I cannot find any peace until I know that he's dead; it's my only wish, my last chance for happiness. My health is bad; the doctor tells me he can do nothing, I exist in agony and anxious waiting. Please, settle things and come home; we have much to discuss. What if I should die without seeing you again! I await an explanation.

Your Father

He folded the paper in on itself and put it back with the others carelessly, causing the whole pile to topple over. Yevgeny hurried to set them right.

"Good morning, Alyosha." Marianne came in smiling from the bedroom, wearing the silk dressing gown he'd purchased for her, a man's gown that was much too large so that, as she walked, it dragged along the rug. She sat down on the sofa, curling her feet beneath her hips, her bare knees peeking out through the opening in front. "Will he bring me tea? What are you doing?"

"Reading some correspondence. Yevgeny, tea."

"You opened one of the letters from Russia? You said you'd let me see what the writing looks like."

He sat and gave her the letter filled with Cyrillic script. "It's curious," she said. "What does it say?"

"From my father. Here, do you see? This word—father. And here—my name." She looked from the paper to him, rolling her eyes as if he were teasing her. "You don't believe me, do you? You're so funny."

It was good—to keep the world of these letters at arm's length and as an object of humor.

But it's a mistake, to allow her to come so close.

"Well, what's it about?"

"I'll tell you the story. I haven't written him for weeks, and he wants to know why and what I'm doing here."

"Oh that. What will you say? You need his money; that's what you told me."

"True."

"Then you must write him—today. Tell him you love him and that you're learning all about Munich—that's it—you're receiving an education here." She laughed and dug her elbow into his side. For a moment they were silent, and she took the letter from his lap and studied it. "And this part" she said, pointing halfway down the page, "what does it say here?"

"He wants me to kill a man—a man who killed my brother in the war."

"It says that too?" Her eyes were steady and clear. "What will you do?"

He rose and took a turn around the room, stopping before the toiletry box on the table. He opened the lid and—ignoring the mirror—began looking in all the drawers and compartments, sticking his fingers inside to see if something might be hidden in the back. His father had mentioned a chance for happiness; could that justify murder? "About whom?" he said. "My father or—"

"The man who killed your brother."

"I've already tried to kill him once," he said, bent over, speaking into the empty drawers. "He's here in Munich, a French officer."

"He killed your brother in the war—but isn't that a soldier's job? Your brother was a soldier."

"I suppose he was."

"So your father wants this death out of vengeance—blood vengeance. Is that right?"

On the left-side bottom drawer, behind his father's original letter, there was a thing stuck against the back, a paper of some kind. He worried it loose with his fingernail and saw that it was a tiny corner of a bigger page, torn off. Curious to see if it retained any message or clue about its origin, he examined both sides.

"Alyosha?"

Both sides were blank. "I'm a bad man, my dear."

"No, if you obey your father's will, then you're good; that's what the priests say. What are you doing with those drawers? Come, write a letter to him. Tell him you love him and you'll do what he wants. Then we'll all be happy."

14.

I had to be what I was in order to become what I want to be.

That night, he had the dream about Durenstein. He'd gone to bed early, feeling tired, but as soon as he climbed into the bedclothes, it was impossible to get comfortable. The room was hot, and he kicked down the sheet and blanket, imagining the rough texture and give of a canvas camp bed in a musty tent. He turned from his right side to his left, then onto his back. Marianne's breathing became slow and regular; she was far away, and his mind pressed in with a hundred things.

There was no lack of money. His father was well-informed: the War Ministry had located him and had just sent on a half-year's accumulation of pay. And when he visited his father's agent, the paternal purse was always wide open. He knew his father. He would not cut off a son because of silence; silence was their accustomed state.

Yet he'd sat for an hour at the table with a blank sheet of paper, pen, and ink. *Dearest Father*, he'd written in Russian, feeling a numbing sense of repetition and disgust. Marianne hummed around his back, anticipating the scratch of his pen, of nib against ink bottle, sure he was about to produce a torrent of words, begging forgiveness, swearing renewed loyalty. But he could not do it.

All his life, he'd not just been Russian; he'd been Russia, his rank and uniform erasing all traces of whoever else he might have become. His uniform—the blue and silver of the Mariupol Hussar Regiment—was an emblem of proud men; to wear it was to enter something grander than one's ordinary mortal life. Every thread symbolized honor and responsibility, demanded respect.

Now he stood apart, naked, off the margins of familiar maps, a stream of unopened letters his only connection with that empty uniform. With great effort, pen trembling over paper, he'd recalled his father's estate, the manor house of timber raised off the ground to protect it from flooding, the fields of rye and wheat, the enormous reach of forest where lone travelers sometimes disappeared.

With a broad, slashing stroke of the pen—the same way he signed an order—he'd filled up the page with his name.

He rolled to his right side, laying the back of his left hand against Marianne's hair.

Perhaps being defeated by the French had caused him to adopt their way of thought, their habit of questioning authority. In his former life, the question of whether to obey authority would never have been posed. Obedience was the cornerstone of life in Russia. But during these past months, the entire natural order of things had been turned upside down. It was no wonder he'd begun to question authority—his father, the generals, the Tsar. He was someone new.

It must have been no more than a few minutes later when he entered the dream—the same dream that had plagued him for months, returning every few nights like a creditor pounding at a back door. The real events that it portrayed had lasted no more than twenty minutes, but the dream jumbled them up like the pieces of a child's wooden puzzle, putting the end at the middle, the beginning at the end, so that it was impossible to know how long it lasted. It often seemed that he woke up before it was over, surfacing for a few moments to gulp air before returning to the depths.

On its surface, there was a place between dream and sleep. He waited there, watching as a lethal mob of two hundred men and horses struggled around a French standard that shook and quivered in a storm, but the scene was flat, the colors saturated with gray, as if what he were seeing was a series of colored handbills advertising a drama. He tried to pull Pyerits's head around, but she was like stone. The awareness of dreaming began to leave him; the colors sharpened. Pyerits stepped forward and seemed to melt by stages into a different place, and from that moment to the very last, he and the dream were one, moving around a few fixed points in time that he would remember later.

His saber was a gory flail, forcing a pathway through the enemy ranks toward the embroidered tricolor. A presence lunged to his right—his sword made it disappear. From behind, a current of air moved against the breeze, and he turned, just in time, to avoid a slash. No longer full of brothers and lovers, the past had become only the moment before the last hoofbeat.

Aware of his advance, the French officer holding the standard cradled it in both arms. He drove toward him and—with his free hand—got a firm grip on the shaft and hacked with his sword at the officer's grip. Just as the flag started to slide free, other Frenchmen crashed into Pyerits from all sides, knocking him half out of the saddle.

Again and again, he cut at the standard-bearer's arms while bullets flew past his head like angry hornets. He brought his saber overhead and down—the most powerful of cuts—and sliced through both the officer's wrists. The Frenchman's mouth was a huge, round hole; past his teeth, his tongue quivered and strained.

The same dream to that point, the same horrifying repetition, but now there was something new. Below the Frenchman's metal helmet, framed by cheek guards of scalloped brass, it was Natasha's face that made a sound-less howl of agony. She held the stumps of her arms up, and warm blood splashed across his face.

The nightmare rode him to a place where blood ran everywhere, off her arms, the end of the French standard, his stirrups, the tips of his mustache. He looked at his palms and saw blood seeping through the leather of his gauntlets. Blood ran down his arms and legs and into his eyes; he couldn't see, and he couldn't hold anything. He couldn't speak because his throat had filled with blood.

"Wake up, wake up, what is it?"

A soft voice, a woman next to him shaking his shoulder, touching his face. Her hands were warm and clean, smelling slightly of soap.

"Alyosha, wake up. Dear one, it's all right. A dream, a bad dream. Lie down, here."

Marianne pulled his head down to her breasts. He resisted, and then gradually, the rigor left his shoulders and the back of his neck. His cheeks were wet, and he pulled back in horror, thinking he was bleeding on her. But the faint moonlight through the shutters showed only snowy flesh.

She pulled him close again. "You were choking. What was it?"

"Nothing—a dream, a soldier's dream, that's all."

In the morning, he slept late, and once awake, remained in bed. Through the half-open door to the other room, he could hear Marianne's clogs moving back and forth—a sweet sound that usually made the two rented rooms seem like home. Today her steps were like a wolf's pacing beyond a weakening fire.

Somehow there must be a way to sleep with her and not have the dream. He'd had other, older dreams of combat, and they'd run their course and gone away, as if the intensity of the experience proscribed a certain number of repetitions. This one would be no different. Perhaps every fourth night, he could sleep on the sofa and have the dream there, and she'd never know.

When he came into the room, she was sitting on one end of the sofa flipping the pages of a fashion journal. "I'll get you tea," she said. "You slept long; are you well?"

He sat on the other end. "A headache."

"Another letter came from your father," she said. "I told him to put it with the rest. Do you want to see it?"

"Not now." The room was hot.

She sat next to him and kissed his cheek. "I sent him out to do the shopping. You had the nightmare again last night—do you remember?" With the back of her fingers, she brushed the hair away from his left temple.

"No." He looked straight ahead and sipped the tea. "It's stifling in here; you put too much wood on the fire."

"I thought you liked it that way. I'll open the window."

"No."

She put her arm on the back of the sofa behind his neck. "Alyosha, the dream—what's it about?"

"I told you—an old battle."

"It's getting worse. You tremble all over, you yell; when I wake you, your hands shake—they're shaking right now. I'm afraid a demon has possessed you."

"A demon—no. It's not worth discussing." He got up and walked to the window.

She didn't say anything, and he turned around to see her sitting up straight, staring at him. Since she'd moved in, he'd learned a great deal about her eyes. They were often clear mirrors that showed his image in a particular way—intelligent, full of desire. At rare moments when she was distracted, he was able to see through them, glimpsing her deep within herself. But at that moment, they'd assumed a new configuration—tensed and half-closed, as if the sight of him pained her—a look he'd never seen.

"The man your father wants you to kill, the dream has something to do with him."

He stared at her a moment, remembering the dream and who appeared in it. "It's not that at all," he said, sitting down again beside her. "Listen, it's about a battle—a skirmish really, near a place called Durenstein, in Austria. I captured an enemy standard there and...and...there was a lot of blood. My brother wasn't present—in the dream, I mean. He was still alive when it happened."

She continued to stare at him. "You're not telling me the truth, Alyosha. This killing, it's the reason you came to Munich."

He glanced at the toiletry box on the table and remembered that his father's first letter of instruction was entombed there, the exhortation held within boundaries of paper and ink. But Marianne could barely read German, let alone Russian.

"Have you written him?" she said, crossing her arms over the bodice of her dress.

"No."

"You said you would—yesterday. You were going to say that you loved him, that you would do what he asked. Why haven't you?"

Like a chain of runaway carriages, their conversation accelerated, each separate part coming faster on the heels of the last. He took a deep breath and stood up. "Enough, all you've done since I rose is question me. My headache, it's even worse. You have no right to make demands on me, to question my behavior, to—"

"I should just be grateful that you took me off the streets, grateful for new clothes and food. Is that what you think? You want me to always wait for you, to stay here and smile and say, 'Ah yes, take me to bed, please.' And I do those things, don't I? But don't ask me not to care about you and worry, because I can't do that. I may be ignorant but that doesn't mean I'm stupid. If you keep ignoring your father, he'll cut you off. And then where will we be? You're like a cat who's forgotten how to hunt, an old pussycat who's growing fat by the fire. Stop being a pussycat and be a man."

15.

I have made a reckless commitment.

All morning, they argued about how he should go about finding Valsin. Marianne, being a woman, thought he should place a notice in one of the newspapers, say that he had something of value he wished to deliver, a letter or a bequest—a ridiculous notion that would only waste money. "Can't you just go to the French and ask where he is?" she asked—a good way to get arrested.

"No, the best course is to do what I've been doing."

"What's that?"

"When I go out in the morning—when I tell you I need some exercise—what I'm really doing is searching for him. And that's why I can't have you accompanying me; because if I find him, there will be a fight."

She rolled her eyes. "But it's taking too long, Alyosha. You've got to try harder. Listen, do you know what he looks like?"

"I'd recognize the uniform. The color—it's nearly the same as mine. And he's an officer, so I'm looking for an officer in a particular uniform."

Marianne rolled her eyes again, but it was agreed he'd begin taking longer walks. So, always in late-morning, he'd leave the building with stick and gloves, moving forward at a steady pace, disciplining himself to stay out of both the past and the future. Instead, he'd notice the great variety of people and horses abroad on the streets. After all, he thought, the hunter who's distracted by what occurred yesterday or might occur tomorrow will never find his quarry today. He didn't see Valsin—of course even if he had, he wouldn't have recognized him. At times, there were French officers about, even cavalry officers, even lieutenants, but no Valsin—he was sure. In his heart, he believed the time was not right.

One afternoon, he stopped before the shop of a military outfitter and spent several minutes gazing through the window at the display of gold lace epaulettes and full-dress swords. To him, it was a familiar world, a place where campaigns began, the beginning—the most exciting part.

He began moving away, and movement caught his eye; he realized it was his own reflection in the glass. A sigh left his lips; used to many campaigns, he knew how each had its own weight and life, a pulse that had to be respected.

Soldiers must wait for the proper moment for action. Until it comes, and the trumpets sound, dismount, get out your pipes—that's the way to stay sharp and prepared.

Marianne doesn't understand.

He opened the door of the shop and was startled by the sound of bells ringing above his head. Inside, two French officers were being fitted for shirts and paid no attention to his arrival. The proprietor spoke to him in German. "I'm sorry to be occupied at the moment, sir. Please look around, I won't be much longer."

He caught all the words and was pleased. A large display case held a variety of interesting objects, including a fine brass telescope, bound in leather, and a set of dueling pistols in a handsome case of dark, lustrous wood.

And a dagger—of course, traveling from Vienna, he'd had a brace of pistols at hand to guard against bandits. However, moving about the city on foot, the guns were too bulky to carry, particularly within the confines of fitted, civilian clothing. He shook his head and sighed; many days had passed since then.

A dagger would be lighter but just as lethal—although it would mean he'd have to close with his quarry to strike. Out of curiosity—once the proprietor had finished with the Frenchmen—he asked to see his stock of daggers.

"Daggers, sir?" the man said. "Of course I have many smaller blades— letter openers, tools suitable for manicure—if the gentleman will tell me the purpose?"

"Hunting."

"Ah, there are a few, yes. Over here." He led the way to a case near the entryway. Inside, there were knives of Oriental design with curved blades and handles of carved ivory—beautiful but impractical for the needs of a hunter.

"Anything else?" he asked. "Something more utilitarian."

The shopkeeper blinked and stooped down behind the case. When he rose, he presented a double-edged blade set in a leather-bound handle with a brass skull crusher fixed to the pommel. The weapon was a little more than a hand-span in length—small enough to be concealed.

He flexed the blade and felt its balance. "Very nice," he said in German. "Not quite what I had in mind, though. Do you have anything for a lady? Not a weapon—something pretty."

He bought a small sandalwood box, inlaid with silver leaves, and left, carrying the gift under his arm. At the next intersection, he turned left. To his right, in the large, ground-floor window of a dressmaker's shop across the street, he caught his reflection. With his coat and hat, carrying the parcel, he looked like a dandy—no, a husband. He imagined the guffaws of other soldiers, other comrades from his past, and turned back the way he'd come.

Alerted by the sound of the bells over the door, the shopkeeper looked up. "Is there a problem sir? The box you purchased—it's not satisfactory?"

"No, it's fine. I've decided I'll take the dagger after all."

✼ ✼ ✼

He heard her voice as he turned onto the second course of stairs.

"I'm saying they cheated you, old man. This bread is mealy; the beer is like piss." It was Marianne's voice, but the tone—sharp and shrill—was far different than the one he was accustomed to hearing.

"Are you listening to me?"

After a brief interval, Yevgeny could be heard saying no.

"I'll tell *him* I should do the shopping from now on. Do you hear? When he returns, I'll fix it, and you can go to hell—what? Don't you dare call me that or I'll—"

His arrival caused Marianne to hold back whatever threat she was about to make. She stood over a seated Yevgeny, who was pulling apart a loaf of bread and holding it up to the light. For a moment, the two of them regarded him open-mouthed, and then Yevgeny sprang up to take his coat and hat. But Marianne pushed him aside.

"Alyosha! My God, where were you? Is that for me? Listen, he's"—she flashed her eyes toward Yevgeny—"been to the market and gotten cheated. Again! I told you, the people see a soldier, and they won't bargain. They won't bargain, and they give him all the stale things, things no one else would want. Day-old, picked-over trash. I should do the shopping." She took one sleeve of his coat, Yevgeny the other, and for a moment, both pulled in opposite directions with surprising strength.

"Stop," he said, close to laughter. Marianne dropped the sleeve she held, yielding possession to Yevgeny, and seized the wrapped present instead.

"It's beautiful, I love it!" she cried loudly, tearing off the paper and examining the box from all angles. "And you got it for me? So sweet. It will be good for jewelry." She kissed him on the cheek and spoke in a low, silky tone. "So, a new plan: you'll give me the money for shopping, and I'll decide what we need and when to buy it."

"Let me think!" he said and pushed her aside. "My God, I'm only gone for an hour or so and return to this uproar. Yevgeny, my pipe. And you," he said to Marianne. "Be silent."

Marianne bowed her head and sat, taking up her embroidery as if nothing unusual had occurred. He sat by the fire and observed how she glared at Yevgeny when he turned from presenting the pipe.

Yevgeny had been his servant for ten years, campaigning with him in Poland and Turkey, attending him at the regimental headquarters in Berdichev. He was expert at foraging, at finding potatoes buried by peasants in the corner of a barn, wine disguised as vinegar, a stray chicken's trail. Upon their arrival in Munich, he'd taken up the duty of going to the market without comment.

Marianne was probably quite correct: she would be more skilled at getting fresh bread than an old Russian soldier who only spoke a few words of German and communicated most often by pointing and shaking his head.

But that wasn't the issue—revolt had erupted in his own household! Except for rare outings with him, Marianne generally remained in their rooms. She'd stopped visiting her girlfriends after he expressed his displeasure. If he allowed her to take over these new duties, it would provide her considerable freedom. Of course, she would never go out alone at night, but even during the day, there were many dangers.

For an hour, he ignored them both. Then he cleared his throat. "I have decided," he said, gesturing with the stem of his pipe. "Marianne will do the shopping. Yevgeny, you will accompany her to carry the parcels."

Marianne worked her delicate jaw and did not smile. "But—" she began.

"I have decided."

Yevgeny was impassive; that was his nature, to accept good news and bad with equanimity. Later, Ruzhensky stepped behind his old servant's screen and began to offer him some coins. "No," he said, interrupting himself. "Wait." He retrieved the dagger from the inner pocket of his coat. "Here, keep this for me."

Yevgeny bowed his head and accepted it with both hands.

16.

I know how to submit to lessons from friends.

His habit was to end his morning walk at the coffeehouse on the Kaufingerstrasse, near the central square, the place where he'd encountered Merseult and Crèpin. It was a calm sanctuary where strangers—both men and women—could sit side by side and not speak. One was among people without being with them.

He liked to arrive by one o'clock, order coffee and a roll, and then read any available French newspapers. The proprietor served the fresh-brewed coffee along with a glass of water, sugar, and a stick of cinnamon. For the price of a single cup, one could occupy a chair for hours.

That day, the air was charged with mountain scent, carrying tidings of rushing spring torrents and birdsong. He'd been late and for the past five minutes, had been stuck on a particular word in the newspaper that he didn't understand, a long word—a noun, he guessed—without which the sentence it appeared in was unintelligible. He folded the paper and put it down.

"Premier Major?"

He looked up. Two men in French uniforms stood by his table, inclining their heads toward him. He reached for his sword, fumbling at the empty space at his left side.

"It *is* him, Merseult, I told you. Monsieur Ruzhensky, we've startled you, please forgive us. Crèpin and Merseult—don't you remember?"

He stood, rubbing his hand in an exaggerated way on his trousers. "Of course, good day, gentlemen."

"It's quite a coincidence," Merseult said. "My God, I was just saying to Crèpin that I'd told Lieutenant Valsin about you. Hah! Perhaps I've conjured you. You are real?" He moved an extended forefinger toward Ruzhensky's sleeve, as if to touch him.

He didn't move but stared at the approaching fingertip until it came to a halt.

"Not a ghost?"

"Philosophy again," Crèpin said. "Don't be rude, Merseult."

"Please sit," Ruzhensky said.

Merseult was already seated and waving at the serving girl. "So, what news do you have?"

"I know nothing."

Merseult had intelligent eyes, dark like lodestones. "How do you find Munich?" he asked.

"It's a most pleasant place."

"It is pleasant, you're right," Crèpin said. "The mild winter, the food. The Bavarians are rather reserved, I think, but—"

"The women, the Bavarian women, they have such generous laughs," Merseult interrupted. "Have you noticed, Colonel Ruzhensky?"

"Premier Major."

"Ah. Of course, forgive me." Merseult assumed a serious expression and looked up, as if he'd prepared a recitation. "In the Russian cavalry, the rank of premier major indicates the commander of the second squadron. It's a position of great responsibility; the second squadron is the finest in the regiment, selected to carry out the most important tasks. A position of honor." He looked down and smiled. "You see, I've been studying things. I'm correct, aren't I. Yes. But you told us you were here on family business. Perhaps when your business is concluded, you'll have time for pleasure—or will you rejoin your regiment?"

"Oh, indeed, eventually. I'm officially on leave." The coffee was cool enough to drink from the cup, and he drank it slowly, eyeing the Frenchmen over the rim. As at their first encounter, the older officer, Crepin, appeared embarrassed by his companion's inquisitiveness, his companion, not at all. The surprise of the encounter and Merseult's immediate mention of Valsin had been jarring, but now he began to relax. "I may not have mentioned it the first time we met," he said. "But I myself was wounded at Austerlitz. Another few months, and I'll be recovered, I'm sure. Until then, I must amuse myself here."

"Then it's a sort of exile," Crepin said.

An exile, he thought, nodding, allowing a small smile to indicate the comment might be taken as humor. It was true; either through death or distance, he was apart from everyone in the world he used to inhabit.

Enough, I must make use of this opportunity.

"So, your Lieutenant—Valsin, you called him—I assume he survived the battle in one piece?" He took another sip, wondering what he'd do if they said Valsin was even now around the corner waiting to meet him. But no, he had his usual sense that Valsin, the real Valsin—not the phantom who stood at their shoulders—was still comfortably far away in the future. "I recall you mentioning his...remorse."

"Yes. Wounded, but fine—the dog," Crepin said, and he and Merseult looked at one another and burst out laughing.

"Now there's another story, Premier Major Ruzhensky, a happy one," Merseult said. "Valsin had a woman with him, a beautiful girl. The brigade commander himself made Valsin dress her as a Hussar to disguise her. At Austerlitz, she rode at his back and saved his life, cut down the Russian who was about to finish him off after he'd been wounded. Poor devil, a woman inflamed by love is a formidable foe. Of course, he—the Russian—had no idea." Merseult laughed again.

"It's the truth, Major—you should see your face," Crèpin said. "They're together now, quite happy, too."

"Together?"

"Yes, she came with him to Munich. Anne-Marie Fröelich—a widow, I believe—a Frenchwoman, quite remarkable. Their billet is close by."

After further attempts at conversation with their now-mute companion, the French officers excused themselves, exclaiming over how pleasant the meeting had been and that they looked forward to the next one—because, Merseult said, Munich is small.

For a long while after they left, he remained seated, making no response when the proprietor asked him if he required anything more. A woman began to mop the floor, slapping steaming water all around. When he shifted his feet to make room, she bowed and smiled, wringing out the mop into a wooden bucket.

He covered his ears with his palms. The past could not be sluiced away so easily; it persisted like the dirt in the water, sticking to him in a suffocating crust. What would he have to do to break free? Without ever showing himself, Valsin kept reappearing in stories told by strangers—the same way the dream kept recurring. The past pressed against him; if he wasn't careful, it would once again become his entire world; an oppressive, drowning one. On his way out, he took care to step clear of the puddles and gave the washerwoman a gold coin.

Flocks of birds swooped along and above the streets, racing to catch the last bits of the day. A sound of singing voices across the square drew him onward. Against a sky lit by a new moon, he saw the outline of the cathedral, its two towers crowned with onion-shaped domes.

Through large, iron-bound doors, he passed into cool darkness that smelled of incense and dust. An orchestra and several singers were gathered before the altar. Their everyday clothes made them appear to be visitors, drawn to the relics bathed in soft lamplight like icons. Their leader rapped his baton against a wooden stand, and the music began—a woman singing a soprano part, her voice soaring above the violin's accompaniment. She paused, and the instruments echoed her phrase twice before she resumed her song. It was—he became convinced—in Italian.

A door to the side of the church boomed shut, and in the silence, a phantom entered. Mischa.

The last time he'd seen him, he'd been dreaming of Natasha. It was just outside Olmütz; while the Tsar prepared to attack Bonaparte, he was asleep on the cot. "I must speak with you, Alyosha," a familiar voice had said. In a panic, he swam up out of sleep to see his brother's bulk darkening the entryway to the campaign tent. A muddy Hussar's cloak hung around his shoulders, and his shako sat crookedly atop his head.

With groaning disappointment, he bid farewell to the dream. His straining tumescence was an embarrassment, but it left quickly, like sleep. "Mischa, where have you been?" he said, pulling on his boots. After being wounded in a skirmish with the French, at a place called Amstetten, his brother had been sent north. "I went to the hospital as soon as I arrived, and they said you never reported there," he continued. That wasn't quite true. He'd taken a day to settle into Olmütz before checking with the hospital.

Mischa lurched into the tent, smelling of brandy. "Speak with you," he said. "I need your help."

"Are you drunk?"

"What of it?" He collapsed backward onto the cot and grabbed at Alexi's hands. "Please, need your help."

"Stop pawing me," he said, pulling his own hands away and noting the look of hurt on Mischa's face. "What is it?"

"Send me back to the regiment. I can't be on Bagration's staff anymore."

He sighed down to his boots, wishing there was some way to return to the dream. Outside, someone began singing about a red fox lost and far from home. "Mischa," he said, trying for a military tone, "I can't send you anywhere. It's not up to me where you serve."

"But if you'll intercede with the Prince, it'll make all the difference."

"What's this all about?"

"I have no more time to idle on the staff; my destiny lies elsewhere. I must fight as an officer in my regiment."

His meager ration of patience ran out, and he scrambled up from the cot. "Your regiment?" he shouted. "It's my regiment, you fool, and you're not fit to serve in it. Don't you understand? You go and almost get yourself killed, and now, with a head full of brandy, you call yourself a soldier? You're, you're—" For fear he'd go too far, he turned away.

"You're finished?" Mischa said in a flat, more sober tone. "I knew you'd be like this; you don't respect me. But you'll see; I'll prove my worth by my actions—if you'll give me the chance. I claim favor as your brother; one favor, I won't do it again." He got to his feet.

"Mischa, Mischa," he said, turning back to gauge the distance between the two of them. "I do respect you. It's just that, you're young. I worry. Father charged me with your protection." At once, his brother's face darkened. "But that isn't important," he went on. "I'll see what I can do—talk to the Prince. Trust me."

Mischa had opened his arms. Within his embrace, there'd been an odor, a man's odor of sweat and alcohol. As he left the tent, his voice had trailed back, "Is the rumor true? That we'll be marching south to find the French? Everyone is eager for a chance at single combat."

In Munich, the soprano part resumed. The song was quite delicate, and he was surprised he could hear it above the orchestra; perhaps the vaulted shape of the church amplified the human quality. The woman's voice shimmered around the pitch but always returned, always pure and exact.

His father believed that he'd been watching his brother, protecting him from danger; he'd failed but was forgiven—provided he'd take revenge. What if his brother had chosen his own path and no amount of diligence would have saved him—from himself?

Truly, the entire sequence of events, beginning with my brother's death up to this very moment, seems connected, set in motion by God's hand or by fate to show me something.

But what? It's a puzzle needing solving; a puzzle composed of living pieces— Crèpin, Merseult, Valsin, my father, even the mysterious Frenchwoman who wounded me—living pieces, not the dead.

Now a different woman began to sing, her voice different, a shade lower, like a darker-hued gold. She rounded the vowels until they were pulsing, lachrymose drops, and the violins echoed her singing with such dignity, such grace, the quivering of their strings finally falling into silence.

What if—by hearing the Frenchmen telling a different version of events—I'm being guided toward a greater truth? The past can be undone, little segments freed and pulled out of sequence in the same way that dreams are composed. If just one action, one leg of the course of things is missing—or another added—the ache of memory could fold on itself like a wave and recede into stiller, deeper water.

A third woman stepped forward—a third soprano joining in, singing a flowing line in unison with the second, with so much art that it was difficult to distinguish one from the other. The first singer stood clasping her hands, listening to the duet with an expression of satisfaction. Her part was clearly over. The orchestra reached a climax, and the music stopped, creating a sensation akin to having one's horse leap clear of a precipice, only to continue, floating high above a deep, sylvan chasm. Before there was any danger of descent, he left.

PART II

Munich, Midsummer 1806

1.

Henceforth, I'm at the sole mercy of fate.

In the coffeehouse on Kaufingerstrasse, he occupied a table set back from the windows. The French newspaper he'd been reading lay open and neglected; he was no longer interested in the never-ending chatter about the threat of war or the illusion of peace. The bells rang the quarter hour; once again, his daily hunt for Valsin had come to an end.

He'd kept to his regular route through the streets around the central square, as if he were conducting a patrol along the boundary between two sectors of a divided city. Munich was no longer unfamiliar. The engineer's hand-drawn map had become like any other old paper he no longer needed to consult; he'd stuffed it into the toiletry box and turned the tiny key in the lock.

Here, on his own, he could admit the truth: his campaign against Valsin was starved for intelligence. Once every few days, he might glance at the pile of unopened letters from his father—whom he had not written—but that had become a formality, like saluting the colors. A reckoning would come, he was sure.

This is what happens when an officer is assigned to a lonely outpost with no superiors to answer to. There are many stories—the most disciplined of men losing all motivation, drinking heavily, developing an infatuation with a local woman.

But it was enjoyable—living in Munich with Marianne, his pretty teacher. The spring was wet but had arrived much earlier than in Russia, the food agreeable. Despite the blustering of all of Europe's emperors, there'd been no notice for him to return to duty—and for that he was grateful. He needed more time, more time away from the military, from Russia.

His cares were confined to particular times and places. When he returned from his walks, there was a moment when she'd catch his eye, and he'd give a tight shake of his head and see disappointment and worry on her face. And then at night, in bed, he still traveled to Durenstein and the dream of blood, struggling out of sleep drenched with sweat and grinding teeth, trying not to wake his lover.

In the mornings, before she rose, he'd drink tea and think about the woman who'd wounded him—a woman dressed as a man. Hard to imagine what sort of woman could behave so murderously, consorting with soldiers in such a way—surely a woman unlike most others, unconcerned with convention and propriety. He'd known women like that, women who followed the army, but they'd always been coarse, their beauty desiccated like flowers pressed into the album of an old maid. Yet the Frenchmen had described this one as beautiful. And dressing like a man—of course it wasn't unheard of, but the idea produced an uncomfortable sensation in the pit of his stomach, fascinating and wrong all at once.

When the past troubled him, he tried to apply his new strategy, adding in the new parts he'd learned from Merseult and Crèpin. It did help, but he wished he had a greater supply of fresh information. In fact, some days he wished he really could find Valsin to learn yet another version of what had happened. Other parts of his past—the ones containing Natasha—plagued him because they seemed fixed, as if they'd been written in stone.

His newspaper was nearly swept off the table. Accompanied by a rush of fresh air from a summer storm, a man and a woman had burst through the door. They stamped their feet and brushed rain off their shoulders, adding to the puddles of water already on the bare floor. The woman said something in French. He took a deep breath and, grasping the newspaper, raised it to hide his face and peer over the edge. The couple's faces were ruddy and shining from the downpour. They sat down two tables away and called for coffee and bread.

The man faced him. He wore a pale blue stable jacket and trousers—the fatigue uniform of an officer of the cavalry. His mustached face was full, his color good, but when he accepted a coffee from the servingwoman, his movements were stiff, as if he were recovering from a wound.

The woman was different than he'd imagined, taller, more substantial, with a fine neck and shoulders. Her hair was combed and tied back, bare of bonnet, gleaming with a luster in the early afternoon light. Surely it was the weather that had put color in her cheeks and a sparkle in her eyes. The man leaned close and whispered something in her ear—some intimacy—and she laughed.

His heart was beating so hard he glanced at his chest to see if it was pushing out against his jacket. With his palm, he covered the lower part of his face and eyed a passage through the tables toward the door, a passage that would take him in a wide arc around these invaders from his past.

Then it was clear: there was no reason to slip away or even to shield his face; if it were Valsin and the woman, they wouldn't recognize him. How could they? It had been more than six months since the battle and only an instant when they'd all come face-to-face. He lowered his hand and turned back in their direction. The officer met his eyes, and he held his breath. But the man nodded and turned back to speak to her. He could hear her reply.

"What? He said that? No, I don't believe you."

The cathedral clock began pounding out the new hour, and as if the whole world were hurrying along, waiting impatiently for him to catch up, a troop of cavalry clattered past on the cobbled street outside. With a sense of the importance of the moment, he pressed it all into his memory, wanting to jam it down with his thumb like a mark in an account book, an account not yet closed.

His chair scraped against the plank floor, causing the couple to glance his way—he'd stood without being aware of it. The pulse in his temples beat, and a small, tingling cloud obscured his vision. It faded, and he found himself maneuvering forward, committed.

Often, in the quiet solitude of late evenings after Marianne had retired, as the fire seethed and rustled, he'd rehearse what he would say when he and Valsin met—if they ever met—trying over and over for the correct inflection, aloud. A flow of words and posture that refused to be evoked now. He stopped before them, feeling that the momentum from walking across the room threatened to carry him further so that he might lose his balance and crash into their table.

"Excuse me," he said, clearing his throat and forcing himself to stand straight. "I'm sorry to intrude." Much to his surprise, the words came to him on the spot—not the ones he'd planned but sufficient. "I couldn't help overhearing you speaking in French. I'm trying to improve my command of the language and wondered if I might talk with you a few moments."

The woman looked up at him, the edges of her mouth lifting in a small, expectant smile. She was pretty and graceful—not at all a rude and bedraggled camp follower. He forgot all else and smiled back, the bells continuing to clang within.

The young officer cleared his throat. "You're most welcome to join us, monsieur." He rose and made a small bow.

Inspiration dry, he hesitated and then returned the bow. "Please, excuse me—I'm Alexi Ruzhensky."

The woman offered her fingers the way a lady would. "Anne-Marie Fröelich, monsieur." For an instant, he was absorbed and forgot about her companion. Their hands touched, and he shivered—the last time she'd touched him had not been so long ago.

"Lieutenant Louis Valsin, at your service," the Frenchman said, still standing. "You're Russian, monsieur?"

"Yes."

Valsin motioned him to take a seat. The servingwoman brought over his coffee, and he was grateful to have something to weigh down the trembling.

"So," Valsin said, "how does a Russian gentleman come to Munich?"

"Business, family business. An acquaintance of my father's—well, it's a long story." He crossed his legs, imagining a theater of insincere gestures. "You're a cavalry officer, are you not?"

"I am, as you are yourself, if I'm not mistaken," Valsin said, looking mostly at his coffee.

He couldn't help smiling. "You're not. How could you tell?"

"Your mustache, your bearing. It would be hard to miss."

"I'm a premier major in the Pavlograd Hussar regiment, a squadron commander."

"You fought at Austerlitz?" she asked.

"Yes," he replied, feeling reckless. "I suppose it's possible we fought each other." His eyes swept from one to the other.

Valsin stared at him for a moment and inclined his head. "I have no quarrel with you now, Premier Major."

"He was wounded there," she said.

"I'm sorry. I myself was wounded—there." All caution gone, he grinned at her. "One of your Hussars put his sword in me."

Shock fixed her face, and whatever theater he'd imagined the three of them involved in was suspended. Not only had he been crude, but he'd also left himself completely exposed. Surely they'd see right through his civilian clothes; they'd recognize the scar she'd made. This woman, she was more than a figure from his memory, his imagination; she was flesh and blood.

"Please excuse me," he said, pushing back the chair. "I meant to say—I was wounded and then taken prisoner. I'm here in Munich to recover. And to conclude some business." His voice trailed off, and he covered his mouth and upper lip with his palm.

"Of course," Valsin said. "You know, your French, it's not bad."

His head throbbed again. They hadn't noticed.

"It's true," she echoed. "Where did you learn?"

Her eyes were like delicate enamel saucers with painted umber centers. "You're too kind. I'm sure my accent sounds dreadful." At this, they both made elaborate sounds of protest, and he smiled. "As a child, I learned your language. My father felt it was important to know French, and he was quite correct. I only wish I could be more fluent."

"And where did you grow up?" she asked with slow and exaggerated distinctness. His French must be worse than they'd given him to believe.

"Near Kiev. Do you know it?"

Valsin nodded and finished chewing a piece of bread. "Great horse country, isn't it? Someone told me that."

"Yes. We're now near Brest-Litovsk; our estate is on the Polish frontier."

"Ah, you must be wealthy," she said. "An aristocrat."

For a moment, he was on guard again, wondering if they were about to begin a political attack. "Modestly so," he replied. "It's my father's property, of course, but someday it'll be mine."

"You have brothers?" Valsin asked.

"No."

Valsin said something about how that was fortunate. "I must ask you," Ruzhensky began, inhaling deeply like a racehorse at the final stretch, sensing the need for additional speed. Her face shone; she nodded as if to encourage him and pushed a loose lock of hair away from her brow. "Just the other day I fell in with two French officers—two Hussars, in fact—and we got to talking. They told me about a lieutenant in their regiment who'd fought at Austerlitz, and his companion, a beautiful blond lady, they said. Could they have been referring to you?"

"Do you remember their names?" Valsin said, glancing at her.

"A Capitaine Merseult and a Chef D'Escadron Crèpin."

Before he could get out the second name, Valsin nodded. "Yes, of course we know them. And they told us about you. What a coincidence."

"What did they say?" Anne-Marie asked. "About us."

"A most extraordinary story, mademoiselle. That you fought at Austerlitz as a man. Can that possibly be true?"

Color went to her cheeks and forehead, and she looked at Valsin and then down at her hands.

"I hope I haven't offended you."

"It's true, Major," Valsin said. "Anne is shy about it, though. Isn't that right, *ma chère?*" Her face shifted as she glanced at him, passing through concern to question, and then, as if she'd reached some decision, she extended both palms and shrugged. Valsin put his arm around the back of her chair. "There's more to the story; she's too modest to boast of it, but she saved my life." Ruzhensky made himself look impressed. "I was leading my men forward when I was shot. A Russian officer attempted to finish me, but Anne cut him down and pulled me out of the mêlée."

That expression again—cut down, as if men were stalks of wheat for the harvest. A buzzing began in his ears, and he felt the three of them taken up from Munich and transported, backward through the months to the battle they'd shared. Again, his throat burned with gunpowder; again, Chernigev, the lieutenant from the fourth squadron, shouted.

"Premier Major! It's him, Valsin!"

Could it be?

In the wild combat of the last quarter hour, he'd forgotten Valsin. The trumpets were signaling retreat. Someone thrust at him from the side, and he turned and fired his pistol, making a face explode in a cloud of bloody mist. He pivoted back around and saw this Valsin—the same man who now sat across from him—strike down a corporal from the second troop, his features drawn into a fierce grimace as he retrieved his bloodied sword.

Is that how he killed Mischa? He looks ordinary—black hair, white teeth, two arms, two legs—just like me. Let's get on with it—if my bullet finds him, fine—if I miss, then it wasn't meant to be.

He drew the other pistol from its holster, and his voice cracked as he screamed, "You, Valsin! My brother!" Without taking aim, he fired.

His target staggered in the saddle, and he felt a wash of satisfaction. Through his glove, the leather grip of his saber was cool, the weight of the blade full of deadly promise. Pyerits moved forward, and he brandished the sword at his victim, who waited like a wounded stag for the huntsman's knife.

But a fierce war cry died on his lips; a sudden image of Natasha, of the last time he'd seen her alive, overwhelmed him. Her voice spoke in his ear, "Has our love meant nothing to you?"

Why think of her now, here—of all places?

He'd felt himself lose momentum, his arms and legs caught by invisible threads, and then another horseman crashed into him from the side. In annoyance, he looked over and saw, too late, the questing sword. The point passed through his jacket and into his side. There was no pain, just a sensation of being struck hard, of losing his breath, an awareness of being interrupted. The last thing he'd remembered was a face, smeared with soot and powder, and a woman's voice crying, "No!"

A clatter of cups broke memory's spell. The other two still sat, Valsin examining his fingernails, and she stirring her coffee. Then she looked up and met his eyes, arching her eyebrows and smiling, and he felt she knew, knew who he was, but chose to ignore it—no—accepted it.

"I'm...I'm astonished," he stammered. "Mademoiselle, I have no desire to embarrass you, but I must salute your courage." And he did feel a swell of admiration for her. Men were trained to be soldiers, drilled and beaten to ignore death, but she had had none of that discipline.

How frightened she must have been.

"No." Her shoulders rose and fell. "Thank you, monsieur, but Valsin is right; I'm uncomfortable about what happened. I'm glad I did it. I would do it again, but not because I'm a soldier—I'm not. I had to protect him, that's all. I'm not sure many understand the difference, I mean between being a soldier and being a...a woman."

So far, it was the most she'd said, and her intelligence and grace dispelled any remaining traces of his discomfort. "I believe I understand you, Mademoiselle Fröelich. May I point out, however, that it's the true heroes who deny their heroism. It's easy to spend years boring everyone with stories of exploits dressed up after the fact. Your modesty makes your deed all the more admirable."

He was being ridiculous.

How could she know who I am? Who could recognize someone from a few instants spent under extreme duress?

Only—she looked at him and smiled and looked down and then up again, as if she wanted to see if he continued to watch her.

"Well, Premier Major," Valsin said. "How do you find Munich? For us, it's good. The Bavarians remain our allies and only resent our presence a little." His flat stare belied his hearty words; it was clear that something had disturbed him.

"Of course," he hastened to respond. "I like it too, although I'm surprised by the coolness of the nights." Had Valsin remembered?

"But surely you're used to the cold," she said. "Being from Russia."

Before he could reply, the young French lieutenant examined his watch. She looked at him, a searching glance he did not return, and then sat straighter and took a sip from the bottom of her coffee cup.

"Major," Valsin said, pushing his chair back, "you must excuse us; I've enjoyed our conversation very much, but I've lost track of the time—an appointment, you see. I hope we may meet again."

"Of course, I too have enjoyed your company." Valsin had risen half-way, his eyes focused on the far side of the room, and Ruzhensky took the opportunity to study her. She brushed a wisp of hair from her left temple and made a quick, nervous smile, which expressed—he was sure—that there were things that could not be expressed in such an abrupt moment of transition.

"May we meet again," he continued. "After all, Munich is not so big."

For some time after they'd gone, he remained, running through each moment of what had just occurred.

Then, after a glance to either side to be sure no one was observing him, he saw them as they'd appeared across the table. He smiled at her, in the same way Valsin had, and pronounced her name out loud with the younger man's inflection. He said it again and reached for the coffee cup she'd used. With both hands, he held it cradled and raised it to his lips but did not drink.

2.

My friend, consider yourself, myself, what we were, what we are, what we must be.

The next morning, he woke to the sound of Marianne's voice, soft and grainy with sleep. "You're awake, Alyosha?" she murmured, pressing her hips into his belly.

With a sigh, she reached into the space between them to grab him in her fist, rubbing him against the upper swell of her hip until he was full and hard. He strained across her and touched the slight, swollen mound between her legs, stroking the petals there until they opened and he felt warm moisture running. Her hair smelled like tea.

She twisted all the way around and swung her right leg over his left, holding her chemise high and putting her knees into stirrups formed of tangled sheets. A pause, and as she bent over, slipping him inside, her hair fell onto his face and tickled his lips. She began to post, closing her eyes, her face half-hidden behind a veil of silver hair. As she arched her back, he reached up to fill his hands with her breasts.

With the rider so absorbed, the horse left its course and the realm of truth by a hand's breadth, enough to veer into a different territory—a different pasture perhaps, where it was also morning, and he also lay on his back in bed.

Everything was the same, except it was the Frenchwoman above him, her skin that was reddening, her breath quickening, her womb enclosing him like a plush purse around a tower of golden coins. Then the reins were tugged, his hips squeezed, and they galloped.

Afterward they both slept a little more. He woke first and considered the idea of a gift for the woman beside him. Last night, he'd returned and said nothing about what had happened, even when she'd complained about him being gone so long and then of how quiet he was—like an old bear.

A dress was sure to please her, although he'd already given her so many. They were jammed into the trunk in the bedchamber, spilling out of the open lid in a riot of color—an extravagance that perturbed Yevgeny, who was accustomed to military order. Jewelry was a good choice—something blue to match her eyes. Natasha's sapphire ring; should he give it to Marianne? No, that would be like mixing gunpowder with flame. Although he no longer wore it close to his skin, the fire in the stone remained alive. Someday he'd have to decide what to do with it; in the meantime, he'd put it in one of the hidden drawers of the toiletry box, out of Marianne's sight.

He sat up in the bed, pulling the pillow behind his back. At Austerlitz, he'd lain in a similar posture, propped against the cold wall of a field hospital. But instead of a sheet of light cotton, thick bandages had been wrapped around his waist. He'd woken to find rough hands rifling through his pockets, so greedy they'd missed the ring hanging around his neck.

The hospital had been located in a church; at first he'd wondered if he were dead and in the afterlife, a sort of purgatory where the dying awaited their final ascent to heaven. Did the afterlife start out in church? No, and in purgatory, the attendants wouldn't speak French. He wiggled his toes and touched himself to confirm that he still possessed both arms. Yes, he was intact, but a heavy ache hung along his right side.

Two voices had risen above the murmurs of the wounded, shouting in French on the other side of the nave. He heard the name Valsin. *Valsin*, he thought, startled. *Here? Could it be the same man?*

I killed him, though.

And then a woman's voice had joined in.

He shook his head. To have to kill Valsin again was disturbing—once was enough.

It's as if I've been an animal being led to slaughter, dragged toward a fate I no longer comprehend. To do my father's bidding, I've had to be a puppet instead of a man, a doll with movable arms and legs that only represents a person, a puppet clad in merchant's garb.

He pushed back the covers and put his feet on the floor. He'd found Valsin, but now that he had, it would be another secret he'd keep locked away.

3.

I don't know if you remember the strange speech you spoke to me last night, and the behavior that you accompanied it with.

Early in the afternoon, she heard shouting outside and recognized Valsin's and Dalhousie's voices. "Bring your cloak and boots," they cried. "We're taking you riding." There was only a moment to wish for a cleaner dress. She put on the old pair of boy's boots she'd found at the market and arranged her hair to spill out behind her bonnet over the cowl of her cloak.

On the street, the two men were laughing and joking, a chestnut mare bridled between their own mounts. "Good day, my darling," Valsin said. "Our parade ended early, and it's so lovely we thought we'd take you for a ride in the country. Let's go." He wore no headgear, and his hair was loose, shining in the sun. She licked her dry lips and took the mare's reins.

"Anne-Marie," Dalhousie said, exhaling a cloud of bluish pipe smoke. "You won't be too bored—coming with us? Is your baking done, your sewing?"

She flashed him a smile and hoisted herself up on the chestnut's saddle in a swirl of skirts, swinging a booted leg over and settling both feet in the stirrups. She would ride as a man would—embracing the animal with her form. With these two, she was past blushing.

Valsin clucked at Lily and led them down the street. Anne-Marie gave a gentle squeeze to her mare's flanks and, passing Dalhousie, moved forward to ride alongside Valsin. She watched him, taking her time, the way lovers do—without the interruptions required by flirting or shyness. In the space between them, the wind blew bits of straw and light, and their animals' iron-shod hooves clattered against the stones.

Some things about him were well defined—a face and a name, a voice—but much remained to be filled in. When would he become familiar?

Well outside the city gates, they passed beneath a shelf of clouds, and shafts of light struck a distant hill, creating golden bars possessing the morning's slant. Mist clung to the lowlands while the sun lit the higher ground rust and yellow. War had not cast its mark here. The fields held neither discarded cartridge bags nor hidden bones. A young boy drove a flock of geese along the lane and froze, regarding the three of them, open-mouthed and still.

"Can we expect the country people to be friendly, Ètienne?" Valsin asked. "I think we look more like brigands than soldiers."

"We'll spread a bit of your money around. That's the best way to make friends. But we'll keep our swords loose in the scabbard."

Wooden wheels from generations of carts and wagons—not cannon—had creased and broken the road, and the recent rains made it awash with mud and pools of water, slowing them to a walk. The air smelled of pine and animal dung, and the mist entered the folds of her already damp clothing to lay close, chilling her skin and putting a curl in her tangled hair. They climbed higher and emerged onto drier ground where, without a word, they broke the horses out into a long gallop.

After a rush into the wind, her mare tired, and only then did she release her grasp of the animal's neck. They slowed to a walk, and she looked up, squinting into the burnished glare of the sky. High above the earth, white wisps floated, shaped by the wind into whorls of lace—tatted filigrees from a wealthy woman's bonnet reaching down to grace the matte-finished earth. Despite the sun's height, trails of mist still wove through a line of trees like small, ancient streams, and she imagined them carrying away toasted, orange-colored leaves, leaves that might travel immense distances to finally be placed gently, kindly, on some older, warmer bank. A dog began barking somewhere close by, startling her into watchfulness. But the three of them were alone, alone with the sound of the horses clip-clopping along, the jingle of the harness, sounds as familiar as the sensation of breath passing through her nose.

In the fields, the last year's dry husks and rotted leaves had been plowed under and the vineyard frames repaired and straightened. A farmer would read these signs in an instant, knowing what had been planted and whether the year held a promise of bounty. But she was no farmer and paid little attention to such things. She possessed a different talent, born from a lonely person's imagination: how to dream a thing with so much force it becomes real.

In the late afternoon, dense clouds crowded away all traces of the sunset, and it began to rain. Far across a field, a man in a broad hat and white smock stood motionless and silent, recognizing them as French, but—she was sure—unwilling to make any acknowledgment. She pulled the cowl of her cloak tighter and hunched her shoulders.

Out of the darkness, an inn emerged as a gathering of light. Its pale, whitewashed walls were framed in oak and busy with the shadows of the stable boys who took charge of their steaming horses. From the outside, they could hear a roar of voices and clattering plates within.

A sea of flushed faces turned up as they stepped through the door. Valsin made a show of his sheathed sword, but there was no danger here—the tavern contained families, the parents eating and drinking while children played at their feet. An old mutt of a dog padded over and sniffed Dalhousie's boots, finally starting its tail in a one-sided wag.

A middle-aged man rose to his feet and approached. "This is my inn," he said to Valsin. "What do you want?" Each word was spoken with great care, as if the extra effort and time taken would help the foreigners to understand.

"Wine, mein herr," Dalhousie said. "It's wet outside and dry within."

The man blinked in confusion, and then, with a slight bow, clapped his hands and issued instructions. Men at a table by the hearth dispersed without complaint, and the three of them were led to the empty seats. A serving girl appeared bearing a clay decanter and three clean glasses.

Throughout the room, conversations resumed, albeit from mouths covered by hands. Still, she heard snatches: "They're French…a woman—she's with them." She removed her sodden bonnet to dry near the fire and shook out her hair, letting it spill over her shoulders like pale straw strewn with tiny jewels. Her blouse was wet and clinging, giving a shape to her waist and breasts. When Valsin pulled out a chair for her, she pressed his arm and laughed, playing to the crowd's sidelong glances. Valsin and Dalhousie also played, pouring the wine, slurping it, holding the half-filled glasses up to the firelight, as if they could see through the velvet opacity. On the wall above where they sat was a print of the Battle of Stockach—a French defeat at the hands of the Austrians.

"That's wrong how they showed that," Dalhousie said, squinting. "I knew men who were there; they saw what happened with their own eyes. Our infantry was never driven back until the very end."

"À merde. What does it matter now?" Valsin said. "Let's not talk about war tonight." With the day's business long since concluded, his uniform was full of wrinkles. He slouched on the chair, loosened his neckcloth, and looked at the corners of the room.

"Then what should we talk about, monsieur—truth, the beauty of women?" Dalhousie asked.

"The beauty of Frenchwomen. You as an example, Anne—what is it?"

"Nothing," she said, smoothing her face. For a moment, she'd seen him as other women did, as she once had—a handsome, reckless officer.

"Maybe you're still mad about Merseult's hayloft party," Dalhousie said. "Oh, yes—I heard all about it." His eyes pierced like a shard of sunlight in a forest glade.

"Shut up, Ètienne," Valsin said.

He wouldn't look at her—from shame, she hoped. "I'm not mad," she said. "I'm happy."

"Sure, now you are, you're with two handsome Frenchmen. Better than those Germans."

The Fröelichs were horse traders who'd kept a stock of blame toward her, as if their son had died not from typhus but sorrow. She was to redeem herself through work. "When soldiers come, hide yourself"—that's what Fröelich said—but she found ways to be seen; it was a kind of rehearsal—a rehearsal only, not a performance as the old man believed. When soldiers did come and saw her, they became enchanted but not tame, staring with shining eyes, assuming the roles of cavaliers just as she took on that of a coquette, learning the part well until, with Valsin's arrival, the rehearsal had ended.

"Are you still glad?" Valsin said. "That we took you away?"

"Thankful, you mean—of course." Why had he asked her? It was long ago that the two of them had appeared, battering in the door. "I was desperate."

"Well, see—anything's an improvement then," Dalhousie said. "Even living with this character."

"Anne and I encountered a Russian officer the other day," Valsin said. "The same one Merseult described—you remember? He'd heard our story, about the battle; Merseult and Crèpin must have told him about that too. He was very impressed—and infatuated with her, I'm sure."

"Ah no," she said, blushing.

"What's he doing in Munich?" Dalhousie said.

"That's what I asked. I don't remember his response. Do you?" he said, turning to her.

"Family business." When the Russian said he'd fought at Austerlitz, she'd felt a chill in the back of her neck. "He was a gentleman," she said. "He looked like Valsin, only older."

"Maybe you have Russian blood," Dalhousie said.

"He—the Russian—told us he wanted to improve his French," Valsin said. "Anne, what did you say—that he looked like me? It's odd when you meet someone like that. Maybe we're not all as different as it seems. Maybe," he said, straightening up and placing his elbows on the table, "in every country, we have a double, someone who resembles us, who—"

"No, no. Not just resembles us, is exactly like us," Dalhousie said. "Exactly, down to the same shade of eyes and hair, and—"

"And you're not supposed to ever meet them, because if you did, it would change everything. The whole world would change." Valsin looked pleased.

"What about scars?" The two men stared at her with parted lips, as if she'd halted them from racing ahead, brought them to earth, and they didn't know the reason. "Scars. If you had this double, would he have the same scars as you? Because that would be hard. You'd have to have had the same things happen to you, the very same."

"Did the Russian have scars?" Dalhousie said.

"I don't think it would be like that," Valsin said. "That your double would be exactly the same. It would be enough if he resembled you in general terms."

"Yeah, maybe if you both shared a few habits, like the way you cut your meat. Or if you liked blonds."

"He did say he was wounded," Anne-Marie said. "I remember, wounded at Austerlitz. So he must have scars—at least one."

Valsin poured them all more wine. "You're right. No one could be exactly the same. Drink up. And we were going to talk about the beauty of women." He reached across the table and took her chin in his palm. "The way you look, you could have no double."

"What about children?" she said, putting her hand under his, keeping it pressed close while she spoke. "They're a kind of double, don't you think?"

"No, children may look like you, but they have minds of their own," Dalhousie said. "Besides, they're so fragile."

The men continued talking, and she thought about fragile, helpless beings.

With their own minds—yes. Do parents make children to replace themselves? To extend themselves out across time, past the end of life—doubling the heart so another keeps beating after your own has stopped? It would be a comfort, a value different from coins kept hidden in a purse.

"Anne-Marie," Dalhousie said, "at Austerlitz you saw the advance of Lannes' Corps—when the Russian cavalry attacked. Maybe the officer you met was among them."

Valsin turned away. Her presence at the battle, her involvement, were subjects he didn't like to discuss. She knew he felt ashamed that a woman had saved him, saw how he often searched the faces of other men for signs of contempt. The other day she'd been surprised at how open he'd been with the Russian. Afterward, he'd been angry and closed.

It was only in public that others might refer to her deeds, as if in acknowledgment that they had been public acts, belonging to others in a different way than other acts did, as private acts like lovemaking belonged only to them. Whenever she contemplated talking with him about Austerlitz, the carnality of what she'd accomplished with her sword arm silenced her; it was a carnality more personal, more private than any physical insertion of himself into her depths.

Sometimes she tried to make sense of what had happened and wished she could talk to him, to have him explain, but since the first few days when he lay in the hospital, those events had become unspoken things between them.

"He's talking about the battle," Valsin said, jerking his thumb at Dalhousie. "A different subject to see if you were listening. She's forgotten."

No.

On the far left flank, she'd been on a hillside among hundreds of horsemen drawn up in columns, so close that each man's knee touched his neighbor's. In front of all the rest, a score of trumpeters stood, their horns reflecting the pearl gloom of the sky.

The horsemen began pointing, and she followed the line of their gestures. On the meadows below, a stream of blue and white trailed out of sight to the south, accompanied by the roll of drums and waves of cheering. But the stream was not flowing away but spilling over its eastern bank like a flood, rolling forward toward a cloud of mist and dust. She stared harder, shading her eyes from the glare; the stream was made of men, arrayed in ranks bright with shining steel.

"If you're a soldier," Dalhousie said, "you must tell stories, reminisce. It's fine if you don't remember things the same way each time."

"Who would know?" Valsin said. "Anyway, she's not a soldier."

The cloud the soldiers faced became a race of wild horses, its leaders pulling the whole herd behind them, trampling and crushing the quaking earth. The sound they made—thousands of hooves beating the ground—came louder and louder until they slowed and drew up in a line, taking the last few steps at a regal walk. All the horses seemed to sigh at once. They were not wild; on their backs, they bore imperious men aboard creaking, leather saddles, their faces flushed ruddy with arrogance. Like creatures with long, segmented tails, other horses pulled cannon into position. A swarm of men surrounded each gun, and then with a popping noise loud enough that it was more a sensation of power than sound, the cannon coughed out plumes of cottony smoke. Spheres of iron hissed toward her like grouse startled out of a thicket, and she cringed and ducked, only to see how they fell short, hiding themselves below in the stream of men.

"I remember very well," she said. "All the killing."

A stir went through the ranks of horsemen. One command was bellowed over and over, and then the whole force drew their swords in a prolonged metal shriek, and the horses stepped forward. Thousands of hooves began to churn the snow-covered mud, turning it to slurry; vibrations traveled up through the legs of her horse and into her teeth. The Russian cavalry was transformed into something greater than the individual lives it comprised; it became a surging river of flesh and iron and brightly colored cloth, regimental flags and guidons sticking out like flotsam in the flood. When the horsemen had come within three hundred meters of their goal, trumpets rang out, and they charged, spurring the frantic, snorting horses and extending their swords, point forward.

Like a machine of many gears, the French infantry stopped. The first line of men knelt, the second aiming over their heads. They waited, the only sound their flags flapping in the breeze, no longer thousands of disciplined men but a feeling, a feeling of dread that made her mouth dry.

She heard the command, "Ready, fire!" Across the hillside, billowing clouds of thick white smoke started, dragging a long, rolling echo. The cavalry froze, as abruptly as if it had run into a wall of glass. Individual riders rode through it, unaware of the catastrophe behind them. Horses crashed into a great pile of wounded and dying men. The living made a frantic retreat, and the French drummers beat their line forward until it occupied the space where the cavalry had been. The fallen horses and men were ignored, stepped over, bayoneted.

"What did you ask me?" she said.

Valsin and Dalhousie laughed at her; they'd gone on again.

"Whoever he is, the Russian has invited us to dinner," Valsin was saying. "Along with Merseult and Crèpin."

"What?" she said, twisting toward him. "Me too?"

"Yes, he sent his orderly by with the invitations this morning."

Dalhousie pushed out his lips. "Typical—only officers get invited to dinner. Will you go?"

"Yes, it should be interesting."

4.

To be able to express all your charms, it would be necessary to paint you at every instance of your life.

After laboring up the stairs for the third time, Yevgeny and the man sent to deliver the dinner entered with their arms full of crates and covered trays. Based on a recommendation from the owner of his lodgings, Ruzhensky had engaged one of the local eating houses to cater the meal. A large table had been brought in, and the men spread a pressed linen tablecloth across it and arranged plates, along with silver and crystal. Soon the room filled with the aroma of rich food.

He'd instructed Yevgeny to deliver the dinner invitations and wait for a reply. Now that things were in motion, he was worried there might be a setback. Military life could be so transient. For all its insistence on routine and punctuality, soldiers might be detained, reassigned—sometimes with little warning. It was only with the greatest effort that he restrained himself from following his servant and seeking assurance that his guests would appear. But Yevgeny had returned and reported that everyone had agreed to come.

Of course, Marianne was not a suitable hostess for this affair. He could admit the French to his lodgings, but some things—his identity, his bed-chamber, and a mistress whose displeasure was eased by a carriage ride to a fashionable hotel—must remain hidden. He explained that he'd run into some old friends—French officers he'd met before the war—and invited them for dinner.

"It would be awkward," he said in a tone that didn't invite objection. "I don't want you here."

The dinner was planned with all the attention given a minor cam-paign—a campaign within a campaign—not only the mundane issues of what to eat and drink but the finer points of conversation as well. He pre-pared several topics, developing his positions with care and making allow-ances for spontaneity.

With regret, he chose a black evening jacket with silk stockings and civilian shoes rather than his uniform, a costume that certainly might lead his guests to unpleasant associations.

At eight, they arrived. Crèpin and Merseult had shared a carriage with Valsin and Anne-Marie. The night was running with rain and wind, and they all came in laughing and joking as they shed their wet cloaks. "When will things ever change?" Merseult said. Candles lit the room with a warm glow, highlighting beauty and hiding imperfection. Yevgeny was scrubbed and dignified in a Hussar's full-dress uniform, without the saber. As instructed, he served them iced champagne, keep-ing his gaze lowered.

She was breathtaking in a dress of pale blue-gray taffeta, the sleeves falling just over her shoulders and puffing out above delicate ribbon ties. Another larger ribbon was fastened below the décolletage, fashionably low and pleasing to the eye. She moved, and the fabric bent in the light and rustled. Her hair was gathered at the back of her head, and in the style of a cavalryman, she wore a single gold earring on the right side.

Valsin, Crèpin, and Merseult wore full-dress uniforms, their pelisses trimmed in black fur and fastened over their left shoulders, their waists encircled by red and silver barrel-sashes.

"Premier Major," Merseult said. "You and Valsin—what a striking resemblance! You might be brothers. Stand together, please."

Valsin—no doubt more accustomed now to following orders than he—stepped up close. Merseult's claim held some superficial truth: they were of the same height and build, both had dark hair clubbed back and the same luxurious mustaches and cadanettes.

"Well, Major," Crèpin said, "this is a happy occasion, I must say. Only last December, we were enemies. Much blood was spilled; many brave men died. Tonight we can break bread together in peace."

"Hear, hear," Merseult said. "A toast, to peace!" The glasses were raised and emptied.

"Yes, a toast—to peace," Ruzhensky said, mimicking Merseult. A sudden rawness surprised him, and he tried to conceal it by signaling Yevgeny to offer a refill. The French had spoken well, but he could only think of Mischa.

"To fallen comrades!" Crèpin barked, and the authority in his voice made all the men stand at attention.

The dead seemed satisfied by the tribute of the toast, and he recaptured his course. "I'm especially happy to see you again, Mademoiselle Fröelich. You've been in my thoughts; your story is quite amazing. I hope you'll allow further discussion of it if we promise not to embarrass you."

It was thrilling to speak with her face-to-face, to have her attention. The candlelight reflected in her eyes, making tiny sparks surrounded by halos of rich golden-brown. Against each cheek, a touch of rouge lay—a rumor of a blush—and her lips colored a deeper shade of pink. When she cast her gaze down and smiled, two dimples formed on either side of her mouth.

Amazing how women can alter their appearance.

The others—including Valsin—also regarded her in fascination, bending from the waist like lithe saplings to come closer, as if she exuded a force as powerful as the sun.

In his chest and groin, an insistent, animal ache pushed against his clothing.

The scene in *Julie* came to mind, the one in which she's reunited with St. Preux at Clarens; how long had their separation been—four years? Still—

No sooner had Julie laid eyes on me than she recognized me. Instantly, seeing me, exclaiming, running, throwing herself into my arms was for her a single act.

Could a book capture a woman? He'd been unsuccessful in involving Marianne directly with *Julie* and had instead purchased several other books they could share, including a well-done set of engraved tableaux. Each one represented a particular aspect of love—flirtation, infidelity, jealousy, surprise, voyeurism—and were rich in symbols. At that moment, it was in the bedroom, along with an absent Marianne. Certainly love—sexual love between a man and a woman—could be organized into these broad categories, humans being such predictable creatures. But were there not many subtle shadings as well? *Julie* makes reference to a dictionary of lovers in which certain things should not appear. Even so, it would need to be quite large.

When dinner was announced, he placed Crèpin at one end of the table and sat himself at the other, with Valsin to his left, Anne-Marie to his right, and then Merseult. The meal began with a leg of mutton, continued with fish, and progressed to chicken à la Marengo, a dish the caterer had particularly recommended. The fowl was cut in pieces, lightly sautéed in flour, and then cooked with mushrooms, onions, and white wine and finally served with small triangles of thin-sliced, toasted bread. Yevgeny was in good spirits and presented the dishes with great ceremony, clicking his heels and bending with a stiff back. At attention, he announced a name for each course in a combination of French and Russian that was sometimes difficult to make out.

"Did he say à la Marengo?'" Valsin asked.

"He did," Ruzhensky replied. "I'm told it's one of your Emperor's favorites. I present it in his honor."

"It's very gracious of you," she said. "Considering how he beat your army."

Crèpin and Merseult smiled and looked down at their plates—defeat or victory weren't things they would have mentioned. However, he took no offense; it revealed a new side to her. She wasn't just some country lass dressed up to amuse the gentlemen.

Merseult steadied them. "Premier Major Ruzhensky is superbly gracious and has excellent culinary judgment. The chicken is delicious."

Polite discussion ensued concerning differences between Russia and France and of the endless attributes of horses. The champagne, and then the Bordeaux they drank, made his head lighter, made it move like a swan through still water. She'd grown silent. "Mademoiselle Fröelich, earlier you remarked on my serving a dish that honors the French Emperor, and I wonder: have you ever seen him?"

The lids of her eyes were plump and generous. "From a distance, yes— it was the eve of the great battle," she said, drawing out the last word in a drawl. She and Valsin exchanged a look.

"Ah, when he made a procession around the campfires? I've heard about that. It must have been inspiring."

"It was, monsieur, much," she said in a low voice. He wondered if she was feeling the effects of the wine, as her words had begun sliding into each other.

"A magnificent sight," Valsin said. "The Chasseurs of the Guard carried torches, and all the men cheered and sang."

"Yes," Ruzhensky said, nodding. "I saw the lights and heard the singing from our position. Of course I didn't know until later what it meant." He paused.

On that evening, before the battle, Colonel Lensky had summoned the officers to issue commands for the morning. Ruzhensky had been the last to arrive; he'd had to squeeze in to stand at the back of the flushed crowd.

While his comrades indulged in bellicose posturing, he'd remained silent behind all the rest, trying to rub warmth into his cold hands. Most of the day he'd spent in his tent, occupied by the sight of Mischa's effects—a compressed gray bundle, delivered with profuse apologies. Strange to miss someone whom he'd lately tried so hard to avoid. All the signs of Mischa's foolishness had been evident in his headlong quest for honor, but they'd been ignored. He should have sent the boy home. Instead, he'd failed him as he'd failed Natasha.

Like a gunshot, the condemnation struck home. He let out a muffled moan, loud enough to turn heads, and stumbled outside, unable to survive one moment longer in such a close space.

At that late hour, instead of the frenetic, spectral leaping of the bonfires' flames, little colonies of embers were strewn like mushrooms within rings of black ash. Dark shadows of horses stood tied to picket stakes while their masters huddled underneath in rough blankets, struggling with sleep. He took a deep breath, desperate for the odor of calm.

A group of officers gestured toward the sky to the west—the direction of the French encampment. At first, he could see nothing and stumbled forward, shading his eyes.

The sky glowed red. Washes of scarlet and gold spilled through the low-hanging mist, infusing it as if great handfuls of herbs were being thrown into steaming water. From across the distance of the night sky a faint, muffled grumble came like that of a river's cataract. The colors intensified—was he dreaming? He seemed to be staring at the inside of a furnace, a forge that worked the entire sky, transforming the dull, man-made shapes below. Within the roaring noise came the rhythmic clash of the smith's hammer.

"Premier Major?"

Along an arc of crystal glasses, shining faces surrounded him. There was a pressure on his forearm; Merseult had reached behind Anne-Marie's back to nudge him.

"I thought we'd lost you," Merseult said.

"I'm sorry," he said. "Please excuse me." He took a moment to compose himself, hiding the effort with a flourish of his napkin. "Bonaparte—please excuse me, your Emperor—is a great man," he continued. "I don't hesitate to praise him. I believe we should be forgiving of our enemies, especially if they best us. Do you agree, Valsin?" It was one of his prepared topics, and he looked across the table in expectation.

"I suppose it's the noble thing to do," Valsin said, laughing. "But as a soldier, I wait for others to tell me who is and isn't an enemy or a friend. It's simpler that way."

"But what of your own feelings? Are you saying you have none?"

"I do, but I keep them in reserve. Things change quickly; one's enemy may become an ally. Flexibility is needed."

"Or a friend may become an enemy," she said. "How do you know who to trust?" All eyes turned her way.

"I suppose the secret is in knowing what true friendship is," Ruzhensky said. "What do you think, mademoiselle?" The conversation had sheared off in an unexpected direction, and he pressed toward her, readying his next comment with impatience.

"I think we've gone from chicken à la Marengo to philosophers' questions," she said. "Or priests'."

"She has you there, Ruzhensky," Crèpin replied with a laugh.

"You, Valsin, what do you say?" he countered.

"Friendship is a process occurring over time. From repeated experience, you learn that you can rely on someone. You become comfortable imposing on them and they on you. Friends are not made in a day, nor do they go away in a day." Valsin looked around at all of them, a pleased expression on his face.

"How much time is needed to make a friendship?" Merseult asked.

"Each case is different," Valsin responded. "It depends on the circumstances and the intensity of what's shared. Soldiers become comrades faster than shopkeepers. The experiences we have accelerate the process."

"Yes," he said, unable to remember what he'd wanted to say. Just at that moment, he looked at Valsin and had a sense of catching sight of his own reflection in a mirror. To hide his confusion, he speared a mushroom with his knife.

Pastries and ices were served, and Yevgeny presented each of the diners with a china cup full of strong coffee. Ruzhensky demonstrated the way the Turks drank it, holding a sugar lump between his teeth as he sipped loudly. After some discussion of how the British blockade was driving up prices on these colonial commodities, he motioned that the glasses be refilled and proposed a toast. "What was our original resolution? That we should forgive our enemies. I say yes—to forgiveness!"

"Bravo!" the men said in unison.

He raised his glass to Valsin and continued around the table until she appeared over the rim, and his progress came to a halt. The glass settled, pulling his arm lower. She held his gaze, raising her eyebrows and inclining her head.

"But you must drink, Ruzhensky," Merseult said. "Don't let her distract you."

"No, the issue wasn't forgiveness," she interrupted, "but trust, I thought. And you"—she turned to Valsin—"said that soldiers trust more easily."

"What about women?" Ruzhensky asked, taking a sip.

"Women are tougher than soldiers, more skeptical by nature," Crèpin said.

"Yes," she said, laughing. "Because we depend on others, we have to choose our allies with care."

✢ ✢ ✢

After a great deal of wine and brandy, Crèpin fell asleep, gently snoring with his head propped by an elbow and hand. She left the room and when she returned, went to sit in the empty place next to Valsin, and they became silent. Rain drummed on the wooden shingles, accompanied by the bells of the cathedral. Ruzhensky loosened his collar.

Only Merseult remained alert. Tonight his inquisitiveness was muted, almost as if he were off duty, but still, something about the man always put Ruzhensky on guard. Merseult, without looking his way, appeared to be studying him.

"Look," Merseult said, indicating Valsin and Anne-Marie. "They're in love. I'm happy for Valsin, a little jealous, too." In a lower voice, he added. "She's quite exquisite, don't you agree?"

"Of course, certainly." He looked to see if she'd heard them and saw how they both sat close together, their heads almost touching.

"I've met many beautiful women, Major," Merseult said, continuing his conspiratorial whispering, "some more beautiful than Mademoiselle Fröelich, but her beauty lies not so much in her face but in who she is, in what she's done."

He flinched, feeling the approach of something that should be warded off.

"No doubt the man she killed—your compatriot, forgive me—would be astonished to know her."

"Know her?" he said.

"Oh, I'm not speaking literally. It's just that I find mademoiselle's ferocity quite attractive." Merseult smiled. "May I ask how you were engaged at Austerlitz?"

He checked his first response and bought himself a moment's reflection by nodding like a sage and taking a sip from a half-empty glass. "Ah, well, the Pavlograds were—"

"But," Merseult interrupted, "you're Mariupol, aren't you?"

He pursed his lips and drained the glass, trying to recall what he'd said during the course of the evening.

"Your orderly," Merseult said, waving his chin at the silent Yevgeny. "He's wearing the Mariupol uniform, if I'm not mistaken. I assumed it must also be your regiment." Not a muscle moved on his smooth face.

"Correct, Capitaine. I didn't think it would matter—one regiment or the other. You're familiar with the Mariupol colors?"

"Very familiar. At Austerlitz, we rode down several of your squadrons."

"Ah, of course. I was in the reserve myself, on the post road."

"But then," Merseult asked, not waiting for him to finish, "how were you wounded?"

The only sound was of Crèpin's ursine snoring. A small smile crept across Merseult's face; neither of them blinked. "It occurred at the end of the day," Ruzhensky said. "While we were covering the retreat of our infantry."

"Please forgive my curiosity, Premier Major," Merseult said, inclining his head.

"I felt for a moment I was being interrogated."

They laughed—too loudly. Merseult covered the awkwardness with a long story about poultry preparation in Italy, and as he went on and on, Ruzhensky decided his intrusive questions didn't matter. He signaled a yawning Yevgeny to refill Merseult's glass. Everything had been a success—diverting conversation, many compliments for the dinner, and all the marvelous opportunities for observation.

She and Valsin were different; they were free, unfettered by memory. It was clear from the way they laughed, closing their eyes and showing their teeth. The memory of how they'd all met, the oddness of it—of being wounded by a woman dressed as a man—was receding; it was a false meeting that had occurred before they'd been introduced.

I have seized the past, molding it and shaping it, almost beyond recognition.

A thought spanned two territories: Anne-Marie—Louis Valsin's beautiful defender—might be Rousseau's Julie—a blond devotee to both love and her lover, willing to do whatever she could for either one. Though he'd only just met Anne-Marie, he felt a surprising rush of intimacy toward her—like finding the tips of tender, green ferns emerging from the debris of a forest floor in late winter. He blushed at the thought and looked around, seeing only Merseult's face, also flushed, still in the midst of a story about chicken.

A success—yet he felt as if he were a sack crammed full of living creatures who thrashed about, stretching his seams to the point of bursting.

5.

If I found a merit equal to yours, if someone came forward like yourself, you would be the only one heard.

"Let us drop you off," Merseult said as they emerged onto the street. "It's almost three o'clock."

With a clash of chains, the hired carriage started up from halfway down the block and began moving their way. She twisted out of Crèpin's grasp; the Chef d'Escadron had stumbled badly coming down the stairs, and she'd moved to support the rest of his unsteady descent, draping his arm around her shoulder. But his hand had fallen too low on her back. She took Valsin's hand and squeezed it.

"It's stopped raining, I think we'll walk," he said. "Thanks."

The gutters ran with gurgling torrents. Like a wash of varnish, a coat of moisture remained on the cobbles. Faint light from lanterns made the street glisten and shimmer, made pockets of mist appear, full of shapes. In her chest, the night air was a rheum of fog. She took his arm, and they set off in small strides to avoid slipping. Against the cobblestones their footsteps jolted with rhythmic pressure, driving the wine and mist from her mind.

"Wonderful dinner," Valsin said. "Ruzhensky was a fine host."

Before they'd left, he'd insisted she call him Alexi Davidych. He'd kissed her hand and held onto it—too long, staring into her eyes until she blushed.

"Interesting conversation, too. Friendship, forgiveness—some valuable sentiments were expressed."

"Mm-hmm."

How closely he'd peered into her eyes—what was the toast he'd made? To forgive one's enemies. He'd looked at her and raised his glass, giving it a small, insistent shake. At the time, she'd been embarrassed and tried to change the subject; she hadn't considered what he'd meant. Was it that she should forgive him because he was Russian?

"I thought I made a good contribution regarding friendship; did you notice?"

She laughed and laughed even harder when she took a careless step and tripped, almost pulling him down on top of her. "Yes, my dear one, I did notice how intelligent you were—no, I'm all right, help me up, please." Valsin had looked so handsome tonight, as had—Ruzhensky.

"Why are you smiling at me that way?" he asked. "Come on, I'm in a hurry to get you home."

Back at their rooms, she took off her gown and folded it, smoothing the material with her palms before closing the lid of the chest. Clad in a thin chemise, she sat before the mirror and washed herself with water from a small basin. Slowly, she removed the pins from her hair. Since she'd made the transformation back to woman's costume, she'd become acutely conscious of its power.

The men like to watch me. And when they do, I notice and pretend not to. I walk past them, laughing, adjusting the play of my hair.

And Valsin, when I pull my skirt up to adjust a stocking, lightly caressing my calf, or when I lean over, revealing the tops of my breasts—he likes that. Then, through delicate eyelashes, light like the powder on a butterfly's wings, I look up at him with a hint of a smile, a suggestion of agreement to whatever he wants.

The mirror—if she looked in it now, who might it reflect? An amorous woman, a handsome Hussar, and—someone else? Smoke breathed against the glass, and she held it there in a particular shape. Out of its dark depths, Valsin, splendid in his uniform, gazed at her. Another figure stood at his shoulder, but whoever it was could not be seen.

At the dinner, the chamber pot had been in the darkened bedroom. A tiny light twinkled, and she'd raised the candle to make out its source. A large wooden box sat atop a small table, and on its raised lid there was a mirror; the light was the reflection from her candle. Next to the box, lay a purple ribbon and a hairbrush inlaid with bone. It was difficult to be sure in the weak light, but the strands of hair caught in the bristles looked pale. She brought the brush close to her nose and sniffed—a floral scent, a woman's scent.

"Have you forgiven me?"

Valsin stood in the doorway. He'd shed his shirt but still wore trousers and boots. She held out her arms to him from where she sat, and he came over and stood before her.

"Forgiven—for what?"

"The hayloft."

When she put her lips against his bare stomach, she thought of apples— an aroma and a taste lingered there from the pipe smoke he'd wrapped himself in. His warm hands embraced her bare shoulders, pulling her even closer. "When the hay spoiled, you mean." With fingers long since shy, she tugged his waistband down.

✻ ✻ ✻

A sound of bells, muffled by the night and all the bulk of the city, traveled down the streets and through the window. A bird trilled, and after a streaming pause, a rooster crowed and was answered by another, and another picked up the call. Then a human sound—a bucket of water dumped to sluice away yesterday's dregs.

They'd fallen asleep facing each other. With one arm and one leg draped over her, he lay on his side, and as the light strengthened, she could make out his features. No crease across his brow; he slept in serenity, mouth closed, blanketed by mustaches. Like a thief with gentle fingers, she lifted free of his limbs and rolled onto her back. The chamber pot beckoned, but she moved to it with extreme care, not wishing to disturb him, not wanting to do anything to cause him to leave. Comforted, she returned with the same caution and dozed.

Hurtled from a dream, she sat bolt upright. She and Valsin had been riding on the road near the Fröelichs' farm. He'd galloped ahead and called to her to catch up. Behind them, there was danger, an enemy who lurked out of sight—it had all been explained to her, but she couldn't remember the details. His horse threw back clods of black earth, and she thought of her skirts becoming dirty but realized she was wearing a Hussar's uniform; it was no longer possible to wear skirts. She began swatting her horse's flank to hurry along, but every time she drew near Valsin, the path narrowed, and she fell back. Over and over, she called to him to wait, but a wind started up, blowing her voice away. The distance between them widened. By the rules of the dream, she would never see him again.

Awake, she was naked and cold, her chemise pulled up, the sheets kicked off. She covered both of them, waiting for him to stir. If she told him about the dream, she knew he'd laugh and tell her it was silly. If she continued to be upset, he'd stroke her and speak in a soft voice. Eventually he'd part her legs, as he seemed to believe lovemaking settled most cares. The dream would remain her secret; she didn't want to be caressed and jiggled out of it too soon. Like an old torn dress she wasn't ready to throw away, she'd keep it, in case she needed it again.

6.

If we are not masters of our sentiments, at least of our conduct.

The next morning, Yevgeny was up early, scrubbing and returning the table and place settings to the eating house, carefully sweeping the floor. When Marianne arrived from the hotel, she stood by the window, sniffing the air; she ran her fingers through the empty space where they'd eaten, as if she could feel the absent crystal, the drape of generous napkins.

"Your dinner—it went well?" she asked.

"Very well, yes. A long evening."

She stopped at the place Anne-Marie had occupied before going to sit with Valsin. "What did you serve?" Marianne said, tapping her shoe on the floor and covering him with cool, blue eyes. "Who was here?"

"The officers, my dear—as I told you. And what of you? How was the room at the hotel? Was your dinner satisfactory?"

"Yes." She chewed the inside of her lower lip a moment. "Everything was fine."

Throughout the afternoon and into the evening, she continued to be distracted and inquisitive. Finally, to satisfy her, he was compelled to create several fictitious dinner guests, complete with names and conversations. When he came to rake the fire and serve tea, Yevgeny kept his eyes averted.

Finally, her questions ended, and she fell silent. Ordinary sounds—carriages passing outside, the pop and drag of her needle and thread—returned, as did memories of the dinner: the nutty taste of the mushrooms, the earring she'd worn, and of course, Valsin.

Although he'd tried to keep to certain topics, like forgiving one's enemies, the conversation had turned instead to friendship; how had Valsin put it? Friendship isn't made in a day, yet the experiences we have accelerate the process.

Friendship, with his brother's killer. Were he to suspect it, his father certainly would disown him, as Marianne feared. In fact, the news—received weeks after the fact—might even kill the old man. Marianne herself would struggle to fit such a thing into a narrow compartment within herself and find it too strange, too unnatural. She'd cast her lot with another man, a man who picked his friends because of shared interests like gambling or hunting—less unnatural bonds than murder.

Her head was down; she was smoothing the fabric within her sewing hoop, brushing it with her fingertips. She was—he was sure—very much aware of him watching her but wouldn't meet his eyes until he made some overture.

"My dear," he began. "May I read to you from the almanac?"

✻ ✻ ✻

The next morning, he ended his walk at the coffeehouse on Kaufingerstrasse. Before entering, he stopped at the glass windows and peered in, looking for Merseult, whom he did not wish to see.

Inside, he ordered coffee and opened the newspaper; soon, he was absorbed in a story about the cultivation of jute. Apparently, efforts were being made to introduce the Asian plant into Europe to provide fiber for the manufacture of ropes.

"Ruzhensky! We wondered if we might see you here; may we sit?"

Today Valsin was in full dress uniform; he explained there was a review that afternoon. She wore her burnished hair. "Ah, please," he said, standing. "A pleasure."

After an enjoyable period of light conversation, marred only by Valsin's comment that—since the dinner—Captain Merseult hadn't stopped talking about him, the three of them fell into that shyness that often precedes further intimacy.

"You know," Valsin said. "You'd be very welcome to visit us at our billet. It's close by—above a tavern called The White Hound. Merseult made such a point of saying the war is over; we are enemies no longer, and I agree."

"It's true, Monsieur Ruzhensky—no, Alexei Davide," she said with a radiant smile. "Valsin and I often have friends over to talk and play cards. We'd be happy if you'd come."

He began to correct her, "Alexi Davidych," but smiled and nodded instead, staring at her until she blushed and looked away. It was clear to him that such a thing would not be possible. There was Marianne, of course, and although he believed that what he'd begun to think of as his disguise was intact, playing cards was a game of chance, as was talking.

"And I think we should meet here regularly—the three of us," Valsin continued. "Late morning, before parade, that's when Anne and I usually arrive, unless I'm on duty. The three of us have work to do." He regarded both of them with raised eyebrows, and she covered her mouth with her hand and laughed.

"Work?" he asked, not sure he'd understood.

"Yes—your French lessons. We must speak clearly—no muttering or mumbling. And you must imitate my pronunciation, not Anne-Marie's. It's too German."

"Oh, *your* pronunciation," she said, stretching the last word out and then hitting Valsin on the upper arm. She blushed again when she noticed Ruzhensky watching her.

"That hurt," Valsin said. "You see, Anne-Marie comes from Mayence, which is next to Germany. She doesn't speak a pure French; hers is under Germanic influence."

He smiled as she struck Valsin again but considered that Marianne was also from an area between France and Germany. Did the two women share the same accent? "I'm eager to learn a purer French," he said. "But truly, mademoiselle, I can detect no imperfection in what you say."

"Aha! Bravo," Valsin said. "I think we must call you by a different name, a French name to encourage your learning." He made a pantomime of studying him, rubbing his chin and closing one eye as if he were purchasing a horse. "Alexandre, perhaps."

"Alexandre," she repeated and broke into laughter, again covering her mouth. He could take no offense at their playfulness; it was infectious. And she was remarkably pretty.

Valsin put his arm on the back of Ruzhensky's chair. "You agree then? We'll meet for coffee as often as the generals allow. And if you like, you and I could go riding and fence. Our friendship will make Munich even more pleasant."

After further conversation, it was decided they'd meet the following day, and Ruzhensky insisted on paying the bill. After the French left, he remained, intending to finish reading the paper. But his eyes drifted between the lines of ink, and he began to think about *Julie*.

Of course, he'd given up trying to read it aloud to Marianne but still read it on his own at times, in silence while she was otherwise engaged. Maybe that was for the best because the letters that held the story, which were the story, made reading them an unusual program in intimacy, one that allowed him to insert himself into other beings, perhaps—he imagined—by crawling into their ears—not the sort of thing to share with Marianne.

It's no good to think about this novel.

No, he thought, struggling to bring his attention back to the newspaper—a piece about some comments of the Prussian king regarding an alliance with Russia.

It was probably true that reading *Julie* made him vulnerable—Marianne had sensed this and instinctively disliked such a sentimental love story, distrusting it for its power to seduce, to bewitch, as she'd said. But a book would not be his master.

It's just a series of words, ink on paper. Julie isn't real; none of the characters are real. A dream. The Frenchwoman too.

A dream I wish to inhabit. Among all of them, all the lovers, who would I want to be? Not St. Preux, who's too sentimental, too weepy and willing to abase himself before the altar of femininity—too French. Bompston's nobility and character are certainly admirable, but at times, he's too good, to an unrealistic extent. Julie's husband, the wise Wolmar, is ancient, elevated above all the others like a creature only half-alive, his bonds with the earth loosened and weak.

He pictured the first engraving—the one showing Julie and Claire with St. Preux in the bower after their first kiss. Claire and St. Preux didn't interest him at all; it was Julie he saw, trying to see more than was there, reaching out to embrace her himself. He closed his eyes and thought of her unclothed, of the way the subtle variation of color on her skin would show her sentiments. Julie couldn't hide from him; he'd learn everything about her: how she blushed scarlet, flushed with the full bloom of desire, and paled alabaster because of dread and worry.

She was devoted to her virtue—well, that's what Monsieur Rousseau wanted people to think, what he wanted the authorities to believe, in order to forestall their censure. But it was a false gloss on a woman of extraordinary passion, one who struggled against the despotism of her father, one who yearned to receive lessons from her tutor not about the physics of abstract forms but of the real properties of a man with a woman, the angle at which hips join, the rate of progress a frantic tongue may make entering a mouth. This was the Julie of the first engraving, feeling not some false, bloodless ecstasy like a saint but rapture and release at making physical contact with a man.

He imagined reading her letters, sometimes aloud, sometimes in silence, running his index finger over the script; yes, he'd crawl into those intimate passages, shoving the others out of the way, tearing through the pages to be with her, close enough that she'd react to the things he said and did. Instead of paper, he'd cut through the delicate ribbons that bound her clothing. Her name was a secret, a name seen like writing beneath the spiraling, transparent layers of an onion, an onion slathered with honey.

The serving woman asked him if he wanted something more, and he stared at her in shock, the blood burning his face. The two images—the one from the engraving and the one in his memory of Anne-Marie—had moved together.

For three days running, he met Valsin and Anne-Marie, entering into discussions of politics and the differences between Russia and France. In that setting, freed from the pressures of wearing elegant clothes, the inhibitions of polite discourse, she was simple and lovely, laughing freely, joining the conversation as an equal partner. Toward him, she was still reserved, casting her eyes down when he spoke to her directly but nevertheless feeling bold enough to correct his pronunciation. They did call him Alexandre, a practice that seemed to amuse them both a great deal. In more serious moments, they called him Alexi, putting the stress on the final vowel.

To watch the pattern of their intimacy became a fascination. It seemed to him that, before his eyes, the two of them often danced together. She would grasp Valsin's shoulder with one hand and his arm with her other, as if he were whirling her ankles above a floor of intricate planks. At other times, she seemed to lean against him for support and then to push back against his bulk, exposing her throat a few degrees more to the light. Like gentle carpenter's planes, Valsin's hands moved over her surfaces, smoothing her hair with his palm, brushing her cheek, her back. And often, their hands intertwined, ten fingers spilling over one another like jets of water from a fountain.

After they departed, he'd remain, entangled by the different stories he inhabited. He was not the person they took him to be; however, it would also be untrue to claim the identity of the person the woman had killed. In fact, he'd begun to think that person *had* been killed and that he himself was someone embryonic, someone developing a new identity, transforming in Munich's womb. It was wonderful; it was unbearable. Taut like the skin on a drum.

7.

If I marry Laura, I said to him, I don't plan to take her to London where someone might recognize her.

Despite the warmer weather, Marianne complained of not sleeping well and the damp. In the first light, he woke to find her staring at him, her eyes girded in gray. A chill overcame summer, so recently arrived, returning him to late winter, a season and a time when one wakes wishing for warmth but must instead wade in and slip across areas of cold, of darkness and ice. He'd return from his encounters with the French, filled with pleasant reverie, and be, from one moment to the next, confronted by the sight of her sitting at the window, her embroidery neglected, her eyes filled with reproach.

He certainly could take her out on his arm—that's what she wanted. Thanks to him, she had the proper clothes. People would assume they were married; gentlemen didn't take their mistresses out for walks, they took them for rides in carriages—something he and Marianne had done, going even as far as the English Gardens. But walking in the city—what if he should encounter Valsin and Anne-Marie?

But she seemed so miserable that he relented. As a precaution, he claimed an eagerness to explore an unfamiliar area of the city, and they set out in a new direction, passing into the suburbs in the early afternoon. On their return, they stopped at a coffeehouse—one in which he hoped he wouldn't be recognized.

She was delighted by the cake he ordered and he by the return of sunlight to her face and of greenery in her voice. Of course she was bored staying in their rooms with only Yevgeny to keep her company. Although, these days, his servant often whistled behind the screen and undertook any chore with little grumbling.

The latest available edition of *Le Moniteur* had an interesting piece on plans to build a memorial to the battle. It pleased him that it was becoming so much easier to read in French.

From behind the newspaper, he glanced at his companion. Clad in a fashionable frock, she made him the envy of all the other men in the room. How were she and the Frenchwoman different? Marianne was younger, although, in truth, when in good humor, she possessed a wonderful old soul and wit. She was more petite than the Frenchwoman, who had a strong grip.

"Marianne," he began.

"Ruzhensky? Aha, I thought it was you! Are you hiding behind that newspaper? I was walking along the street—it's a fine day—and I spied you through the window." Merseult gave him a huge grin that broadened even more when he noticed Marianne. "Mademoiselle." With a short bow to her, he pulled out a chair and removing his shako and gloves, began to sit.

"Would you care to join me?" Ruzhensky said with an inward groan. "I was just catching up on the latest news."

"Military news? Thank you, I will sit. Truly, this is a happy coincidence; I've been looking forward to seeing you again. But please, will you introduce me to your charming companion?"

"Of course," he said. "This is Mademoiselle Marianne."

"Marianne—I see," Merseult said, curling his lips inward as if the name had provoked him to impolite laughter. He rose again, taking Marianne's hand and kissing it. "A pleasure," he said. "Ruzhensky, it seems you're a magnet for beauty. You're not Russian too, are you, my dear?"

"No, monsieur. I'm from—"

"Capitaine, please excuse me," he said, covering Marianne's hand with his own to silence her, a gesture Merseult's dark eyes didn't miss. "I don't wish to keep you from your business."

"Ah, well—I don't have any, at the moment. But I thank you. Is there—"

"What about parade?"

"Parade—no, we're done for the day, nothing to report, the colonel says. Later the junior officers will drill the men; you know how it goes. Is there news from Russia?"

"No."

"Valsin tells me you've become friends."

"Yes, I'm fortunate he was able to forgive me." He took a sip of coffee and finding it still too hot, poured a little out into the saucer to cool. "That is, it's unusual—to have been enemies and then find you have so much in common."

"Soldiers who have been enemies have more in common with each other than they do with civilians of their own land. That's what we said at your dinner—do you remember?"

"Of course."

"And Mademoiselle Fröelich, you've gotten to know her as well."

He glanced at Marianne, marking that this was the first time she'd heard the Frenchwoman's name. It didn't seem to affect her; she smiled and nodded, as if her only wish was that he and Merseult continue their conversation.

"An extraordinary woman," Merseult was saying. "Imagine—a few twists of fate, and it might have been you she'd killed." The man's eyes were twinkling. He'd heard the expression before but had never seen the phenomenon so clearly; sparks seemed to dance from Merseult's dark pupils to his mouth, making the grin he displayed even broader. "If your squadron had advanced up the post road—I mean, isn't that where you said you were? In reserve, you said."

"That's correct; it was another topic we discussed at the dinner party."

"Yes, of course, but we'd had so much wine."

He shrugged. "I bear both of them nothing but friendship; it is as you say, we've more in common than anything else."

"Until our next war."

Laughter eased them away from serious topics, and Merseult told a story about a masked ball he'd attended. "Mademoiselle," he said. "Do you like to dance?"

"Oh yes, monsieur," she said, glancing at Ruzhensky. "But dancing at a ball—I've never done that."

"I'm certain you'd be a quick study. Have you known the Premier Major long?"

"Long?" She faltered and looked at Ruzhensky.

"Since the winter," he said.

"Ah," Merseult said. "You know, mademoiselle, every time I ask you something, it's your grizzled companion who answers. I'm beginning to suspect you're a ventriloquist."

"A what, monsieur?"

Ruzhensky drank off the coffee and put the cup in the exact center of the empty saucer. "Merseult, Mademoiselle Marianne is my mistress; she lives at my lodging, lives with me. Does that satisfy your curiosity?"

Marianne, her face red, excused herself.

"Pretty girl," Merseult said, looking him in the eye and smiling. "Forgive my teasing. We all must love the ladies, eh?"

"I'd prefer you keep this matter private. I'm sure you can understand. It's my own affair. Even Valsin doesn't know."

"Of course, a private matter, say no more." He took a sip of coffee. "I will say I envy you getting to know Mademoiselle Fröelich. I wish it had been me she'd rescued. It's funny—she keeps herself apart from all of us; I believe you're the only man who's gotten to know her besides Valsin."

Hot blood raced to the top of his ears. "Oh, no. We are not—I mean, I know her only through the Lieutenant."

"Oh?"

"Please excuse me, my skills of expression in the French language are sometimes inadequate." Within his discomfort, he was forced to acknowledge Merseult's ability to provoke him into blushing just as he'd done with Marianne.

"In you, there are few signs of inadequacy," Merseult said. "She's warmed to you—is that it? You thought I was joking earlier, but I believe women are drawn to you."

"Truly."

"Yes—animal magnetism," Merseult said, stirring sugar into his cup. "In all seriousness, I'm concerned about those two. Valsin's name has come up in discussions of promotion, even transfer out of the regiment. Marriage would be a hindrance. The mademoiselle is the one I worry about. She has no family, I'm told. She'll need a patron." He looked at his watch. "Well, my Russian friend, I salute you and bid farewell. Thanks for the conversation. And please give my regards to the young lady. She's exquisite."

After Merseult's departure, Marianne returned, full of questions about how he knew Merseult and who he was. "The dinner he mentioned—it was the one you gave?"

"No—a different affair."

"And the man he mentioned—Valsin. Who's he?"

He shook his head. "A mutual friend."

Just when he thought he'd satisfied her, she asked another question. "Who was the woman you were talking about?"

"One moment." He ordered her a fresh cup of coffee. "Woman? No one. Before I met you—someone I knew. More cake?"

"She killed someone? What did he mean? I didn't understand."

"Not killed literally, it's an expression, a new French expression." He shrugged. *What was meant by patron?* he wondered.

And that I show few signs of inadequacy; damn the man, he's so difficult to understand.

"Well, then what does it mean?"

"Uh…that the lady was quite attractive, that's all."

In his indirect fashion, is he telling me something, something important?

"And you asked him about parade. Do they have parade every day?"

"What? Yes, a military routine."

"At this time?"

"More or less. I'll get the bill—you there, waiter!"

She tugged on his arm. "What is parade? I know what a parade is. Is that what they do—march around a field?"

"It's more than that. The whole regiment must report for inspection. Everyone draws up in formation and—"

"On their horses?"

He stared at her a moment. She was leaning forward over the table, her eyes bright and shining. "No, dismounted—unless it's a formal inspection by a general. The roll is called to make sure everyone's present, and the colonel makes announcements of important news. It's usually over in an hour or so. Are you ready to go?"

"And what time is it at?"

"You just asked me. Noon, around noon."

She took a deep breath. "Then Alyosha, why don't you just go to their parade and watch for him—your brother's killer? It's no wonder it's taking you so long to find him; you're looking when he's not there."

He shook his head. "I couldn't just go to a military parade and—"

"But other people do; I've heard that. You can go and watch them drill."

"At a distance, maybe, but what good would that do me? And even if I did see him—think about it—what then? I couldn't just rush up and kill him."

"No, but—"

"I'd be struck down, killed myself. Is that what you want?"

"No, but you could follow him."

"Listen, I'm not so sure I'd recognize him anymore. And I can't just ask; it would arouse too much suspicion."

"But you've got to do something. Your father's letters—one came just yesterday; you didn't read it, did you? What's he going to think? I'll tell you—he's going to think you're dead and stop sending money. You'll go to that bank you go to and they'll say, 'Sorry, sir, that account's closed.' I'm right, aren't I?"

8.

Pretty women don't like to lose their tempers.

That night, as he entered the doorway, she rushed at him with greedy hands. "Valsin, ah God, where have you been? Take me to eat!"

"What?" he said, laughing and grabbing her by the shoulders. "Ambush! To arms! Where's my sword?"

"I'll draw it for you if you feed me. While you've been out, I've been going mad. Where were you?"

"Our drills ran late, and I spoke with Merseult for a while. He's—no, stop!"

Her hands were busy, pulling at his clothes, snaking into his pockets. "What's this? A love letter? And this?" A pistol was tucked into the waistband of his trousers, and she drew it out. "Ah, so you *are* well armed. Is it primed?"

"I've told you; weapons are not for play, women shouldn't—"

"No?" She gave a shriek that was mostly laughter. "Women shouldn't be allowed pistols, certainly not. Pistols or swords, eh? Come on, don't be so serious. Let's have some fun." She put the gun on the table. "I'm sorry I was so mean earlier. Let's go. I want you to take me out, right away. I've been sitting here for hours. Change your shirt and wash a bit. Let's go."

She'd been near weeping; all the hours of the afternoon and early evening had become massive, silent bars of stone in which she'd sat imprisoned, studying an almanac as if it were a school lesson, reading every paragraph, each letter. She'd thought about the phases of the moon; it was said the moon affected people and—using the almanac as a guide—she'd tried to go over recent events to see if there were any connections with her moods. It was often cloudy at night, though.

America: there, the almanac said, a modest amount of work produces a bounty all out of proportion to its effort. Peasants have clean shirts and eat chicken every night. The poorest man can speak to the wealthiest without fear of retribution or dismissal. Philadelphia is the city of brotherly love, where the streets are laid out perfectly straight and sickness is unheard of. Philadelphia—the word itself is fascinating. Philadelphia. Perhaps—

But during the last hour, she'd begun to fill herself with emotion, as if she were a book that could be over-written, a blank book in which to inscribe her sentiments. The first one—love—was familiar, too familiar; she felt restless writing in love. Jealousy was a good one; by thinking about Valsin and the hayloft, his women with marked buttocks, she made the words so big on the page that she had to get up and pace the room. The paper had become inscribed in acid, etched deeply and rubbed with salt.

She'd turned the page. The Russian—he was an interesting subject; what might he evoke? Jealousy in Valsin?

Ruzhensky: he makes me blush. I'm a rose he might pick, and beneath his fingers—instead of pricking him—I'd withdraw all thorns and enclose him in moist, crimson petals. Wantonness is written across the book; that ink flows freely.

"All right," Valsin said. "Ready."

☆ ☆ ☆

The tavern was crowded with noise and heat, and she couldn't wait for the wine to be served. "I have a great thirst tonight," she said. "Like a man, my love. Let me drink your glass too, and order us more."

"You know, Merseult thinks Ruzhensky is mysterious, dangerous even—no, save some for me!"

"What are you talking about?"

"Ruzhensky. Merseult thinks he's involved in some sort of intrigue. Perhaps because he's Russian. But I'm not concerned."

At the edge of her attention, a horseman in blue with empty eyes shot a gun, firing a bolt straight at her heart. "I'm going mad," she said, blinking. "Every day, there's nothing to do. If the day were only shorter, half as long." She squinted into the glass. "I'm too restless, I know. When you're absent, I feel like a dog chained in a yard, and I pace and whine." She clacked her teeth shut at him.

"No—you're getting drunk."

"What, are only men allowed to drink? I do—feel that way. A bitch, one whose master will one day give her a scratch behind the ears and never return. Oh, sorry, sorry—I'm not supposed to say things like that. I should never complain—never, never—because I was saved by a handsome officer. I'm terrible."

"You're drunk, and you're clowning. Let's get something to eat."

He doesn't see. Or hear. I'm shouting at him, and he thinks it's the wine. Why can't I just tell him? Not to go.

The need was there, but somewhere between her heart and her tongue, it got all mangled and interrupted, squashed and sat on.

Valsin, I'm going mad.

She watched him, waiting for a reaction; he took her glass and drank it off. Had she said the words or just thought them?

✠ ✠ ✠

Blood rushed through her temples like a mountain cataract. A half step behind him, she trod on the back of his boots and laughed. He pulled ahead, talking about the Russian. "If anything, I believe he's uncomfortable at times—because we've been enemies," he said, tossing back words from one corner of his mouth. "But that's all over. Do you remember when he said that—"

"Will you wait? Don't walk so fast."

Ruzhensky—his hands are smooth and powerful; his nails cut square, making his fingertips thick and blunt. The hands of a wealthy man. I've never touched a wealthy man's hands before.

"À *merde*. I'm tired of hearing about Alexi Ruzhensky. Do you think he'll give you money?" She came to an unsteady halt.

"No, of course not—we're becoming friends." He stopped and turned to face her. "What's this about? I thought you liked him."

"What made you think that? He's no better and no worse than any of them. That's what bothers me—that you're always going on about these men you admire, Crèpin, Merseult, and now him—the Russian. You think they'll help you—but they won't. You don't see it; you're blind."

He turned his back and stepped forward.

"You're—" She wanted to say something more to hurt him but couldn't think of it and lunged after him.

Valsin was silent until the door to their rooms closed behind them. "Tomorrow when we see Ruzhensky—"

"Mon Dieu, do we have to see him every day? Why don't you ask him to move in with us? You go; I've had enough friendship for a while. I don't want to—"

"Fine. I'm going to bed."

She sat down on the chair, and the room began to roll upward. It was a strange sensation, and she wanted to tell him about it. "Valsin—"

"Do you know—what you said about Ruzhensky and the others— you're wrong. I spend my time with them to get away from your grasp. You hold our love close like pieces of gold, making sure I'll pay all I owe you."

"Owe me?"

"You think I owe you my life," he shouted. "I didn't ask you to save me. I'm going out."

☆ ☆ ☆

Later, the shape of the basin wavered in the candlelight. The flame pulsed, and she looked up into the surface of the mirror, searching for the reflection of the slim, tallow taper. She made herself entirely still so as to hear the first moments of his return.

But in the room beyond, there was only more stillness.

This room is not still; it beats with anger, as if the two of us were still colliding within it, blundering into one another. If he'd just come back, I'd make him understand, make him see I forgive him for calling me grasping.

Anger was alive. It was a part of her from a nightmare, as if somehow she could turn into another thing, a figure in shadows who never forgave, who wanted to strike, to hurt. Just before he'd walked out, she'd said that he had the mind of a junior officer, that he lacked that spark of strength that made generals—men who commanded and led. The others, Merseult and Crèpin, were glad to have a lackey to lead their drills and carry out their commands. "And your Russian, too!"

The way he'd looked at her—it was more than letting her see she'd struck home—she had. It was saying he understood she wanted to wound him, that he knew she was hurt and couldn't make it go away. In the mirror, she could see him now, pressing his mouth together as if he were regarding a naughty child.

There was something wrong with her; that was why Valsin loved her only to a point. It was something that couldn't be named, a shadow following her around—the figure from a nightmare. She reached out slowly, frowning, and held her open palm over the flame, lowering her hand by stages until the burning stopped.

9.

In sacrificing myself to duty, I can't avoid committing a crime.

Marianne refused to drop the subject of parade, and he finally said he'd search for Valsin in the evenings, when the French officers were at the taverns, and this seemed to satisfy her. That night, he set out after dark, walking for an hour through the streets surrounding the Marienplatz. The next morning, he accompanied her to a dressmaker's shop.

The next night, he set out again, following the same route. He hadn't really expected to meet Valsin—who had good reason to stay at his billet—but a figure approached from far down the street, walking on the opposite side. Twenty paces more, and the flare of a street lantern revealed the outline of military costume, and he knew: out of the all the possibilities and choices in the divided city, they'd been drawn together. He crossed to the other side so they were walking toward one another along the same path.

"Hail, friend," he called as Valsin stopped. If their encounter surprised the younger man, he gave no indication. The light from a lantern overhead showed his face creased with care, a dullness in his gaze, as if the backs of his eyes were lined with dark cloth. "What a coincidence," Ruzhensky continued. "I'm headed for the tavern back there—the one you just passed. Have you eaten?"

"No," Valsin said, turning around.

"The food is good, unpretentious, and solid—like Munich itself. The beer is better. Will you join me?"

Their goal was a doorway flanked by glass windows glowing orange. The entrance itself was weather-tight and opened with a slight inhalation of the night air. After stepping down over the threshold, they entered a low-ceilinged room that smelled of cabbage, bread, and tobacco. Clusters of men clad in somber civilian clothing sat smoking and drinking. With polite nods and downcast eyes, a party of four made room for them at one of the long trestle tables.

"I wasn't able to go to the coffeehouse today," Ruzhensky said, settling onto the bench. "I hope you didn't wait long."

"No. I didn't go either. I was the duty officer."

"Your beautiful consort—where is she tonight?" He looked around in irritation. A draft had blown onto his neck, as if someone close by had compressed their lips and exhaled, trying to extinguish him like a candle.

"At our rooms." Valsin nodded at a serving woman, who brought mugs crowned with foam. "Ah," he said and then drank, wiping his mustaches with the back of one hand. He cleared his throat and seemed about to say more but looked away.

It was the first time he'd been alone with Valsin; perhaps without distraction, he could see the man more clearly. "Please excuse me for being so direct, but you seem troubled. Is there something wrong?"

A corner of Valsin's mouth turned down, and his nose twisted to the side. "A foolish argument." He shrugged and drank again, his eyes fixed on the bottom of the mug.

"I see."

"It's nothing, I'm sure," he said. "Let's talk about something else. Tell me about Russia, about your home."

"Today I saw a crane flying," he began. "And then heard church bells; in Russia, the bells sound in a different way. You've never been there, have you. Even now there's snow in the deep forest; we could go riding and not see anyone hour after hour, hearing only the sound of the wind in the trees and the crunching of the horse's hooves. A meadow of stars fills the night sky. Sometimes the air becomes so cold, it hurts your throat to breathe."

"Where is your home again?"

"My father's estate is near the town of Brest-Litovsk, east of Warsaw. When he dies, it'll be mine. And he's dying. I've had no news, but I sense it. To tell the truth, I don't care much anymore. His death—it seems far away, in the past." He paused to clean his pipe. It was almost true; he'd had no word of an end to illness. In fact, the unopened letters were silent. But from the east, there was a pall in the air, like smoke from gravediggers' torches. A murmur of funeral chants.

"A death in the past—I don't understand."

"It's just that—my father and I aren't close. I do miss Brest-Litovsk, though. My memories of it are inseparable from those of a woman. She died long ago, and I still talk to her; I mean I remember talking to her, remember her talking to me." Eyebrows raised, he looked up. "Foolish, eh? I wouldn't expect you to understand." He banged the pipe against the table leg; when he straightened, he felt the draft of cool air again.

His companion shrugged. "Women are our other halves; they express all that we cannot—not something to be easily forgotten."

An image arose of Natasha within the depths of a kind of mirror. He reached for her at the same time she reached for him so their fingertips almost touched but could not, being separated by a thin veneer of glass. A wash of longing for something he'd missed swept up to his ears, nearly choking him, and to hide the turmoil, he took a drink and saluted Valsin with the mug.

"A wise comment. I wish I'd understood that when Natasha—Natalya Ivanovna was her name—was still alive." The sound of her name seemed to force away any remaining traces of propriety. He would speak now as he would to a brother. "Valsin, please excuse me, but Anne-Marie—you love her?"

"Of course. She saved my life." He laughed, and Ruzhensky joined in, forcing out guffaws. "I have a confession," Valsin continued, his eyes shining with small specks of reflected light. "I haven't said this to anyone before. It's been on my mind."

Even more alert, he put down the pipe.

"What I mean is," Valsin continued, "right now it's good with us. I have a lot of time to spend with her, as you can understand. We've been happy..." His voice trailed off, and again, his mouth twisted.

"But you're not sure about the future?" He felt like a judge who watched and listened—a judge who'd forgotten nothing but was now pulled between two different trials, exiting and entering one of two different courtrooms, only one of which was in the present.

"Yes, that's right. Sooner or later the regiment will leave Munich, for where I don't know—France, Austria. But whether it's this summer or the next, I'll be off again. What will she do; or rather, what should I do about her?"

"Marriage?"

Valsin smiled without engaging his eyes. "No, I'm afraid I have to choose between her and the cavalry. I don't see how to put the two together. The day I receive orders to leave on campaign will force a decision."

"You're unwilling to resign?"

"I don't know what else I'd do. And I have every reason to expect further promotion and opportunity."

"What would happen to her if you were to leave? She has no family?"

"No, the revolution and the wars have scattered everyone. That's true for me also."

"She needs your protection then. Without you, she'd be in real trouble." *Unless,* he thought, *someone else could help.* He shifted his posture on the uncomfortable plank bench and looked over his left shoulder. The whole exchange suddenly felt artificial to him, as if someone else were feeding him lines to say; he spoke like an inquisitor, only to lead the younger man along for someone else's benefit, a third party listening behind a screen.

Valsin looked down, pulling one end of his mustache with his right hand.

"You do love her, don't you?"

"I'm not sure."

He pulled on the pipe—too hard, and choked on a wild plume of smoke; those same feelings, those same thoughts—he'd had them, the same, years ago. And acted on them. Damming testimony—against them both. "Ah, if you're not sure, it means you probably don't...love her, I mean. That's a fine fix to be in," he said, controlling his voice, forcing it to rise above the tumult of the past. "When we have a woman of value, who's worth keeping, we scratch our heads and wonder if we're in love, and when we're alone, we wonder how we could have let her go. True?"

"You're right again. It's hardest for me when I feel she has only me to rely on. I want to escape; then I pity her and feel like a bastard."

He licked his lips—not so much by choice as by dread. He was mute. The judge's careful world had melted into his disguise; he couldn't maintain the two as separate realms. How could he condemn Valsin for something he himself had done? For a few awkward moments, both of them looked in other places.

"She's...she's—difficult at times," Valsin said. "I do my best to please her, but I have duties, other cares." He drained his tankard. "I've said too much," he muttered into the empty space. "Shall we go? I'm stiff with sitting. By the way, I'll look for you tomorrow at the coffeehouse."

"Fine."

"I don't think she'll join us."

"No? Please express my regrets."

"She's…indisposed."

On the way out, Valsin walked ahead. Just over the younger man's left shoulder, set into the door, the wraith's dark eyes watched them both. *Little witch,* he thought. He stared straight ahead while Valsin opened the door, and the surprised eyes turned aside.

10.

Julie, let me breathe. You make my blood froth; you make me tremble, you make me throb.

The sun grew stronger, and he stopped his promenade to stare up at the sky's milky brightness. Dazzled, he moved on, remembering the sun at Austerlitz, how he'd been directly beneath it, mounted on Pyerits, waiting to attack. Since then everything was changing: enemies to friends, despair to hope—the plane of his world tipping in response to—cosmic forces? Was he fate's puppet, or was this sequence of his life an expression of his deepest, truest self—an expression he alone directed?

Philosopher's questions—that's what she would call them.

The White Hound was on a small lane off the Kaufingerstrasse, which accounted for the French couple's frequenting the coffeehouse around the corner. The third floor—that's where Valsin had said their rooms were when the two of them met yesterday. The narrow lane was from the oldest surviving part of the city, a passageway whose cobbles were worn flat. It was shaped in a long curve so that, as he approached from a block down, he would be concealed from anyone watching from above.

In the noon hour, the business of the city seemed to pause, its tempo slowing before a promise of rest and the midday meal. Workmen walked with hands emptied of tools, shopkeepers pulled shutters closed. He glanced up at the row of windows on the third floor. Had Valsin returned from parade? Perhaps he and Anne-Marie had already left their rooms, making their way to the coffeehouse. Or did they remain within, engaged with one another, intertwining their thoughts and words, interweaving their histories with looks and gestures that occurred in the present, not the past?

How vulnerable lovers make themselves; any ecstasy, any true communion of souls, becomes a precious possession at risk of being lost or stolen.

A carter's wagon—filled with boxes and wooden crates of many sizes—rumbled past. The driver stopped, checking the address against an order in his hand, and began untying the ropes that held the load in place. Ruzhensky stopped too, pausing by a doorway to observe, wondering whether anything might topple over.

"Monsieur—Alexi?" She'd come up behind him, laden with several wrapped parcels, cloaked by the crowd and the sway of his thoughts. Like any proper lady in Russia, she wore a bonnet and a stylish jacket over her dress. Even so, he would recognize her anywhere.

"Julie—please excuse me—Anne-Marie," he said, making a bow. "Is the Lieutenant...? Here, allow me to help you." His face was burning, and he hesitated to straighten for fear she'd notice. Finally, he took hold of a sack and slid it off her arm.

"Thank you. I've been shopping. Today Valsin is on duty."

"Ah, then you must also allow me to buy you a coffee to amuse you in your loneliness."

The carter had finished his delivery, and the wagon pulled away without mishap. Beneath the hot sun, the edge of her bonnet made a line of shade across her brow, and she extended it, placing her hand above her eyes and peering up at him. He noticed how the flesh on her palm was red and swollen—as if from a burn.

Finally she nodded. "Very well."

"I've missed seeing you these past few days. Valsin said you were indisposed."

"I have missed you as well."

Such a direct statement. He glanced at her in surprise, feeling again a rush of blood to his face, a sensation in his belly not unlike the effects of a single glass of vodka. Her eyes were downcast but rose, pinning his own for an instant and then looking away.

Idlers occupied the coffeehouse; they sat near the window, watching the street, eager, no doubt, to see someone familiar with whom they could engage in conversation. Satisfied that Merseult was not among them, he guided her to the back where a table was set apart. "Please, order anything you like," he said, removing his hat and gloves.

"You must enjoy walking; you're pretty far from your rooms," she said. "Don't you miss riding?"

He considered this. "I'm able to enjoy both, having so much free time. Sometimes I hire a horse and sometimes not. Walking is a fine activity, an exercise for the body and spirit."

"How so?"

"The benefit to the body is clear, yes?" He felt settled again and smiled. "The spirit is nourished by the slow pace that allows considerable time for reflection and observation; one sees things one wouldn't see on horseback, being distracted by managing the beast." He inclined his head. "Do you understand?" He noticed the dark depths of her eyes, churning, he judged, with curiosity. "I also have not taken the time to purchase a new horse. I lost my mare at the battle. Pyerits was her name—it means pepper—and I find her hard to replace." He paused, watching, anxious to see what might cross her face. But she merely bobbed her head.

"Pepper. Men are so attached to their horses," she said. "Valsin would sooner part with me than Lily."

"Ah no, you're joking." For several moments they were distracted by the arrival of coffee and a plate of sweetened fruit tarts, covered with powdered sugar.

"These are good," she said, licking her fingers with a charming lack of self-awareness. "I could get used to this life." She sipped at the coffee and then leaned forward. "You and Valsin have become friends; he told me about your conversation the other night—some things at least. Did you tell him what to do?"

"What to do?"

"Yes, you know—give him advice. I know he respects your opinion. There are things he probably wants to discuss with you—in private. I think it's good for the two of you to talk."

"About military matters, you mean."

She frowned and took another tart. "About me."

How bold she was, direct like a man would be, as Natasha had been and Julie was. She was interrogating him, trying to discover secrets.

She persisted. "Did he say anything?"

He wiped his mouth with the napkin. "Gentlemen don't talk about ladies; I don't understand what it is you want me to say."

Her mouth rippled, and she ducked her head like a bird trying to hide beneath a wing. "I want to know what his plans are." She hunched her shoulders. "He says he loves me and then the next day talks of leaving. I can't live like this anymore. What did you tell him?"

A bird captured by love, a lovebird at risk of pining to death. "I will not say your name didn't come up in our conversation. When it did, it was in the way of admiration, and of—on my part—envy of Valsin's fortune."

She shook her head. "I want to know what he says." Her tone was strident; in fact, their whole encounter, which had held such a pleasant promise of mingling, had become oblique. The sudden shifts and twists in her conversation made his head ache.

"What is it you wish to know?"

"I already told you; when he talks of leaving the army, is he sincere? Or is it just a lie, and when he says he loves me, is that a lie too? Find those things out for me." A spot of color had risen to her cheeks, and she took a deep breath. "About love." Her voice cracked on the last word.

"Love—I'm sure he loves you," he said, hoping to soothe her. "The rest—it may take time."

Her eyes were squeezed shut as if in pain. "You won't help me; you're just like him. I'm going now." She gathered her things and made for the door, and he followed.

Outside the coffeehouse, she said she needed no escort to return home, but he was unwilling to let her go. "Valsin would want me to accompany you."

"No. I can't see you anymore."

"But why? We're friends, and—"

She shook her head. "No, it's not right. Good-bye," she said, tearing away.

He pursued her, but when he reached the corner, just after she'd turned to the left, it was as if she'd disappeared. With reluctance, he gave a last, searching look at the façade of the building where they lived and started back to the Kaufingerstrasse.

She's come and gone, as if Julie had stepped out of the pages of the book, alighting on the streets of Munich to eat cake and drink coffee, opening herself to me in a different way than Valsin did because men and women can't loosen themselves to each other the way a man can to another man. When a man and a woman come together—no matter what the circumstances—there always has to be a check on their passions and their gestures. Everyone knows that.

☆ ☆ ☆

When he returned to his rooms, Yevgeny reported that Marianne herself had gone out during his absence, refusing to permit an escort, as had been decreed. When she returned, laden with parcels, Ruzhensky confronted her. She looked at him angrily, saying she'd only gone to the market to do their shopping. "I don't need his help," she said, referring to Yevgeny. "Tell him to mind his own business."

A disturbing dilemma: if he forbade Marianne to go out at all, he risked her sullen anger or even defiance. If he let her go, he'd have to trust her. A third possibility occurred, and later when she was changing her clothes in the bedchamber, he approached Yevgeny. "Listen," he said. "When she goes out to shop, you wait a moment and then follow her—at a distance. To see if she's telling the truth."

11.

But one thing to note is that I began to see a different aspect of the same object that had never left my heart.

Munich was dark like a mine, its matte surfaces sucking away the feeble glimmers of the streetlamps. At this hour—ten o'clock—the few people who were out hurried past him, their faces buried in stiff collars. The air was dry and carried scents of mountain pine—no portents he could read. For several blocks, he walked slowly, followed a lamplighter, pausing whenever the other man did, watching from the shadows as the lamps were checked for flame.

At the next intersection—the lane Valsin lived on—a man in uniform crossed in front of him, and he hung back, pressing against the cool stone wall of a building. By the time he turned the corner, the anonymous figure had entered shadows farther down the street.

The first floor of The White Hound was awash with French soldiers and young women, hanging out of doorways and windows, arms around waists, legs around legs, singing and laughing. Away from the torches and candles, solitary, silent couples embraced in alleys and under eaves, some face-to-face, some front-to-back, moving together in an elemental, familiar dance.

Darkness covered the second floor; on the third, all but one of the windows glowed with yellow candlelight, wavering as if seen from much farther away, and he wondered if their chamber was the one unlit.

He'd told Anne-Marie he envied Valsin; could it be that he felt a stronger, darker sentiment? Whenever the three of them were together, he was reduced to employing a thief's strategy, stealing glance after glance, seeing how the younger man regarded her, touched her hand, her hair, intimacies that were endless and infinite. It was true: he resented how they sat together with no space between them.

From time to time, he'd overheard the other officers in his regiment discussing a sensation that tortured them into a sleepless, joyless state, a sensation caused by some infidelity of their mistresses. It seemed absurd to him, that men could be so weak. Surely—he'd always concluded—the answer was never to become so vulnerable.

Jealousy—was jealousy the sensation he felt when he thought about Marianne being with other men? Like mice gnawing at an unreachable itch—it was at once horrible and pleasurable. Alone, his thoughts often turned to imagining all the details of her most private moments before she'd met him.

It's as if we—Anne-Marie and I—are married but she's taken a lover. I'm like an old cuckold, obsessed by the pleasures they share at my expense, dreaming of the time she'll tire of him and come back to me.

The smile on his face galled him. He was already keeping too many secrets; should he also hide Anne-Marie—the way he felt about her—from Valsin?

I should break off all contact. But a Munich without them wouldn't be whole.

The best course would be to admit my feelings to Valsin, at least those of envy. I envy you, I could say. Her beauty has made me have certain thoughts that I hope to dispel by taking away their secrecy; by telling you, apologizing, I hope to receive your pardon. That would be best: confessing the attraction, unburdening myself—except it's no burden to dream about her.

He turned away from the silent building full of noisy flesh.

Across the street, a different figure wearing a cavalry shako stood motionless. He froze—was it Merseult? Merseult, who seemed to inhabit the edges of other encounters, interfering, provoking, but always only to a point. Whoever it was began striding toward him. Valsin.

"Alexi! A surprise. Let's walk together."

They talked about the weather, how it would no doubt be hot later in the summer. They spoke of the merits of equipping the cavalry with lances, a practice he was quite familiar with, having served often alongside Cossack squadrons. "Very effective against infantry," he said, and Valsin related that the Emperor Napoleon himself had been so impressed with the Poles' use of the weapon that he planned to outfit an entire brigade of lancers.

A patrol of gendarmes approached them, but their initial curiosity gave way to salutes when they saw Valsin's uniform in the light of their torch. Down certain streets, women called to them; otherwise they were alone.

"This is the second time we've met in this neighborhood," Valsin said. "Do you often walk at night? You need a woman to draw you home." They entered a small square and walked across, passing a small fountain. "Natasha—the woman you mentioned," Valsin said. "What happened?"

He brought one hand to his head, pinching his temples between thumb and finger. The past was nudging him again. "She killed herself. Threw herself in a river because I left her. You're shocked—but it's the truth. Listen, it was just a year ago last spring. We had a huge fight over some silly matter. I don't even remember what it was about." He looked at the toes of his boots appearing and disappearing with his stride. "That's untrue. I told her I was leaving. I was so angry I just wanted to get away for a while. She said she would die without me, and I laughed. The next time I saw her—she'd kept her promise. I wasn't that surprised," he said, and then his attempt at nonchalance failed. She deserved no false bravado. "I regret it, Valsin. Don't make the same mistake." The younger man didn't respond, and they walked on a further half-block.

"And since then, there's been no one?" Valsin asked.

"No." As they passed under a lamp, he glanced at the younger man's face and noted the absence of creases. "When I was your age, it was too difficult to be a soldier and a husband, just as you said the other night. My father urged me against marriage. I always believed it was a step that could be taken the following year. If I could go back somehow, I wouldn't delay; I'd rush to marry Natasha. My life would have been much better if I had. Instead, I kept putting her off until it was too late."

It occurred to him that this was a part of the truth. He might blame his father, he might cite ambition, but there had been other reasons. She'd frightened him as much as she'd attracted, and he hadn't been sure he was strong enough to bear her dependence. Again, he darted a look at Valsin; why not tell him the truth?

"What—what is it?" Valsin asked.

The past pressed on him so that he felt he must fall to his knees. If he could just tell Valsin all that had happened—then the younger man might understand and redeem them both. They rounded a corner, and he gazed up at the double towers, capped with onion shapes. A notion tugged at him. "I know this place. Let's go inside."

A rectangle of light lit up the entrance; the main door was open, and he wondered if the musicians he'd once heard in rehearsal might be performing again. But except for the scratching of an old woman's mop, the church was quiet and empty. Clouds full of incense and prayers were still gathered above the altar, and candles guttered before still, varnished images. He and Valsin moved halfway up the aisle and sat in a pew.

"This is a Catholic church, isn't it? Are you Catholic?" he asked.

"When I was a child."

He wondered aloud about confession; could sincerity really bring grace?

"That's the idea," Valsin said. "You go into those closets against the wall and talk to the priest through a screen. Repent your sins, renounce them. And yes, you have to tell the truth or...God knows."

He eyed the confessional, trying to imagine. "Do you believe that?"

"It's good to unburden yourself of the past, certainly, but I think the more important thing is to live your life with excellence in whatever you do. Of course, it's necessary to serve many apprenticeships, but once you achieve excellence, you can only sin against yourself."

He nodded, trying to digest what was surely an important idea. Then, facing the altar with its wounded, hanging man, he began to speak.

"Valsin, I have to tell you about something—someone. It's been troubling me, and—"

"And here we are talking about confession. Go ahead."

"Yes, well, I...you see." He clasped his hands and plunged forward. "That day—the last day I saw her, Natasha, her father had just died."

Valsin looked at him in silence and then leaned forward to grasp the back of the next pew with both hands.

"It affected her more than I thought it would. She wouldn't eat, didn't sleep. Each day I tried to encourage her, divert her; I read aloud, from the favorite book we shared, looking up at her in expectation after reciting a familiar passage.

"That day, it was glowing and spring. From the market square, two streets away from her house, sounds of cheerful laughter could be heard, and from the river, newly cleared of ice, came a wonderful, fecund aroma. Sunshine warmed the earth; mud had begun to compete with snow. Pyerits tossed her head, and I walked her around in a tight circle."

"Pyerits—your horse?"

"Yes. When I got to the house, I told myself, *I'll insist on opening the windows—all of them. After I hand Pyerits off to the porter, the first thing I'll do, I'll tell Irina*—Natasha's maid—*let in the wind, let in the light.* The house was musty, and it was past time to rein in the pace of mourning. You see, I was thinking about opening windows in order to avoid the truth."

"Uh-huh."

"The day before, I'd sent a note to my father asking that inquiries be made on my behalf regarding a staff position because, well…it was too soon after her father's death to propose marriage, but meanwhile, the world was stirring, glory was being amassed for distribution to the bold. When I returned, I thought—perhaps in a year or so—things would be different. I knew I had to tell her."

"I understand—go on."

"A quick inspection of her darkened bedroom showed everything as it had been the day before—heavy curtains stained with dust and weeping, eyes ringed with shadows and drooping with fatigue, as if they'd been exhausted in a vain search for one departed into oblivion. 'Natasha,' I said, 'soon it will be Easter, you must be ready.' I kissed her cheek and spoke in a hearty tone I hoped would provide encouragement. 'Wouldn't you like to walk around town? You can wear boots against the mud; if you like, we'll go to the bathhouse.' 'No,' she said.

"I paced the room, rehearsing a thousand things I wanted to say: that I loved her, that I hated her, that I would feel the same from afar. I stopped and faced her. 'My dear, I—'

"'I know what you're going to say,' she broke in, pausing to brush a curtain of hair away from her face. 'And you're right,' she continued, 'you've been patient. It's just that I feel as though I've lost myself.'

"A familiar tide brimmed her eyes, and the hair fell back across her brow; I turned to the window, thinking, *how can the woman possess any more tears?* 'I may be called away on campaign this spring,' I said. The sobbing stopped; silence wormed its way between us. 'It's just that I want you to be prepared, that's all. I haven't received any orders yet.'

"'And you want to be sent away,' she said after a moment. 'Then you'll be free of me.'

"'No, I have no choice; you know that. It's not that I want to go.' Within me, a worm squirmed around the lie. *I should treat her like a normal human being, not a child. I owe her that. Why not tell the truth then?* That's what I thought."

Valsin nodded.

"'I'm nothing but a burden to you,' she continued. 'It's because I need you that you want to run away.' Her voice, that beautiful instrument that had so often been a loving hand, easing my cares, kneading tense muscles—enticing me—had become harsh and grating, the twang of a nag. 'You feel obliged to marry me,' she said, 'and you don't want to, I can see it in your eyes—when you have the courage to show me your eyes. Every day, you're here; your body is here, but not you, your soul. It's as if I've received an official visit from a uniform with no man inside. That's the truth, isn't it?'

"I turned on her; I told her I'd never said I'd marry her, that I didn't know what I wanted.

"She crossed the room to stand in front of me and grabbed at my hands. 'Has our love,' she said, 'meant nothing?'"

He paused, aware of the echo in the vault of the church. Valsin seemed nearly asleep, but the silence stirred him. "Go on," he said.

"'I can't survive without you—please,' Natasha continued. 'Let's leave here, go anywhere, Moscow, Kiev. We'll be together, and we'll be happy. It doesn't matter if we marry.'

"And I snatched my hands free and made for the door." He spoke the last word and turned toward Valsin, waiting.

"And then?" Valsin asked.

"And then she asked me where I was going. And I told her I needed time to think.

"All the way down the stairs, I felt I was pulling against a long band of silk. Tighter and tighter it enclosed me, but I pulled back even harder and at last, tore free. At the door, the maid regarded me with frightened eyes. I paused on the porch outside, surprised at how the struggle had made my heart race. It was good that we'd argued, I told myself, good for her to be angry. That's what a person needs to be able to grieve, everyone says that. Then, moving off down the street, I twisted around on Pyerits's back and looked up. Ever since her father's death, the drapes in her room had been drawn, but now they parted, and for a moment, a slim, wraith-like hand touched the glass."

Valsin leaned back in the pew and pushed out his lips. "And that's the last time you saw her?"

"Alive, yes," he said. "She gave me everything—her house and the servants, all her money. Everything and nothing. So Valsin, you see? Do you understand?"

The next day, he'd received a message from Colonel Lensky. He was to end his leave and rejoin the regiment as soon as possible. The Hussar who delivered it said there were rumors of a summer campaign against France. He told Yevgeny to prepare for the trip south to Berdichev, the regimental headquarters, thinking how the plans of the emperors had freed him from having to make a decision.

In the midst of this relief, Natasha's porter—Pavel—appeared, his leathery face swollen from weeping. "Your Honor, it's the mistress!" he announced. "She sent us away—we didn't think anything was wrong. She was weak, poor girl, but she got Chorny saddled by herself and she must have taken him up the river, up where the current is strong...turned him loose...we found him—later." The porter gave a great sob. "The water— she threw herself in the water. They found her in the city, she...her body caught against one of the bridge pilings—swept downstream all that way."

A tunnel formed, a narrowing black tube into which Pavel shouted. At the other end—his end—the porter's voice was a hollow croak, making sounds in an exotic language, like a Tartar. He mouthed the word *no*, and his own voice sounded just as foreign.

"Your Honor, it's true. Maybe she fell off Chorny, an accident."

The tunnel constricted, choking him. He grabbed Pavel by the shoulders and pushed him out of the way, then rushed outside and began running toward her house. If she'd thrown herself into the river below the town, the current would have taken her far away; they might never have found her. *She wanted me to know.* Then he understood—beyond any doubt—not just that she was dead but that he'd killed her.

A coffin had already been placed in the parlor of her house, and on halting steps, he approached so that she came into view by stages. Her body had been washed clean. The beautiful, thick hair that he'd so often twined in his fingers was now combed and covered with the lace bonnet she'd last worn at the New Year. On her bruised face, he sought signs of reproach. No, there was nothing; she wasn't there. The hands he'd often kissed were cold and dry, the sapphire ring she always wore a harder shape above hard bone.

There was nothing from her—no letters, no gifts. The flowers she'd given him months ago were more than faded. With little resistance, the ring came off and fit around his little finger.

On the way out, he told Irina to inform the priests he would pay for the prayers to be sung, for her body to be anointed. "Tell them—whatever the cost."

"Your Honor, she left this," she said, handing him a folded note. He opened it with shaking hands.

You're free now. Remember me.

N.

It wasn't enough. Couldn't there be more? More than a solitary initial. While Irina sobbed in the hallway, he tore the room apart, finding nothing but bottomless drawers full of her scent.

Valsin was talking. "And you're saying you blame yourself?"

"Of course, if I'd just stayed with her." He covered his face with his hands.

"If you'd stayed, you would have saved her? No. How can you possibly know that? It sounds to me like she was an unhappy person, probably her whole life. How long did you know her? A year—that's all? And you take responsibility for everything? You treated her badly, but you didn't kill her."

He gestured at the confession booths. "I wonder, is it possible to judge oneself and be free of doubt?"

"No—then there'd be no need for priests."

Valsin began laughing, and he stared at him. It was as if the younger man knew what the older was thinking—all of it—and still, was able to laugh. Laugh while they both waited in the prisoner's stall. He thought of priests in satin robes, waving smoking censers, singing a ragged line of chant deep in their throats. Was that their purpose—to tell you if you were justified in feeling righteous or sinful? Could others free you from doubt?

"I think you are a priest," he said, gulping air and wiping his face with a handkerchief. "I've just confessed something because I wanted you to understand."

Valsin smirked. "Do you feel better? If I were your priest, I'd give you an act of penance to perform like climbing the steps of the cathedral on your knees. You see, that would demonstrate publicly that your repentance was sincere."

Disturbed, he shook his head. "Isn't there some other way?"

"I'm joking—shall we go?"

✻ ✻ ✻

An hour later, the glow of the oil lamp revealed it was just before midnight, a time of transition, a time for important thoughts and resolutions. He put his watch back in his waistcoat pocket and threw himself into the armchair. Besides the settling fire, the only sound was Yevgeny snoring from behind the screen.

At the church, instead of telling Valsin what he'd intended—that he was infatuated with Anne-Marie—he'd been confronted with himself. What had made him offer the story of Natasha's death? It was as if he'd set off in one direction and wound up in another.

On the table was a letter; this one he would open—tomorrow. He knew what it was—a short note from the lawyer in Brest-Litovsk and a bank draft representing the year's rent on Natasha's house.

Why had Valsin introduced the image of climbing up steps on one's knees? It was disturbing, not because he had any aversion to pain—physical pain was simply something to be endured. It was its public nature. To do such a thing would be a waking nightmare of exposure.

Of course, in Munich no one knew him; better to be shamed here than in Russia. He slumped in the chair. No one knew him any longer in Russia either—he'd disappeared, like a boot that steps and passes out of sight forever. He rose and went to the table. The small mirror on the toiletry box was dark; he moved the lamp closer, and in the gloom, the flame appeared like a watch fire. To its side was half a mustache, lips, a nostril—all in deep shadow, as if his face were a sculpture of hard, exaggerated edges. He strained into the shadows, searching for the wraith who'd accompanied him for so long, so far. *She must show herself now,* he thought. *Tonight—at this moment.*

But on one side of the room and then the other, there was nothing.

The cathedral clock began tolling, and he moved to the window, counting twelve strokes.

12.

The young man, blind to the changes made in his mistress by the advance of time, loved her the way he had seen her and no longer the way she was.

She'd been well into her first sleep when he returned, banging against the doorframe in the darkness. "Valsin?"

"Sorry. Didn't want to wake you."

She rose and lit a candle in the other room, checking out of habit to see his image, softened and indistinct in the penumbra of swooping light. He sat at the table and took off his boots. "I was with Crèpin and Merseult and then, as I left the tavern, there he was again—Ruzhensky. We walked for a while."

At the sound of his name, she glanced at him and then away. Should she say she'd seen him the other day? She poured out the rest of an uncorked bottle of wine into two glasses, remembering how the tarts had tasted of sweet fruit and cream. "It's strange how you keep meeting him."

"Thanks. Yes. He told me a story. I don't think he intended to; it just fell out between us."

"What story?"

"About a mistress he had in Russia. Apparently she died, and he blames himself." He took a drink and smacked his lips. "I don't know. He seemed upset, but it didn't make sense to me. He said that the woman's father died, and then he—Ruzhensky—was called away on campaign. When he told her, she drowned herself in a river. It seems to me—"

"Everyone left her."

"What?"

"Everyone left her—that's why she killed herself."

He shrugged. "What choice did he have? Anyway, people don't kill themselves over one or two misfortunes. It takes a whole series of blows. Listen, it's not so unusual in the military—suicide, I mean. And the ones who do it—it's never a surprise to those who know them. God, this wine is sour."

"Was Ruzhensky surprised?"

"I don't know. What I'm saying is that people like that—well, they plan their deaths for years, and their comrades know it."

"Did he say what the woman's name was?"

"Natasha—one of those great Russian names, eh? I bet she was a beauty. Why?

"Just curious."

He stretched and yawned and said he was going to sleep. Soon, in the next room, a torrent fell into the chamber pot and then a rustle of clothes on the floor. For some time she sat hearing the creak of the bed as he settled, staring with unfocused eyes at the candle's tiny, wavering light. She finished the wine.

Before Austerlitz, she'd never met anyone from Russia. Her knowledge of the land was confined to stories about Cossacks raping and pillaging. At the Fröelichs', the maids said they'd kill themselves rather than be taken by a Russian, whom they claimed were half demon. Many of them had been at the battle, the still and dead, the disarmed prisoners pleading for mercy. And the wounded—at the hospital where they took Valsin, most of the men were Russian. An image flashed through her mind like a winter squall, an officer in blue and silver frozen at the end of her saber.

All those men, including the one I killed, were nameless strangers, only partly real. Ruzhensky—he's becoming too real.

She imagined him riding a horse bareback across fields full of grain, bursting seedpods with a whip, sending their powder floating through sun-lit air. She wondered how he would smell, whether his bare skin would be pale or tanned. What scars *did* he have? So his lover had died from his neglect. Of course Valsin couldn't understand such a thing because it was too close to him. It was clear enough to her what had happened. The woman's father dies; she has no one else, and to him, she becomes a burden, too great, and so he rushes away, and she despairs.

But alive—Ruzhensky's mistress had ridden as a man. In her vision, a beautiful, dark-haired woman joined the horseman in the meadow and she watched—a little jealous.

From the other room, Valsin's breathing was slow and regular; she wanted to fall asleep too, to not think anymore, but her mind was working on something, like a bird weaving together sticks and bits of stolen cloth to make a nest. She snubbed out the candle and sat forward, clasping her hands together and touching her fingertips to her lips.

I have to get hold of this thing that's going on. This thing between the three of us—Valsin, Ruzhensky, and I.

She'd realized it the day she met him on the street.

On the surface, he's an older version of Valsin. His eyes are darker, though—more piercing. With him I have to work harder at hiding myself. And he's in love with me; I can see it in his look, in the moments of silence between us. His desire makes me too aware of him; when we're together, he surrounds me, and then later, lingers like smoke in a close room.

When we left the coffeehouse and he said he'd escort me here, my heart was beating so fast; I was afraid I couldn't stop him. Because I knew Valsin wasn't here, that he'd be gone for hours. I could have asked him to come, I could have...I ran to get away from him. How many times will that work before I say yes?

She resolved never to be alone with him again. If she met him on the street—even if it was midday—she'd excuse herself and hurry away. And it wasn't even good to see him with Valsin; it was too uncomfortable.

But she could not settle. Sleep wouldn't come because Valsin had told her the story of the Russian woman drowning herself. In a river. All she could imagine were drowned kittens, the way their fur matted, how they looked to be asleep. A river, she thought, would be so cold. There'd been times when she'd sat in the kitchen of the farm where she'd lived with her dead husband, watching bread dough rise, wondering how things would be different if she didn't exist. Without her, she'd thought, all the routines of the house would continue, the floors swept with bundles of rushes, tides of firewood and buckets full of water coming in, going out as ash and steam. But she'd see none of it; those routines were nails driven into wood to shape a coffin. She'd given her life till the end of that year, and in that time it must prove that miracles could happen.

Miracles did happen, and she was still alive, but routines and waiting were again beginning to crowd around like crows at the battlefield.

13.

Human souls want to be coupled to express all their worth.

In the morning, he resolved to go directly to Valsin and tell him what he'd meant to say the previous night. He gave a brusque farewell to Marianne and headed first for the bank to deposit the rent money on Natalya's house, thinking he would ride to Valsin's quarters and catch him before he left for the coffeehouse.

However, the banker kept him waiting and finally requested he come back the next day. When he went to hire a horse, the apologetic stable master asked him to return in a half hour as all the animals had been taken.

So it was past noon when he arrived, and he left the horse at a stable and walked the last block through a summer rainstorm. In front of the building, there were no soldiers and none present when he crossed the threshold, and he regretted all the delays that had probably caused him to miss Valsin.

The stairwell smelled of equal parts turpentine and mildew; his tread provoked creaks and groans, making echoes dart across the dark, dusty space above. Rainwater ran from the ends of his mustache onto his jaw.

When he reached the landing, he imagined he could hear, on the other side of the wall, a clacking of heels as she hurried to let him in, smoothing her skirts with her hands. If Valsin were gone to parade, she'd no doubt have walked to the market to buy bread and wine and then found nothing else to do. She'd be bored, just as Marianne was.

He knocked, and the door opened quickly, as if she'd been right there, waiting. She took a step back, staring at him as a child would, in silence, her hand pressed against the doorframe. Light poured through the window into the room behind her, obscuring everything but her shape and her eyes—dark, wet, porcelain saucers, shining and opaque. For a moment they stared at each other. "Good day, mademoiselle," he said at last, removing his hat and bowing his head. "Is the Lieutenant here?" If Valsin were out, he'd have to change his plans.

"He's not," she said, holding her ground and regarding him—he could make out her features now—with the same drowsy expression she'd had on her face at the dinner party. Perhaps she'd been sleeping.

"Ah, I was out riding and hoped I might see him. I wished to…discuss something."

"Today you're riding; I thought you preferred to be on foot so you could think."

Her face was perfectly smooth like a statue, giving no sign of what she thought or felt. Only her gaze, direct and unwavering, spoke of a defiance he wasn't prepared for. Was she angry with him? They continued to face each other in the doorway.

"Mademoiselle, I don't wish to trouble you, but do you suppose I might come inside for a moment?" He'd just begun moving forward when, to his surprise, she pushed the door hard as if to shut him out. His boot had already crossed the threshold, and the toe made a solid thump against the narrowing panel. He frowned, looking down at the point of contact, and she continued to push, also regarding his boot and also frowning. Then with an inclination of her head, she stepped back from the doorway, and the door was released.

"You're most kind," he said, entering the room. "I think I may have misjudged the weather; it's raining hard. There aren't many people out. The Lieutenant is...?" She pulled a second chair up to the table and sat down. "I thank you, mademoiselle," he said, encouraged by her gesture.

"Why do you keep calling me that? Call me Anne-Marie the way you usually do. Your coat's all wet; take it off if you want."

He stood and removed his coat, the activity allowing him a moment's reflection. Being alone with her—not in a public place but in these rooms that he had often imagined—had imposed a formality on his words. In such a free space, to call her by her name seemed too great a liberty.

"Valsin is at parade; this afternoon they'll be drilling."

"Ah," he said, sitting down. He could easily imagine what Valsin was doing—suffering like a beggar in the storm. "I hope he wouldn't object to my being here."

She looked away and shrugged. "Want a glass of wine?" Her voice, usually so sweet, sounded nasal, as if she had a cold.

"Please," he said. "I also hope you don't mind my being here." In what he concluded must be silent acknowledgment of his candor, she glanced at him from the corner of her eyes and then came closer, standing at his side while she poured. The wine gurgled, and a scent of rose water filled the space between them. She wore a striped skirt, blue on white, and had a pale rose-colored handkerchief tied over her breast like a shawl. In the sunlight, her hair was loose, golden, glorious. But her sullenness frustrated him—she must not be mute like some anonymous serving-girl. He'd provoke her. "Well, do you?" he said.

"Do I—what—mind that you're here?" she said with a slash of her eyes. She sat down again. "What good would it do? You forced your way in."

He looked down and sipped the wine. "Yes, I suppose I did, but what I mean is: do you mind my being here at this moment?" He widened his eyes in a manner he'd once seen an actor do.

"I neither care nor don't care. Today, at this moment, I'm indifferent to you."

It was said with just a hint of drama, enough so he felt encouraged. She crossed her legs and began twisting a lock of hair between her fingers.

"Ah, you're neutral then. I recall the other day—when you surprised me on the street—you asked for my help, to find out what Valsin's plans were regarding...the military—is something wrong?" All through this speech her color had increased in an ascending, scarlet bloom. In her eyes, steel collided with flint.

"I don't need to know about that; I don't care anymore," she said, speaking in a rush. "Talk about someone—something else. And I didn't surprise you on the street."

He drew himself up, offended at her tone—as if he were the servant. "Just what is it you wish me to speak of? Tell me, please—and be more pleasant." She sniffed, twisting her hair faster. Something about him seemed to elicit the worst sort of behavior from her; he certainly hoped that would change soon. At least she was no longer sullen. For the moment, he must gentle her, treat her as he would a wild mare. He took a deep breath. "Do you enjoy riding, mademoi—" he paused and smiled. "Anne-Marie. I understand you ride well."

"For a woman, you mean." It wasn't said as a question. "Why are you being so formal today, Alexandre? If you're going to ask me to go riding, I don't want to."

"No, of course not," he continued, trying for a sweetened tone. "You've ridden for a long time?"

"No."

He was pleased she'd actually responded. "Really! I'm astonished. How did you learn so quickly?"

"My husband was a horse dealer. Day and night, I was surrounded by horses." She poured more wine for herself and muttered something. "Sick of them," was all he could make out.

"Day and night, I see. Well, you're quite skilled to have ridden as a trooper. Military standards are high." He paused. "I wasn't aware you were married."

"I was. He died."

He'd forgotten about that. Strange to think of another man besides Valsin possessing her. "I'm sorry."

"How do women ride in Russia?" she said.

"Oh, ladies ride as they do here. Some women, though, ride as men do, as you did." He grimaced at his crudeness. "Please excuse me," he began, but she did not seem to mind or notice.

A memory erupted of the horseman at Austerlitz, who had not ridden sidesaddle. "Made—Anne-Marie," he said, his mind plunging, "I don't know why it's hard for me to call you that today. I think it's because we're alone."

She stared at him and blinked.

"The other day, you said you couldn't see me anymore. I didn't understand why because there's nothing to be ashamed of. We're friends, you and I, and I enjoy talking with you. I was going to tell you that I too lost someone whom I loved. Not a wife—as I've never married—but a woman who wore trousers or full-cut pants like a Cossack when we went riding. Where I live, there are vast forests. You'd like it, I think."

"Did people think she was strange?"

"For wearing pants and riding horses? No. Besides, she didn't care what others thought of her. The company of women, the fashions of women—dresses and stockings—confined her. She was never happier then when she could ride a good horse all day, through sun and rain."

"What was her name?" Her tone was softening, her voice drawling.

"Natalya Ivanovna."

"Natalya Ivanovna," she repeated, making the name sound more musical, drawn out like a melody of bells. "And how did she die?"

He looked off to a corner. "She fell ill." Natasha's real death couldn't be spoken of here—why had he even brought her up? It was her; her jealous spirit had inserted herself into their private conversation. His eyes swept the room.

"I haven't ridden since—we came here," she said, looking directly at him and coloring, as if she were surprised by the effect of her beauty. "I miss it. Valsin never wants to go anymore. I think he only wants me in dresses and…stockings." She poured more wine into his glass, and a few drops spilled from the neck of the bottle onto the table, glistening for a fraction of a second before being absorbed by the wood.

"Ah, well—sidesaddle then." Within his shirt and waistcoat, he'd begun to feel hot and immobilized. Now that she seemed calmer, there were important things to say; he must bring their conversation back around to her fears of Valsin leaving. "You know, I've meant to ask you if you enjoy reading. I have a book, a book I treasure, *Julie*—"

"About the lovers? No, I've always wanted to…to read it. I know how to read."

"I'll lend you my edition; it's been an inspiration to me. We could discuss it. It's all about life, even though—at the end…"

"Don't tell me the ending!"

"No, I assure you."

She smiled at him, and he smiled back, noticing how her smile pressed two elegant lines of dimples below her cheeks. All at once, he felt pleased and ridiculous. Why had he mentioned *Julie?* Should he now say she reminded him of the main character? No, she was more than a reminder. "I'll say again how pleasant it is to talk together," he continued. "My thoughts have often turned to you as I've gotten to know Valsin. I wish we could become better friends. I know how important you are to him and—"

"He said that?" The dimples retreated.

"Of course, many times. Please excuse me for being so direct, but I believe he worries about your welfare should he be called to duty. I understand only too well how such a thing could happen." Now he felt he had some momentum. "Have you given this much thought?"

"What are you saying?" she replied, narrowing her eyes. "Why are you asking me such personal things, especially when I've told you I don't want to discuss them?"

"It's just that I believe I'm in a unique position to be of help. You see, years ago, I was in a similar situation." He paused, hoping to get a sign of encouragement from her, but she'd not only crossed her arms but had re-crossed her leg and had begun making the foot jiggle with furious energy. "It was the woman I just mentioned; I was very much in love, but because of my military career, we had to endure long periods of separation."

"And what did she do?"

"Ah, it was difficult, but she consoled herself by writing letters; we consoled each other that way."

"But you said she died."

"Yes. She was…not consoled." Like a punctured bladder of air, what he'd said lay flat on the floor between them.

"I don't understand you."

"No—I'm being too indirect. What I want to say is how difficult it is to express the depths of love to someone, to make them understand your innermost feelings. I've always been clumsy at it, and Valsin is like me, I think. You must know how he loves you, and that whatever comes to pass, you can rely on him, trust that he only needs a little more time to under-stand himself."

On her face it was clear that the anger and impatience that had been present were gone; she seemed to focus beyond him in confusion, a film across her eyes. He'd won through something, passed her outer defenses. "We're all—"

"I wasn't supposed to be there," she broke in. "At the battle." For a moment, her shuttered gaze flickered, as if she'd allowed him through but then had closed it tight behind him. "I was supposed to wait, behind the lines, wait while the men fought," she continued in a flat voice. "They dressed me as a soldier because a general complained about a woman being present." She grimaced. "It seems foolish now, as if it were about someone else, someone you hear about in a story. You see, I just wanted to be with him, with Valsin, and then I was in the war."

"I do see," he said. Why had she begun talking about Austerlitz? He shook his head, knowing what was to come. It seemed that this was his penance—to hear the tale told again and again.

Better than walking on my knees.

"An officer saw me—once the fighting had begun. He thought I was a straggler and sent me forward, and then my horse got excited, and I was caught up in the charge. And then, I saw this man shoot Valsin." She glanced at him, with reproach, he thought. She became still and folded her hands in her lap but seemed to be looking past him, as if he were an image lacking dimension, not fully flesh and blood.

"I can still feel the sword going in his side," she whispered. "Ah God, I dream about it! Don't you understand? Damn you." She took a handkerchief from her sleeve and touched her mouth, hiding the damage.

"No." He reached for her across the table. After a moment of recoil, she allowed his hand to stay atop hers. "I understand you," he said, feeling warm silk. "You were trying to protect the person you loved." He understood more: her terrible gaze was not directed at him but at the violence, the killing. "Please, it's all right, the battle is far in the past."

Chance put us at odds. We needn't be enemies any longer.

With her free hand, she swiped at the passage of a tear down her cheek. "When I first met him, I knew that whatever love we shared wouldn't last; loving him would be like being inside an hourglass emptying. But he took me with him, and for that, I felt I owed him my life. That's why, when that man was going to kill him, I didn't think twice. I wasn't afraid. I should just feel grateful for the time we've had and not hang onto it. It's driving him away faster; I feel it. I don't want to be grasping. But when he leaves, I'll be alone."

Who was speaking? Of course, it was the woman before him, but she was expressing things over which Natasha could have claimed ownership. He shifted in the suddenly too-small chair. Could Marianne? Here was a glimpse of another world, another half of the world he and Valsin inhabited. "No," he said. "You're not driving him away; it's something else, something inside him that he can't let you see."

"What? Why not?"

"It feels like a weakness."

"What is it?"

"That he needs you to be complete."

She stared at him, her brow creased, her head beginning to shake back and forth. "He told you that? But it doesn't make sense. If he needs me, why leave?"

She was like a princess in a tower, and he'd climbed all that way to see her, groping through their conversation, finding a toehold with his boot, getting closer and closer. He caught himself leaning halfway across the table, bending toward her like one of those straining young saplings.

With her other hand, she lifted his off, taking both hands back and folding her arms across her breast, hugging her ribs with her open palms. "I love him with all my heart. If that means accepting that he must leave me, then I'll accept it. I'm not grasping." She shook her head more quickly and squeezed her arms.

"And afterward?"

"When he goes? What are you saying now?"

"Nothing. Just that if he does leave, I wonder what you'd do."

"I don't know." She shrugged and looked down. "I have some ideas. Life goes on."

That was it: the affirmation he'd sought. By her simple statement, she'd freed him in a way she couldn't possibly comprehend. He rose, intending to embrace her, but caught himself. "Very happy then," he said. "I'm very happy. You know, I hope that every day Valsin tells you how pretty you are. When you smile, dimples crease each side of your mouth, and you appear generous and lovely." Why had he said that? Her eyes tugged at him, and he saw how lonely she was. After clearing his throat, he looked at his watch. "I've intruded long enough; I must leave you with many thanks for this conversation. I don't think Valsin will return anytime soon."

"Do you have to leave?" she said, rising too. "Where will you go?"

Her directness was like a child's question. "To return the horse I hired, get a good supper, and think of how pleasant it was to have your anger at me melt."

"I wasn't angry at you. Just unsettled. And a little dizzy."

He intended to kiss her hand and stepped forward, but his motion seemed to set her moving as well. In the next moment, they were pressing together, as if they'd both gestured, and made the distance between them disappear. In her mouth, he tasted wine. Only a small part of him was unoccupied with her, and it shouted in his ear—stop!—and he seized her upper arms to push her away. But didn't let go. She looked back with widened eyes and shook her head. Was she saying no to what they'd begun or no to being pushed away? It was clear they couldn't speak. Against his grasp, her arms strained—toward him and her hands slipped free and reached for his hips to pull him closer. He tore the handkerchief free from her breast and the blouse from her shoulders, ripping the fabric. Another kiss, and they moved backward until the corner of the table pressed her thighs apart and her legs embraced his.

He lifted her up to the surface of the table, pulling away bunches of trousers and skirts.

14.

If I can get back up again, I will force you to forget my fall.

All around her, voices floated above the loping melody of a hurdy-gurdy, and aromas of tobacco and roasted meat hung in the tavern's thick air. With the blade of a large, wooden spoon, she skimmed the surface of a bowl of potato soup.

"What's this thing called again?" Valsin asked.

"A Chinese shadow show."

He looked pleased. "Is it—"

"You ask me every time—I don't know if it's from China." At one end of the room, a gauzy screen of scrim had been set up, lit from behind to create a warm, golden color. Every other moment, shapes glided across its surface—the puppeteers' preparations. "Probably."

"So, what did you do today?"

"Same as always," she said into the bowl.

I allowed him in because of boredom—that and too much wine. When he first arrived, I was spiteful. He was right to think I was angry—angry at his friendship with Valsin, for the way he'd just assumed I'd be welcoming—as if he knew I wanted to be alone with him. I struck a balance between meanness and provocation, teasing him, making his skin red like certain morning skies.

But then, the things he began to say were not things any man had ever said to me before. A priest, maybe. He's no priest.

"I know—you get so bored. I'm sorry," Valsin said. "That's why I wanted to bring you here tonight—to atone for it." He cracked his knuckles. "I worked them hard today. We did everything exact, worked till the drill was perfect. Like Prussians. The generals will be pleased."

They'd done it twice; the first time he'd come quickly, and she'd hung onto him with her legs and arms, laughing until he began kissing her again. When he was hard, she put him back inside her and moved against him in a slow grind that finally burst like a hot flower whose petals she could still feel.

Then, before she could do much more than climb off the table, pulling her skirts down, he'd turned away and re-arranged his own clothing. He did have a recent scar—below his ribs; she'd seen its white and pink trail through his open shirt, and he'd seen her seeing it and turned his back. When he was once again dressed, she brushed a long blond hair off his coat, thinking it was her own, but she saw it was a lighter shade, and she'd held it up, looking at him and canting her face to one side. But he'd turned away and at the door, stopped and said, "We must never—" in a hoarse voice. And he'd gone, leaving her wondering what it was he'd been about to say. Never tell, never love? Never be enemies—again.

A short, dark-haired man, whom she recognized as the puppet master, emerged from behind the screen to survey the room. He cleared his throat. In response, there was a gradual diminution of conversation, giving way to the rustling and scraping of chairs against the floor. The man clasped his hands together in front of his chest. "Ladies and gentlemen," he announced, "a new offering—*The Lady and the Hussar*. Please gather 'round."

Up until the moment when Valsin stepped into their rooms, she'd had every intention of telling him about Ruzhensky's visit—at least a variation of it. Because part of the truth is better than none.

He came by today, looking for you. We talked for a while.

Her hesitation hadn't come until, after kissing him, she'd opened her lips to speak. The words had hung at the brink, and she'd trembled, frightened at what she'd done. What, she thought, if he should become angry even at the idea of Ruzhensky calling? She'd done something very wrong, bad. If Valsin learned the truth, one of the two men would kill the other, and it would be her fault. No, better to say nothing.

Her mouth twisted.

Sinful.

Valsin glanced at her, and she quickly turned the twist into a grin.

The hurdy-gurdy lurched into a wheezing military march that made the audience laugh. From one side of the screen to the other, a shadow minced, then reversed course. The candlelight was adjusted, and the outline of a horse and rider became visible. The horse pawed the ground, and over his head, the rider brandished the tiniest of swords.

The music became a wistful, pretty melody, and the silhouette of a woman appeared, wearing a bonnet and carrying a basket of flowers. The horseman lowered his sword and drew near. The horse pranced and capered, and the rider preened, presenting first one profile and then the other to the audience. He dismounted and—after bowing to one other—the couple broke out into a dance. Every now and then they stopped to embrace, each embrace becoming longer and more passionate. The music soared.

She studied Valsin's profile. He beat the song's rhythm on his knee, on his face, an idiot's smile.

With much more speed than she'd ever imagined, she'd become a soldier's wife, and like one, she would soon be left behind. Perhaps she should ask Dalhousie for another uniform and join the regiment as Witowski had said others had done, other women unwilling to be abandoned. Would Valsin want that? Lately he'd seemed preoccupied. That was it—it was his preoccupation that had allowed Ruzhensky entry. Despite her brave statements about love and life going on, she was also too full of spite.

The horseman was bent over, kissing his lover, when the hurdy-gurdy gave a passable imitation of a trumpet call. At the sound of this call to arms, the man's head snapped up. The horse reappeared and nudged his master in the back, and the audience burst into laughter. To sudden melancholy strains, the rider passed off the edge of the screen.

The woman bent down to pick up her basket. When she straightened, her belly bulged. The audience cheered, whereupon both horse and man returned to join the woman for a bow.

"Amazing," Valsin said as the applause diminished. "The puppets look real, don't they? And they're just made from paper and leather, maybe some ink. I must tell Ruzhensky about this; he'll be interested. What is it?"

Her cheeks were like fire in a forge. All those in the audience, she was sure, were sharply aware of her; in the next moment they would whisper and glance at the shape of her belly. Nods would pass, winks—then an unclothed laughter.

Ruzhensky. He was with her still, this time not as flesh but as a word from her lover's lips. From the very first instance when he'd introduced himself, she'd felt jealous of his influence on Valsin, of the time the two men spent together, time so clearly of value. But today she'd realized that—after his visit in the long hours of the afternoon—she wouldn't feel jealous of him again. Instead, there would be a curiosity about someone who'd caused a shift, a shuffle in a realm where the things she cared about swam in large, opaque shapes. She needed time to name them.

"The soup is cold," she said. "Can we go?"

15.

We have the upper hand, charming Julie; our friend's mistake has restored him to reason.

During the early hours of the night, the wind—which Marianne referred to with dread as the *föhn*—began. It caused, she claimed, people to become irritable and strange things to happen. Under the eaves of the house, the air moaned and shrieked, scouring the walls and roofs and making a legion of wary dogs bark. And she slept in the moon's glow, curled toward him on her side, her left hand clutched close to her lips, her knees pressing against his thigh.

He'd washed and gone to bed early, claiming he was tired, but away from the softness of the other woman's flesh and the hard edge of the table, he couldn't sleep. How had it happened? He'd gone to Valsin's intending to confess his feelings about Anne-Marie and instead had made things a hundred times worse, as if his efforts to free himself had only ratcheted his shackles tighter. It wasn't like him; he was used to discipline and self-denial, an ordered life.

It was just that, it was so sudden—like a well-planned ambush.

At a certain point in the conversation—at the end when he'd been most sincere—it had occurred: that shift in her affections that had been evident in her eyes, and the way her mouth had become fuller.

And there had been a delay in his departure, filled with many moments of caress. Under her blouse, her arms had been silken ropes bracing herself against him, giving him purchase on her, as if she were a lovely boat holding fast with its anchor against the tide-driven sea, bracing ever harder as that sea raged and foamed.

The Frenchwoman's anger had melted, anointing him, transforming him into something more than a reminder of violent death and war, but still—even as they coupled—she'd watched him with dark, curious eyes, not speaking. Like any good soldier, she'd kept something in reserve, and that realization made her even more attractive. He was like Julie's anonymous lover who, after their tryst in the chalet, was not satisfied but only desired her more. The book's words came easily to him:

No one knows you; you don't know yourself. My heart alone knows you, feels you, and understands how to place you where you belong.

A stab of pain made him hurry his palm below his ribs where the sword had gone in—her sword. Weeks had passed since it'd troubled him. He took a deep breath, but the movement caused a pulling sensation around the scar.

How can I face him?

He pulled the sheet higher around his chest, and Marianne murmured and laid her hand on his shoulder. The tryst had been an error—an exquisite one, but one that must remain an isolated event. To keep it so would not be difficult; he was far too experienced a horseman to lose his seat twice.

He'd just have to act as if it hadn't happened; the two halves of his whole world in Munich must not touch.

The bells rang the hour, and he rose. He would return to the bank—a gentleman's business of a serious nature. He hoped to get away without waking her, but while he finished a cup of tea, she entered the room, yawning. Behind his screen, Yevgeny polished his master's boots, banging brushes and heels, and then shifted to sharpening the dagger. The sound of the leather strop was like a serpent's hiss. Next, he was sure, his servant would wind the clock, raising the pitch of time higher and higher.

He stood. "My dear. The wind started last night; I recognized it from your description. Very unusual. Well, I'm out for a while. Yevgeny, my gloves."

"Where are you going?"

He sighed; her tone and posture were too familiar. Intolerable. She was unhappy, and her unhappiness refused to be contained. It threatened to overflow and carry away a part of his life in a flood. Not a flood of tears—she was too strong for that, and besides, tears were easy—a flood of bitter anger. *Wretched maid indeed,* he thought.

"Marianne, please don't start; I told you, the bank. I'll return by early afternoon."

"Take me with you. If you're so ashamed of me, you could just pretend I'm your wife. Besides, what difference would it make? You don't know anyone here except for all those French officers."

He caught Yevgeny's eye, but the old man bowed his head and withdrew behind the screen. Had there been a smirk on his face? "How can you speak to me like that?" he said. "My God, you're not even up five minutes and you're complaining. It's quite impossible to act as if we're husband and wife—we're not. Don't bring it up again. The next time I go out, smile and say good-bye; when I return, smile and embrace me. That's what I expect."

"You're going to the bank to get your father's money even though you ignore and defy him. Then you'll probably spend it on some new whore while I wait for you to finish. Just go; get out!"

She screamed the last word, and he hurried down the stairs.

✻ ✻ ✻

"Monsieur Ruzhensky, forgive me for not being able to see you yesterday. Your account will be credited immediately."

The banker—a Herr Montag—was an older man with the smooth skin of one accustomed to neither smiles nor frowns. Until this point, their dealings had been quite limited; they'd shaken hands and exchanged a few pleasantries in French before conducting their business. But today, Montag looked down at his desktop, his gaze moving over a pen and a bottle of ink, a small jar of pounce, and three leather-bound ledger books, their edges aligned with each other and the edge of the desk. He cleared his throat. "I must speak to you about a private matter," he said, frowning at a sheet of thick paper, creased in two places and covered in a delicate script that lay across the top ledger, awkwardly, as if it didn't belong there.

"I'm sorry," Montag continued, "I have received a letter from your stepmother. Apparently," he said, picking up the paper and adjusting the pair of eyeglasses he wore, "your father is not well? Your stepmother fears that—ah—you have not been receiving his letters." Montag looked at him over the glasses. "They've had no word, it says."

"Yes."

The banker blinked twice. "I see. Well, she's written me to pass on important information. I'm sorry to tell you, but she says your father is near death. And that there are problems on the estate requiring your attention. She asks that you return to Russia at once. Please forgive me for being thrust into this personal affair."

For a moment, he couldn't tell whether the last sentence was part of the letter. Indeed, his father's wife might well apologize for involving herself in the struggle between the two of them.

Montag put away his eyeglasses. "I regret the intrusion," he said.

"Of course," he said. "Forgive me for causing you this embarrassment."

"Please, how much money will you require?"

☆ ☆ ☆

The street was a blur of white buildings and curious faces. Although his wallet was again full of bank notes, his heart had been rifled by an expert thief. The letter may have been written in Ekaterina Feodorovna's hand, but the real author's identity was clear. Sham filled that single page; his father had deliberately neglected the estate to ensnare his surviving son. From the brink of the grave, he was preparing to make him do his bidding.

Despite all that had happened in the past few months, he'd have to assume the role of master of a Russian manor, putting it on like the uniform he'd discarded. It was the exact thing his father had always planned, and he'd spun a scheme to make it real.

What am I to do? If I ignore this letter, I risk losing my income. That would mean, at the very least, having to return to the military, at worst, financial ruin; no, the very worst thing would be to lose her—Marianne. She depends on me, and without my protection, the city will destroy her. But the mask of responsibility I must wear, the burden of wealth I must bear are articles in a sentence of death. I've been condemned for treason. That's it—as if my father has known all along everything that's happened—all of it, as if I've responded to every unanswered letter with a full accounting of how I've betrayed Russia, the Tsar, and God.

For a moment, he found himself cowering, expecting, after all these years, to be beaten. A fast-moving carriage rushed past, and he realized he was at the curb, feeling the draft from the horse's passage, clapping his hands over his ears to muffle the roar of his cascading thoughts.

After walking several more blocks, he stopped and looked around; he was once again in the square before the cathedral. Overhead, above the twin spires, the sky was a brilliant blue, deep and thick, not at all like a regular sky but as if the city had been covered in an enormous, seamless blanket, a king's blanket marked with the richest of indigo dyes. The double spires caught his attention, and he peered up, shading his eyes with his hand. Odd—they weren't doubles as he'd thought; they were subtly different, one higher than the other. He continued up the steps toward the entrance.

At the doors, a crowd of beggars had massed; they watched him without looking, aware of his presence—he was sure—before he became aware of theirs. One beggar in particular caught his attention, a young man who knelt with downcast eyes, holding a bowl above his head and exclaiming in a high-pitched voice, as if in prayer. But he had no coins to give away and parted the throng with his stick, ignoring the imploring hands.

Inside, the church was an enormous white cavern, different than it looked at night. A double row of pillars ran toward the altar, a score of them to each side. High overhead, the ceiling was gathered in arches that seemed to strain and groan under an incredible weight, one greater than that of the whitewashed stone. *What is that odor?* he wondered. It was of dust and decay; it was the smell of age, of things persisting for centuries. But the air was clear; there were no motes suspended in pathways of sunlight. Where were the windows?

"It's beautiful, eh?"

A priest had approached him. "I'm sorry, I don't speak German well," he said.

"Ah, you are French." The priest switched to that language. "You're standing on a special place; do you know the story?" He gestured at their feet, where the floor was covered by stone tiles in a checked pattern of red and black. But his right boot had touched a different tile, a white square that bore a black mark within its boundaries, like a footprint with a dot behind the heel.

"The Devil's Footstep, it's called," the priest said. "You see, long ago, when the cathedral was under construction, the devil made a pact with the builder that no windows were to be fashioned, so that the devout would be left in darkness and confusion. But the builder was a good man; he tricked the devil. Come with me."

The priest led him to the side aisle, and there, hidden from the central area of the church by the screen of polished stone, beautiful stained glass windows, set into the outer wall, let in a palette of red and green, blending with the stone to make a soft, gray glow.

"When the devil realized what had happened, the church had already been consecrated; he couldn't do anything about it. He was so angry, he stomped on the stone near the entrance and left a mark there with his tail and foot, his cloven foot. It's a wonderful story, don't you think? And the light, enjoy it; just sit in one of the pews and see how it shines in with the truth of God. And enjoy being away from the wind."

On the way back to his rooms, he bought a bouquet of Alpine flowers. The room was still when he entered, and for a moment, he feared she'd gone. Yevgeny appeared, taking his gloves and hat, and nodded toward the bedchamber.

"Marianne," he called. She was lying on the bed, and at her side, *Julie* was open. His first reaction was alarm that the book might reveal things he'd thought well hidden. But she twisted around and sat up, and he realized she was preparing to embrace him as he'd demanded she do. "No, no, stay," he said, holding up his palm. "Please. I brought you these."

"Did you finish your business?" she said, receiving the bouquet with downcast eyes.

"Yes—no. You're reading *Julie?*"

"Reading? No. You know I can't make sense of the words. But I was looking at the engravings, trying to imagine the story, trying to understand why you like it so much. You do like it, don't you? I see you reading it sometimes. It's special." She closed the cover and glanced outside. "The wind—it's making everyone unhappy."

"Yes." He went to the small window and heard the cooing of pigeons beneath the eaves. Dense and golden light pressed into the chamber through the space between the wooden shutters. He cupped his hands; the weight of what was captured there made an acid spike ascend his throat. Right now, he could turn and face her, tell her the truth: he needed more time, more time with Valsin, his confessor, his physician of the soul, his brother. And more time with Anne-Marie; he needed a few more afternoons with her, parting her long, white legs and digging his fingers into her hair. Marianne would accept it or not, but either way he'd free himself of deceit, like a porter able to put down half his load.

No, Anne-Marie was from a different country, a different time—a time that existed outside the window, across the tiled rooftops, a midday time the two of them had to remain inside of, like children in a womb. When they were together, he could allow himself certain indulgences, certain affections; feelings might arise in him that could not be translated into a language others could understand. To keep things so separate was a burden but one he must carry and not spill out across this late afternoon. "Marianne," he said, sitting down beside her on the bed, "I'm not ashamed of you. But we are not married, and walking the streets is something married couples do." He switched from French to German, giving each word equal stress. "I was unkind. I am sorry."

She met his gaze and pressed her lips together. After a moment, she took his hand and kissed it. "What did you do when you were out? I know you went to get money, but you were gone a long time. I was worried."

"I went and sat in the cathedral for a while, to think. There was a letter from my stepmother; my father is near death, and I must return to Russia."

"Russia…"

It was very clear. He could bargain for a little more time, but he would have to leave, carrying memories, good memories he wouldn't have to work to change. He squeezed her hand. "I own a house in the city—in Brest-Litovsk; you'll like it. It's made from logs and clean timber and has real glass windows. There's a stable, and we'll have horses; I'll teach you to ride. We'll live there together."

A clattering noise came from the other room, as if Yevgeny had knocked over a stack of bowls. "When will we go?" Marianne whispered.

"Soon. There are some matters I must finish."

Her eyes freed themselves from looking at his and drifted somewhere else. Finally, she nodded. "Lay down with me—here."

✧ ✧ ✧

That night, he dreamt he was again in the church, gazing down the long path of white columns toward the altar. This time, when the priest approached him and spoke, his voice was familiar, and he looked up in surprise to see it was Valsin, dressed in a priest's cassock. He understood that he must not comment on the Frenchman's change of uniform.

"So you're in Munich, eh?" Valsin said, smiling. "It's a good time of year, with the light so strong. The devil's foot, do you see? The light has to be let in because the devil loves darkness."

When he looked down toward the floor, Valsin snatched his robe closed, but not soon enough. In the bright light of the vault, his bare feet peeked out beneath the hem. They were cloven. He covered his face with the cowl and hurried away.

16.

Know then that your dream isn't a dream at all, that it's not your friend's shadow that you saw, but him, that this moving scene, constantly in your imagination, really happened in your chamber.

"Anne-Marie."

A man's voice calling her name, an urgent signal emerging from a mid-day stir of sound—whinnies, wheels groaning, a work crew's rhythmic chant. She looked to the right and then the left, unable to place its origin.

When it came again—familiar and yet alien so close to The White Hound—she stopped so suddenly that the person behind her, an older man wearing a smock, stumbled into her back. He cursed and grabbed her arm above the elbow, spinning her around. "You stupid whore, watch where you're going," he said and drew back his other hand as if to strike her. But as she began to wince and cower, his glittering eyes refocused over her shoulder, and his face turned pale. He released her just as a whipping sound came from over her head, and a walking stick slammed against the man's left ear.

In shock, she turned to the left and saw a different man's face very close, a line of mustache below the brim of a hat, lips pressing together, eyes almost shut as if he were judging whether to continue his attack. The man in the smock, holding his ear, disappeared into the crowd, leaving her with a sensation of pressure on her upper arm, a feeling of being soiled by a stranger's touch.

A hand—less strange—pressed against the small of her back. "Are you all right?" The voice was familiar.

Not sure what to call him, she nodded, rubbing her arm.

"I must talk with you. Alone."

"Yes."

He turned and strode off toward The White Hound, and she followed him, keeping her eyes cast down. As they approached the entrance, she checked for the presence of anyone who might recognize her, but at this hour, all the soldiers were gone at parade. Inside, a boy was washing the stairs with water and a large brush, and they stepped around him, still not speaking. At the darkened landing on the third floor—stifling from lack of air—she stopped, and he turned back toward her, very close. "Alexi," she said, finding his name despite the heat. "What is it—you want to talk?"

Instead of answering, he took off his hat and pushed her against the wall. Through a kiss, he spoke, all out of breath so that the words came in little gusts against her mouth. "I need to...talk to...you. I need to...tell you...you don't understand." The sound of the brush scrubbing in circles made everything else indistinct. "You don't know who...I am."

Shaving had made his chin slick; he smelled of cologne. She pulled him toward the door. As the latch clicked shut behind them, the cathedral bells rang the half hour, and he ran his hands down her back and hips, smoothing her curves and lifting her dress, and she pulled him into her arms, wrapping one thigh around his. Together, they advanced to the bedchamber like a three-legged creature with two joined heads, stopping in stages to remove a boot, a sash, a stocking. His hand crushed her bonnet, and her hair fell loose. They kissed, and whatever words he was speaking were dammed by lips and tongues.

At this hour, it was dark in the smaller room. The sun shone on the other side of the building, and only a thin panel of light from the main room stretched across the floor and up onto the lower end of the bed. She moved backward until her thighs caught at the bed's edge; she sank down and looked up at him, and he pressed himself against the wall, watching her. In the stillness, he took a deep breath and sighed. It was the first pause since he'd called her name on the street, and it worried her because she thought they'd been moving fast so as not to think, that thinking would force them into words and then sentences, into reason that might stop whatever was happening.

"We're alone...for hours." She pulled her blouse away from the waist of her skirt, keeping her eyes on his.

He came forward and pushed her shoulders down and her legs up so that she lay flat. His other boot hit the floor, and he removed his waist-coat and trousers, leaving only his billowing white shirt. She started to pull her skirt up, but he shook his head and put his right knee between her thighs, pinning the fabric to the bed. His fingers began to unbutton her blouse, pushing the tiny buttons through the holes; he leaned over her like a tailor to see what he must do. He pulled her forward by one arm and set the other arm free, and she started to reach for the remaining sleeve but he held her hand and shook his head. It was when he pulled the shift over her head, that she understood he would undress her completely.

Maybe it was a Russian custom, she thought. She was rarely without clothes, certainly not while making love. The costume for lovemaking consisted of shirts and shifts pulled up or down, or even regular clothing lifted and opened. Being naked was a state of transition; it occurred at morning and night, day clothes to sleepwear and back again. Being naked meant risking sickness—that's what everyone said. People were naked at birth—and at death.

But—he held her breast in his palm and kissed her nipple; his shirttails were thrust apart by his erection, and she understood that undressing her was a way for them to slow a frantic pace but still without speaking. She took him in her hand, feeling his heart beat against her palm. At the soft skin at the tip, her thumb moved in a circle, smearing warm, sticky seed. He released her skirt and pulled it down her thighs, lifting her knees to free it from her feet. Then he rolled down the stocking she still wore and ran his hand over and between her thighs, pressing his palm against her mound.

"Take this off," she said, touching his shirt.

He shook his head.

She lifted her thumb, and a strand of semen stretched out like a glistening thread of honey drawn from the comb. In her mouth, it was salty; the skin on his cock was dry and white like marble. He was doing things to her, kissing her thighs, opening her purse with the tip of his tongue. He was making her dizzy, and she grabbed onto his hair with both hands and hung on. Then he was above her, pushing all the way inside. At first he didn't move; he was just there like the hilt of a sword against a scabbard, and she looked up at him. Naked.

When he pulled away, the bed creaked, and she was like wet sand running after the tide. When he pushed back inside, there was no sound; she was full of him. Inside him too, inside his ear and his throat and his skull. She could see herself in his eyes. The emptiness was gone. And the bed creaked faster, running away all around.

Afterward she wrapped her ankles around his calves, pulling his weight close with her arms while he shrank by stages inside her. Her fingers explored under his shirt, feeling bone and hard ridges.

"A lot of scars," she whispered against his neck, keeping her eyes shut. "No, don't move. I want us to stay this way as long as we can. I wondered if you did—have scars. Will you tell me about them? I don't know much about you...maybe it's better that way. I'm talking too much, aren't I. Sorry. But what was it you wanted to tell me?"

He twisted up and ran his forefinger over her lips. "Now it doesn't matter. I didn't intend for this to happen. I'm glad, but—"

"I know."

"I just wanted to...I only wanted to see you, from a distance. But we can't—"

"I know."

All the resolve she'd felt about not seeing him again—which had been easy to forget and not think about—was back, waiting, accusing. She turned her face away and pushed against his chest. "You should go."

After he left, she straightened the bedclothes, reluctant to dress, to go from one thing to another too fast. She turned around, and the mirror caught her; she turned away, as if it were a giant, ogling eye, covering her breasts with her hands. But that was silly; she was alone. It was just a mirror, and she faced it, letting her arms fall to her sides.

In the time since her husband had died, she knew she'd been thin and dry, but now—after six months of living and eating with Valsin— her breasts were full, her arms and thighs soft and plump. She'd felt this bounty beneath her hands, and within her tightened clothes, but seeing its reflection made her feel beautiful and aroused again.

But also stupid. She was risking everything—for what? Because Valsin would leave her and she had to arrange a way to live? No, it wasn't like that. She wasn't like that, so sinful as to plan it all out, to use men to survive. To sell herself. It must be that she loved him—Alexi. She loved Valsin, and she must love Alexi too.

No, she was a fool. There had been no thoughts of love; no thoughts at all. Her mind had stopped working. She'd felt confused, like a simple country girl with round heels who's easily tipped into bed.

It was something about the man on the street, the fear I felt, and then Alexi slashing with his cane. All of a sudden, the fear became puzzlement over what was happening. He was transformed from a violent intruder into a rescuer, and then into a memory, a memory that nags me still, sitting just out of reach in the back of my brain.

His face, she'd seen his face somewhere before, long ago; it was an echo she couldn't place.

17.

Consider that you still have another Julie, and don't forget what you owe her.

That night, there were periods when everything made sense, when nothing was different, just an ordinary evening by the silent summer hearth. Yevgeny was out on his night off. Marianne worked quietly at her sewing, and he took up *Julie*. Then, sometimes at the end of one of the letters, sometimes in the middle, she'd break through the page and be there, alive beneath him, grasping and pulling with her flesh, her breath heaving inside his ear.

It was true—he'd sought her out, and at a time he knew she'd be alone. He'd stationed himself along the street where he knew she'd walk, hanging back in the shadows of a doorway, waiting. He would—he'd promised himself—not speak. He only wanted to see her. But her name had burst from his throat, and then—what choice did he have?—he had to reveal himself to protect her from a brutal assault.

He'd almost told her who he was; the words had caught between his teeth, his breath coiled to release the message.

I'm the man you killed.

He'd wanted to put them inside her, speaking into her mouth so that the meaning would lay dormant until she was ready to accept it. Then they could be together—really together, not stealing a furtive hour away from others. In Russia, it wasn't so unusual—for men to have foreign mistresses. She could live in Natasha's house, have her own maid and porter. He'd spend every possible moment with her.

"The man your father wants you to kill; will you do it?"

He looked up, blinking. His finger stopped its tracing of words. Marianne kept her eyes focused on her needlework, and in the silence after she spoke, he wondered if he'd imagined what she'd said.

"I mean, before we leave for Russia?"

Her questions emerged out of a past conversation that seemed to have continued within her.

"But I forgot, you've never found him, have you?"

"What are you talking about?"

"The man your father wants you to kill."

He cleared his throat. "The truth is that I've stopped looking for him. Since we're leaving, the whole thing doesn't matter. My father wouldn't understand. Everything has changed."

She looked up but not at him. "Everything?"

"Yes. I've come to believe that when he fought my brother, it was nothing personal; he took an equal chance and was the victor, that's all."

"So if you were to find him now, you wouldn't kill him."

"No," he said. "I just said that—"

"Do you love me?"

He forced himself to meet her gaze. "I do, of course."

"I think I believe you," she continued. "Yevgeny says you'll take me to Russia and sell me to a Cossack, but I don't believe him. You do care—it's hard for men to say such things, but it's true. I know all about you." She brought the needle close to her face and squinted. "But then, I'm just a poor girl," she said. "And simple. Sometimes I think, how could someone like you love me?"

"Pay no attention to Yevgeny. It doesn't concern me at all what others think. There was a man in Russia, a very wealthy man, a noble, and he loved a serf woman and married her—a huge scandal. And I loved a woman who was of lower rank. I've told you the story—my father hated me for it, but I was prepared to give up everything to be with her. Everything, and—"

"No, stop."

He looked at her in surprise. Her pale skin had become mottled with patches of scarlet, like areas on a map of a foreign country, uncharted areas, and her eyes were two, hard pits.

"That woman—the one you loved—yes, you've told me about her, but not in this way. You said you failed her, and that she died from sadness."

"No, yes. What is it?"

"You're full of stories about people. It's easy for you to say things that aren't true; because you're wealthy, words cost you little. It's different for me; I'm afraid. I'm afraid someday, I'll become someone in the stories you tell, and you'll change what really happened to suit the weather."

His tongue rolled around his upper teeth, delving into the spaces between his gums and cheeks. "My dear, please, I'm sorry. I didn't mean—"

"What's going to happen to me?" she said. "Is Yevgeny right?"

"No, don't let him distress you. I told you, we'll leave soon. Together."

"I don't think you're ready, Alyosha. To truly love me, there's something you have to give up."

"What are you asking me for?"

"You know."

The witnesses to this demand—the hearth, the table, *Julie*—were muter than his absent servant. "No, you're speaking in riddles. What do you want from me? I tell you I love you, I've told you the truth about

Valsin." In horror, he watched the name flash across to her like a bolt of lightning igniting a field of dry grass.

"Who's Valsin?" She stressed the last syllable of his name—the same way that Anne-Marie did—and rolled the end of it in her throat. "I know that name, Valsin," she continued, a cruel smile on her lips. "It's the same name the French officer spoke at the coffeehouse—the same name, Valsin— he killed your brother. You told me he didn't. You've hidden him for a long time. You don't trust me, yet you expect me to trust you, to give up every- thing and go to Russia. And there's a woman." The hoop shook in her hand.

"What woman? I've never told you about a woman."

"You said she killed someone."

"No."

"She's like me. She looks like me."

For a moment, he held an image of them together, Anne-Marie next to Marianne, letting the two overlap, as if he'd cut a shape out of pond ice and fitted it back together, sealing open water. "How can you say that?" he said, struggling to keep the two apart. "You've never seen her." Julie was there as well, beneath the surface.

"I know about her." She shrugged. "You're lying again."

There were footfalls on the stairs and a cough. Marianne went into the bedroom, closing the door behind her. Yevgeny entered, and after exchang- ing a few words with him, Ruzhensky rose and followed Marianne, finding her lying face down on the bed. She twisted around and regarded him over her shoulder.

"If you've decided you won't kill him, then why stay here any longer? Answer me that—what's the point? What's keeping you here?"

He turned and left the room. He'd blurted out a secret name, and she'd put it all together, a skilled surgeon stitching together the two parts of his world.

Later, she seemed to fall asleep right away, but he couldn't be sure. When he spoke to Yevgeny about their return to Russia, his chest and throat tightened, and he had trouble finding the words. He was like a swimmer who realizes he's gone too far out to sea, who catches glimpses of people on the shore at regular intervals as the waves swell up and down. People who can no longer see him. A man already drowning, given an intermittent, fading vision of the future he'll no longer inhabit.

Life goes on, she said.

18.

Because I fooled him once, I have to fool him every day and feel myself forever unworthy of all his kindnesses.

In the late afternoon, she lay against Valsin's back, holding onto his upper arm with her right hand. Her nose pressed against his shirt, smelling cologne; her shift remained pulled above her hips and below her breasts, covering her middle like a sash.

Although he was—she was convinced—on the point of leaving her, the knowledge seemed to have freed her. At a time when she'd expected to feel sorrow and guilt, she felt lazy and generous. It made her want him inside her, as if a tiny part might break off and stay forever.

Yet at times she couldn't bear his touch. His whiskers made her skin red and irritated; the sound of his voice set her teeth on edge.

What she'd done with Ruzhensky—that was the name she was trying to use when she thought of him—had become another layer of clothing between her skin and Valsin's, one she couldn't discard. Even after whole afternoons spent in bed, till they were both sore and laughing and limp, she couldn't be naked with him, couldn't change what she'd done. And there was no one to confess to. She couldn't tell him, not now, when he was going to leave; it would seem she'd done it all out of spite.

No—she had to rid herself of the guilt. It was horrible and silly; Ruzhensky was something that had happened between other, more important moments, like the third act of a four-act play. She wouldn't see him again; already he was becoming nothing more than a name Valsin mentioned.

She nearly squirmed off the bed in shame. If Ruzhensky were so unimportant, why had she done it? For pleasure, for spite, excitement? Was she that horrible?

Love was her redemption; if she loved them both, it would be all right. She had to keep saying that to herself.

"Let's do it again," she said, and clutched at Valsin's shoulder to make him turn toward her.

He rolled away, breaking free of her fingers and leaving the sheets askew. Trousers were hoisted, braces snapped into place. With a knife that lay on the chest by the bed, he cut open a fresh-smelling bundle of laundry tied with brown string and began pulling out clothes. "There's one missing," he said after a moment, half his face twisting in the afternoon light.

"What's missing?" she said.

"One of my shirts."

His shirts were old and patched, and it surprised her he could be so saddened by the loss of any one of them. She rose from the bed and pulled the shift up over her breasts. "Here, let me look," she said, touching his shoulder again.

"No, listen—it's gone." He shrugged her off.

For a moment, they stood next to one another, looking down at the pile of clean white shirts and linens. Valsin seemed to reach some decision; he leaned forward and darted his hands at the clothes, and pulled forth all the things that belonged to him. With all the clean clothes gathered into his arms, he went into the other room, leaving hers separate and alone. A single, white blouse fell from the bed to the floor—a blouse that had been recently mended.

"It's just a shirt," she said, following him. "What's wrong?"

"It's nothing. I've had it for a long time, that's all; I'm sure it's gone for good." He put the pile of clothes down on the table and walked to the window. "I wore it during most of last year's campaigns—when we met."

"I'm surprised you remember."

He spun around. "Don't you think I remember everything about you?"

He was angry. A chill went along the back of her neck; could he have learned the truth? "What's that supposed to mean?" she said. Why had she provoked him?

"It means the shirt was important to me; I thought it brought me good luck. It's really too ragged, but I wanted to keep it even so."

She understood: he was thinking of his future, disappointed at the loss of a memento of the time he'd carried a woman off in the middle of war—a fine story to tell around the campfire. She filled her chest with air, straining, until small explosions of light danced in the periphery of her vision. "I forgot to tell you—he came here the other day," she said, leaning against the doorframe. "Alexi—I never know what to call him."

"Alexandre, that's the name we used." He grinned at her, and then his expression shifted back to the business of costume. "It brought me good luck," he said. "But now—maybe I don't need it." He began re-folding the laundry.

"You don't care, do you?" She imagined an angry confrontation flaring between two men accustomed to killing, friends who could easily remember how to be enemies. An image of them circling one another with bloody swords refused to disperse, and she held onto her breath.

"Mind? No, I'll buy a new one."

"He stayed for a while. We talked."

"He didn't mention it. What did you talk about?"

"Oh…many things. About Russia, his home." She stepped toward him, index finger against her lower lip.

"Anne, what is it?"

"Nothing." She choked out the lie, watching for the exact moment his rage would begin.

"Whenever you do that—put your finger to your mouth—you have something to tell me. Ruzhensky was lucky you let him in. Have you forgiven him now?"

She looked away. When she was a little girl, a giant balloon had landed in a meadow outside Mayence. Filled with hot air, it had come to rest on the earth, and then as she'd watched, the canvas bag—as big as one of the old willow trees by the river—had begun to deflate, sagging away until it could be folded into a bundle and stowed away on a wagon. She remembered wondering where the strange air inside had come from and where it had gone—how could something so enormous disappear?

Valsin was going on. "I've always believed you liked him a little."

"I never said that," she said, taking in another breath and blowing it out through her fingers.

"It's obvious. Remember the dinner party he gave? The way you flirted with him?"

"No—stop accusing me of things."

He frowned at her. "I'm not accusing. Why are you acting so strangely?" He closed the trunk lid and stood up. "He's a good man; he's fond of you."

A certain rigidity in his posture, an angle of his chin let her know what was coming. He was like one of those semaphores set up to communicate the Emperor's wishes over long distances so all the necessary preparations could be made beforehand.

"We received orders today," he said, his voice muffled by his collar. "The regiment is to prepare to withdraw to France."

"When?"

He shrugged. "We're just ordered to be ready."

For weeks the talk had been about when and where the army would go. The newspapers and taverns were full of stories about the Emperor Napoleon's struggle to avoid war with the Prussians but—as Dalhousie said—the Emperor Napoleon was not known as a man of peace.

"But when we go, I won't know where we'll be, and I doubt if we'll stay there long."

A knot burned in her stomach, and she crossed her arms to keep it from loosening. "So you're giving me to him?"

"I didn't say that. He'd be glad to help you, that's all. Listen," he said, taking her by the shoulders, "wherever fortune takes me, you'll be at my side, in my heart. I'll send for you as soon as I'm able."

She studied his face to memorize every pore.

I am a part of Louis Valsin's past, already a memory.

19.

I have always noticed that hypocrites are sober, and great reserve at the dinner table too often heralds feigned morals and duplicity of soul.

"I'm glad you wanted to meet," Valsin said. "Much has happened."

"Yes?" he said. "What is it?"

Across the span of the trestle table, he waited, aware of the sheathed saber at the man's side and the length of his arm. Valsin had sent a note asking to meet at a tavern on the far side of the Marienplatz. A friendly note giving no hint of outrage. By luck, it was delivered after Marianne had gone out, insisting she had to shop, alone. He'd considered tearing it to pieces and stuffing them into his waistcoat pocket for later disposal, pretending he'd never received it, but that would have only postponed the inevitable. No matter what had happened, he wasn't ready to leave; he had to see Valsin again. In any case, if Valsin did know the truth, he wouldn't seek a confrontation in a crowded public place. Still, he'd dressed slowly, as if facing battle, and crossing the square, his feet had dragged against the smooth stones.

"I'll tell you, but tonight, it's you who look troubled—a woman?"

Two women, he wanted to say, marveling at the younger man's intelligence. He measured the distance between them again, wishing that if Valsin really grasped the situation, he'd understand. After all, an older brother was allowed many liberties. For an instant, the lightness of the thought warmed him, and then, another glance made him shift on the bench as if he'd realized he were sitting on a pile of nettles. "A woman? No," he said, shaking his head. "I remain on my own. I haven't been sleeping well—that's all."

"There're lots of girls around Munich," Valsin said. "Many would be glad to offer companionship to such a distinguished gentleman."

Valsin grinned at him and raised his eyebrows, and for an awful moment, it seemed he did know what had happened—all of it, both about Anne-Marie and Marianne. Merseult could have told him—at least about Marianne. Anne-Marie might have confessed. Maybe Valsin knew of one and not the other. But which? "I'm certain you're right. But I don't think I'm ready for such a complication. Unlike you." He stretched his lips across his teeth in an imitation of a smile and buried his face in the tankard of beer. "How are things with…with…" He couldn't get out her name.

Valsin laughed. "It's been easier between us lately, almost as if she's accepted that I must go. She'll be well taken care of; I'll make sure of that. That's what I wanted to tell you, we've been ordered to prepare for a fall campaign. Of course, there are a lot of rumors, but—"

"You told her, and she doesn't seem unhappy?"

"No, distracted, bemused almost. Ha! Perhaps she's found a new lover."

Merriment was all over the younger man's face; the older man covered the lower half of his own with his hand. It seemed to him that large objects—battalions of primitive infantry, phalanxes from different realms—

were about to crash into each other. A shiver went down his spine and on into the chair, the floor, the earth.

"So, a fall campaign," Valsin said. "Some say against Austria again, but I think it's Prussia. The thing is—"

Valsin spoke of rumors, rumors of war in the East, feints and counter-feints, supply depots and ultimatums, and Ruzhensky began to relax. All around them, the trestle tables were occupied by soldiers—drinking, smoking, filling the space of the long room with the funk of soldiers' tales. Two old men played a violin and a hurdy-gurdy in one corner. Although there was nothing authentically Russian in the room, he felt a growing sense of being at home, a home where men sat before the hearth and told stories. One where he could be himself. Within the time it took to drink a mug of dark beer, his initial wariness disappeared, and the two of them were soon occupied in eating roasted potatoes and drinking a second mug, speaking as old comrades.

"Tell me," Valsin said. "If you're ordered to join your regiment—what will you do?"

"It would take so long for such an order to find me, the war might end before I ever received it."

"Does that concern you?"

He wanted to shrug again, to put off a question that didn't seem terribly important. "If I receive an order, I'll obey it."

"It would be that simple? How could—"

"The truth is," he said, "tonight, my thoughts are more on women than war." Valsin raised his brows and pushed out his lips. "Yes, a woman is essential," he continued. "Our discussions have made me realize that. Yet I wonder: if I become more involved—I mean, should I meet someone—how will she change me? Will my horizons expand or narrow?"

"Both," Valsin said. "But the process of expansion will be much more pleasant. You have someone in mind?"

"What must I give up to have her? She'll want me to give up something, and I don't know what it will be. Do you understand?"

"I think so; we should talk more about this. But listen, what of the military though? Despite what you say, you're still an officer; that status will not fall away like apples on an untended tree."

"No, but—"

"If Napoleon orders us east, how long before your Tsar objects and expects you to express those objections with the point of your sword? Will he allow us to dismantle Prussia? Free Poland? What will you do?"

He took a drink and met Valsin's eyes.

"Well? Are you lost in thought? What will you do?"

Tonight some truths could not be released; like Aeolus's winds, they must be kept corked away to avoid disaster. "You're right to press me; the subject is troubling, so I avoid it. I also have news of a journey: soon I must return to Russia. As I've said, my father is dying, and there are business matters to settle. But I keep delaying my departure because I appreciate having the French army between Munich and the Tsar." Valsin began laughing. "This way, he can order me all he likes but I have a good excuse for disobeying him. You see, here, I'm a free person."

"We've liberated you then. So stay. Find a local girl."

"Who knows?" He laughed but felt a renewed discomfort that Valsin was not joking. "No, you're correct; as I say, I must return to Russia and face my responsibilities. Only—"

"Ah, my friend," Valsin said. "We've come full circle, you and I. When we first met, here in Munich, it was I who was unsettled, unsure of my path. Now it's you. I want to give you the same good counsel you gave me. Let's consider your situation a bit more. What awaits you in Russia?"

He shook his head. "To be a landowner in a remote province, an owner of serfs—you know what a serf is?"

"A slave?"

"Yes, but it's not what you think—or maybe it is; they're all so dependent, everyone depending on me. For bread, for work, for life itself."

"People depending on you—sounds like the military. I think you're taking your difficulties too seriously. You wouldn't have to stay there for good. Couldn't you set things right and then return here or travel?"

"Perhaps," he said. "Yes, that's possible."

"Of course, our Emperors will have the last word. By the way, I hope we never face each other across a battlefield, but if we do, I'll see a worthy enemy."

He began to reply, inhaling and opening his mouth but instead reached for the tankard of beer with his right hand. Valsin did the same thing so that they moved in synchrony, raising the tankards up, smiling, and saluting one another. He wished he could provoke other things in Valsin, provoke them by thinking about what had happened, the whole chain of events, beginning with Mischa's death—no, Natasha's—if he could think about it all, and how he'd tried to kill this man and realized what folly it was. He wanted to hold all that in his mind and then pass it into Valsin's mind in the same way, in the same order, so that he'd understand all of it—the regret, the guilt. If that were only possible.

"I have to confess I'm eager for campaign," Valsin said. "I want to add to my laurels."

He looked at him and smiled. "I'm sure you've covered yourself with glory."

"I'll tell you, if you like—about what I have and have not done, and perhaps you'll understand why I feel I'm not finished. But to hear this tale, we must not be Frenchmen or Russians. Are you prepared? In the woods east of Vienna, there was a place called Amstetten."

Mischa had fought at Amstetten. Was this to be another eerie story to stitch the cloth that bound them together? He took a drink and waved his hand, as if feeling smoke.

"We were pursuing your army and came upon the rearguard drawn up to fight, surprising us as we debouched into a clearing. The situation was unfavorable. Our infantry extended far to the rear along the forest road; we had less than a squadron with which to defend ourselves."

"Prince Murat charged with his escort company and was soon turned back by a large force of cavalry. I entered the clearing with less than a hundred men and saw a mob of horsemen galloping straight for me, swinging their weapons like a thicket in a storm and roaring—a swarm of creatures in white and green chasing Murat's gallant followers the length of the field." Valsin drained his tankard and waved for more.

"I knew I had to act, to make decisions and issue commands, but fear pithed my arms and strangled my voice. If we didn't move, we'd be overrun and the Prince captured or killed. I tried to swallow and then felt something deep inside me, something ready to break out, wild and frantic. Turning in the saddle, I caught the eye of the trumpeter who'd come up close behind, holding his horn inches away from puckered lips. My scrotum tightened, and I wrapped the sword knot around my wrist.

"'Company, charge!'

"The fear I'd felt was gone; I was like a ship under full sail the moment after its cable is cut. There was my horse Lily, alive beneath me, the plashing of hooves in the muddy slush, the heft of the saber in my right hand, and a wild screech of trumpets. Exhilaration grew like a fire's bright flame, and a deep, red mist gathered at the periphery of my vision. I plunged into the enemy ranks, screaming, '*Vive l'Empereur!*' and broke their line in two."

Ruzhensky licked his lips; his eyes searched from side to side. He wanted to pound the table with his tankard, to join this soldier's story. How he loved the cavalry! For months he'd not felt such an affection, but now, it coursed through his blood, cracking the rigor of dormant, peaceful limbs like a February thaw. How could he give it up?

"An enemy horseman," Valsin was saying, "resplendent in green and silver, slammed into me, his sword straining for my heart. Lily reared up, ears flat. Like a dragon, she sank her teeth into the other horse's neck. The motion whisked me out of danger, and with a slash of my saber, I struck back, also drawing blood.

"My opponent was a good swordsman, better than I, and the cut on his arm had done nothing to discourage his ardor. The seconds passed, and I was put on the defensive and forced back among the trees. Despite the cold, I panted, sweat ran down my face, my right arm tingled from the ringing of our blades. Death was hunting me, I was sure, drawing near.

"I wondered: Would it all end here? Would I see the final sword stroke as it came to cut the thread of my life? Feel the air pushed aside by its swift passage? And this man who wielded it, would he later boast of having killed an officer, of how he'd separated me from my horse and sent me to an ignominious death on the snow? Or would he be indifferent? If I'd led my men to sacrifice, I hoped it wouldn't be in vain.

"With all my strength, I parried.

"All at once, there was a tremendous explosion, a herald of danger and pain. Huge icicles, dislodged from the trees above, crashed to the ground, and the horses reared in terror. In astonishment, I watched as a large clump of snow and ice fell onto my opponent. Like a thunderbolt from an unseen god, it stunned us both, but I was the first to recover. I held my saber aloft and drove it forward, piercing the man's heart. He sagged against his horse, the reins slack, blood spreading under the green tunic.

"Our soldiers had hauled two cannons forward, bringing them into action just behind and to the left of where I fought. After loud warnings to clear the way, the gun crew fired again. This second discharge, loaded with grapeshot, made a bloody shambles of the enemy, and their surviving trumpets quavered the call to retreat.

"And I was hailed as a hero, the man who'd saved Prince Murat. But I knew the Prince had been saved by luck or whatever it is that causes falling ice. Real courage would have spoken the truth: I was only playing at being this hero, this Lieutenant Louis Valsin. The real me was someone else—still a scrawny sixteen-year-old receiving his first uniform, so nervous he couldn't tell the brigadier his birth date. Still the same trooper who, later that year, hung back when the Tenth charged the Austrian infantry at Neerwinden, when each flying bullet slowed my progress more and more, until I arrived behind all the rest and never swung my sword. Later I made up a story—feeling my way bit by bit—about how I'd galloped to the fore, screaming *'Vive la République!'* and sabered my first man; I didn't know why no one had seen me."

"No, no—stop," Ruzhensky said, holding up both palms and shaking his head. "Enough. You're being too hard on yourself; you did act with bravery. Accept it and be done."

"But that's just it—why do I keep torturing myself with the past? And why does that young man's fear—a fear of death soldiers aren't supposed to have—still persist? Even at Austerlitz, I felt it. The man who wounded me, I saw him advancing and only felt fear. And then to be rescued by a woman." He shook his head. "You know the story. Many a time since Neerwinden, I've kept my place in the line and killed many men. No one sees my failings except me. No, the real Valsin is not the person others see."

While the younger man spoke, Ruzhensky listened and nodded, while another part of him copied a woman's quick hands, piecing together past and present. He tapped his right heel on the floor.

Valsin shook his head. "But you, I'm sure you know what you've done and exactly who you are, regardless of what others believe."

"You think? Perhaps. I know that for every good act, there's one I'm ashamed of. The scale balances." Pressure rose inside, pushing against the roots of his hair.

Let in the light.

"I have a different problem," Valsin said. "I act in ways that seem necessary to me at the time but that others then call courage. I can find no courage in myself, and I'm embarrassed by praise that feels false."

He snorted. "There are worse fates than that. Maybe you're wrong about yourself." It was Valsin's turn to snort, with enough force that he had to wipe his mustache with his sleeve.

"Are you ever afraid?" Valsin asked in a quiet voice.

"I haven't been for a long time, no. But I don't think that's due so much to courage as to boredom. Throughout this last campaign, I craved the excitement of battle; I hungered for it. Away from combat, my existence was dull and bleak. I had nothing to live for but to be close to death."

"And now?"

"Now every moment seems brighter and more precious." He leaned forward. "Do you know, Valsin, getting to know you and...Mademoiselle Fröelich has been quite significant to me." With raised eyebrows, Valsin looked up from the work of selecting a potato and began to interrupt. "No, wait, there's something I must tell you," Ruzhensky went on in a low voice. "Something I've kept secret, and now, I'm ashamed. I've deceived you."

"What are you saying, my friend?"

"It's that—you see..." He swallowed and looked away from the face that was so like his own. "I...it's just that...so many of my comrades were killed at Austerlitz, and at other battles—that at times, I've had difficulty forgetting that we've been enemies." He grimaced; what he'd said was true, but it wasn't the truth.

Valsin stared at him a moment. "I'm glad you said something; I didn't know. You've always seemed friendly—from the first. I've been insensitive, going on about the skirmish at Amstetten." He took out a pipe and lit it from a candle's flame. "Tell me, where did you fight? Austerlitz, you said. We've never even talked about where we—"

"It's not so important," he said, raising the tankard to drink. "Yes, of course, Austerlitz, and a place called Durenstein."

"Wischau?"

"No," he shouted, slamming his tankard onto the table. Not only Valsin but some of the other drinkers looked up in surprise. "My God, I tell you it's hard to talk with you about such things, and you bring up even more!"

"What are you so angry about?" Valsin smirked at him, his hands hidden beneath the table. "Ah, I see, you can't forget you're Russian. Maybe it's easier for me to talk about our battles because I was on the winning side."

He could feel his chin straining against his mouth, forcing its ends down. His pulse thudded through his neck. Valsin was provoking him; was this affair to end here, in a tavern in Munich where civilians would later crowd around a battered, bloody corpse and begin to tell a tale of murder?

Down the table, two arm's lengths away, a large butcher's knife lay at rest amid bread crumbs and a heel of cheese.

It will serve—this Valsin will never be able to draw his sword in time.

But the man was talking.

"You must forgive me," Valsin said, shaking his head. "What I said was wrong; I beg your pardon." He put his hands flat on the table. "Please. We are more than Russians and Frenchmen. You see, I too lost comrades in our wars."

Long tendrils of blue pipe smoke drifted around Valsin's head so that, in the murk of the tavern, he began to resemble a figure in an icon, a figure who also began to float toward the ceiling, only to be replaced immediately by another below. Ruzhensky squeezed his eyes shut, trying to concentrate, trying to decide who was real—the enemy or the friend. "Very well," he said finally, reaching for the tankard. "I also apologize. The truth is there was someone in particular, a fellow officer, whose death I blame myself for. It's been an obsession. Can you understand?"

Instead of providing any affirmation, Valsin stared at a corner of the table, and Ruzhensky wondered if the emotions were too strong, if the younger man would again lapse into provocation. But instead, he looked up, blinking. "Of course, I too blame myself for the death of someone—not a comrade, though. Like you, I have no one else to blame. It's a burden I carry alone." He wiped at a puddle of beer with his sleeve. "For me, the scale won't balance."

"No matter what you do?"

"I must always hide who I am. I can't let others see my shame."

Shame. Yes, he's right. Shame devours me. I never imagined Natasha would kill herself, that Mischa would be so foolish. And I made it worse by trying to kill this man.

He looked at Valsin, who slumped in his chair, regarding an almost-empty tankard.

"Valsin." The sound of his slurring voice made him realize how drunk he was, but that didn't diminish the importance of his words. "Valsin, I think you and I have shared more than we know. Despite all the things that separate us—my brother's death, our loyalties—"

"Your brother's death? What—"

He waved his hand. "No, no—that's not important. This ale—it's confused me. A long time—I did have a brother who died—a long time ago. I was saying—despite these things, we're destined to be friends, good friends. Do you agree?"

By way of response, Valsin raised his tankard. "To your brother and to us." He drank the dregs and cleared his throat. "Listen, the man I mentioned was a Russian cadet whom I fought a single combat with—at Wischau, that's why I brought it up. I thought you might know the story, because Merseult said that he told you—but what is it? You've gone so pale. Ah, I see, I'm doing the same thing again, and you've asked me not to. Sorry. I just want you to know; even the lives we take can be precious."

Silence fell by stages; they declined any more to drink, and Ruzhensky got out his pipe. He inhaled the smoke and tried to relax the muscles encircling his eyes.

This is my true friend, a good man whom I've imposed on in the worst way, loving his lover. I can never confess it all to him; the only solution is to depart. Anne-Marie won't tell him, and no one else knows; it will be over, in the past. Forgotten. I can't see her again.

I'll take Marianne to Russia—as soon as possible, before she sews together any more of the truth. If only she could first meet Valsin, see how good he is, how sincere.

He imagined instead the two women together, sitting across a table, perfectly still, staring. Anne-Marie's eyes were deep, velvet brown—Marianne's as blue as the northern sea. Then, instead of being separated by the width of a table, they moved closer, face-to-face with their heads lying against two pillows, their gold and silver hair streaming behind them like flames. It was a pane of glass between them, and he realized, turning his head, that both sides of it were mirrors. The perception made him dizzy.

"We should go," Valsin said.

He looked up and blinked.

If he knew the truth, how would he judge me? Was there a way he'd merely think me tardy in telling?

"Wait," he said. "A final toast."

"Very well," Valsin said, signaling to the yawning serving woman. "A toast to—what?—your Tsar, my Emperor?"

"To women, to Anne-Marie—a worthy woman who saved you," he began to say, lifting the charged mug. "Let's—" It occurred to him that it was not only Anne-Marie but another woman—Natasha—who'd sent her disruptive memory across time, staying his sword and saving them both. He looked at Valsin in confusion. "Let's drink to her."

"I wanted to talk to you about Anne-Marie. With me leaving, she won't have anyone here. Is there a way you could help?" He grimaced. "But you're going too. It's fine; I'll give her money. It's just that…I want to say that if affection ever grew between the two of you, I'd be happy."

His mug was suspended between them. "Let's drink," he said, nodding.

The tankards were knocked together and beer deeply drunk. They both wiped their mouths with the backs of their hands; he knew he needed to say more. "Valsin, I've been wrong about many things. Can you accept my apology?"

"For what? Let's go."

The tavern disgorged them onto the street. Just as Valsin raised his hand and began to turn toward The White Hound, Ruzhensky grabbed his shoulder. "Wait."

"What is it?" Valsin said. "Are you ill?"

"No," he said. The middle distance filled with the sound of the cathedral clock wafting along the night air, beginning with a sharp, violent act that became a gentle reminder of the insistence of time.

We both walk the same path, in parallel, like two men trudging along either side of a riverbank whose flood separates us by ten years. The river is broadening, its banks shrouded in mist—when will we meet again? Some might say tomorrow, might assume a pleasant rendezvous could be arranged with little effort, but it's dangerous to assume, to take for granted those things that fate can snatch away.

"Listen," he said. "You must understand how alike you and I are."

Valsin laughed. "There are certain similarities, I agree. But you haven't yet been rescued by a woman. Farewell."

Outside the open window of his room, a night bird settled onto the orange tiles of the sloping roof, but the noise did not alarm him. He stared hard, widening his eyes, forcing the greenery to resume its climb across the paper on the wall, forcing the truth to shape the past.

My brother was bent on glory and followed his own course. And I was relieved by his death; it was his death—not Valsin's—that freed me from my old life. At Austerlitz, it was too soon to admit that truth, and I played a deadly charade. How selfish; death is final and absolute. Already, Mischa's memory recedes into the past—the dark ship he sails on has swift sails that obscure. All my bargaining with fate has been nothing but a further abandonment; I approached Valsin's death as a game of chance.

Across the wall there was a play of shadows, branches of the tree outside thrown into relief by moonlight, twitching and dancing with the breeze. He stared at the movement of shapes, wanting to believe they were more than random, wondering if he stared hard enough, that he would see something new, read a message sent in a language only he would understand at that particular moment. But the engine of the wind shook the world outside; boughs flexed. All nature's energy drove down in a great eddy, and whatever meaning the light and shadow had held was scattered. Tears came to his eyes, a rare inundation.

20.

There are a thousand secrets that three friends must know and can only tell each other by twos.

It was market day; all around the central column with its image of the Virgin, clustered stalls of canvas and lath were jammed full of rugs and wool stockings, iron cooking pots and glass vials. The flower seller's stand overflowed with delicate blooms—big carmine and yellow roses packed in tight rows, the symmetric layers of velvet petals presenting themselves like vain, human faces, aware of being admired. Others formed bells, their curving lines inviting only the gentlest touch. A type of small blue flower caught his eye; it was the same color as the Mariupol uniform. With some of the Bavarian coins he'd amassed, he bought a generous bunch. It would be a suitable present for Marianne. The thought of pleasing her began to dispel a slight anxiety he'd felt since leaving his rooms. She'd looked at him so coldly when he left, as if, from him, she'd learned to expect disappointment.

Late in the afternoon the day before, a message had arrived from Colonel Lensky, ordering him to join the regiment in the Ukraine. Make all haste, it said. He'd told Marianne to prepare for their departure the next day, that he'd take her to Brest-Litovsk. She wanted to buy some things for the trip, and after she left, he called Yevgeny. "Listen," he said, "go to the Frenchman, Lieutenant Valsin—here's the address. Ask him to meet me tonight at the tavern." But his servant had returned with the message that it would be impossible. Tomorrow, Valsin had said, tell him to look for me tomorrow—at the Marienplatz. After parade.

Just as he finished paying for the flowers, Valsin appeared, not ten paces away. Clad in fatigue uniform, he walked with his saber held off the ground to keep it from dragging. And behind him, she wore a bonnet, a plain blouse and skirt, and carried a wicker basket. As soon as they saw him, she pulled at Valsin's arm and frowning, spoke urgently until he shook his head and broke away.

It was more than he'd hoped for—that she'd come as well. A return to the intimacy of the days when they'd first met, before the development of other intimacies—that's what he wanted now. Valsin clasped his elbow; she didn't offer her hand, and her eyes remained cast down. He wiped his face with a handkerchief and glanced at her again, noting a bloom on her cheeks that— he understood—was not just due to the heat. In his fingers, the bouquet was awkward, as if he'd become a jealous suitor, surprised by a rival's presence. "I was browsing in the market and bought these." He brandished the flowers. "They're familiar; I think we have them in Russia. I thought that—if you both came—I could give them to you." When he pushed the bouquet into her hands, she recoiled and stared at him, her eyes starting a little from her face. "Valsin, with your permission? They complement her hair. Please."

"Of course," Valsin said. "They're beautiful."

She passed her palm over the very top of the blooms, and the color in her cheeks darkened even more. "Thank you," she said, speaking to the flowers.

"I didn't tell her you'd be here," Valsin said. "A surprise."

He felt light-headed, as if it had been days since he'd eaten. "What have you got in there?" he said, inspecting her basket. "I see a loaf and a bottle."

She pulled it away. "A few things for the larder."

He imagined a picnic in the English Gardens or down by the river; how he wished he could be included. Anything seemed possible. She was, he could tell, shy with him, angry even, and it was understandable. Still, she was a jet of beauty shot against the summer sky.

"I've received orders; we're to leave in two days," Valsin said. "You've heard the stories? The Prussians sharpening their sabers on the steps of our embassy in Berlin. What about you? I'm not asking you to reveal any secrets, but—"

"I've received similar orders. Just yesterday."

"Fate steps with big boots—isn't that the saying?" Valsin said, laughing. "I've given her some money, borrowed it against my pay. She can stay here or go elsewhere. Right, *cherie?*"

"*Mon Dieu*, will you shut up?" she said. "I'll be fine."

"Let's head for the wine seller's," Valsin said. "It'll be cooler there. Let's go." He moved between them, taking both their arms in his, and they set off.

Down a side street, many empty carts stood with their shafts canted upward. Cages held hens and pigeons, peering out through the bars like convicts longing for the freedom of light and air. Just ahead of where they walked, an irate and profane butcher chased a pack of dogs away from his stall. At times it was difficult to hear anything but a sibilant roar, and then—all at once—silence would break out in equal measure.

They passed a teeth-drawer's tent and an apothecary, then a vendor selling wildflowers—their colors squashed by the midday sun. Many conversations rose above the square, like the sound of harvesters gossiping over their scythes. When they reached the wine seller's area, a man called out from a nearby stall. "He's asking us to come and have the new wine," Anne-Marie translated, not realizing he'd already understood.

At a small table, they sat and watched the flow of the crowd. The wine was refreshing and clear. Presently his pulse began to hurry; a tingling touched the back of his knees.

His summer had been quite full—populated again by the living. He wanted to tell these two, to make them understand. While Anne-Marie whispered with Valsin, he studied them both; Valsin was alive, excited about glory and piles of laurels. But she was tense, like a tree in a storm.

He wanted to tell them about all the other parts of his life, about the traveler's toiletry box—how one drawer contained his long-ago business with his father, many sealed letters, another, his friendship with Valsin, how another held Anne-Marie.

Of course, a fourth was hidden from the last two. It contained Marianne and his private feelings for her; that one was well locked.

At that moment, it seemed quite important to tell them almost everything. Even—yes, couldn't he just confess now?—about the long-ago battle; Valsin would understand.

"No." A modulation in Valsin's voice caught his attention. "I told you—I don't want to talk about it," the younger man said to her, and his tone made her recoil as if she'd been slapped. "Can't we just enjoy being here, the sun and the air?" Valsin's mouth twisted in a frown. "She's worried about me—in the wars," he said.

"Of course. It's only to be expected. After all..." There must be some way to tell them. "Have you ever considered," he began again, hunting for the right words, "that things can happen within us, things of great importance? We're so accustomed to momentous events, political events— war and all the business of emperors. But I'm talking about changes in our hearts." They were staring at him. She widened her eyes and shook her head—just enough for him to see. "Things that once seemed quite important, feelings we had, can become trivial."

"I understand," Valsin said, nodding. "Like our rivalry…why are you both looking at me like that? You know—we used to be enemies; that's what I mean."

"Things can change inside us," she said after a moment. "That's true."

Truth. He smiled at her, wishing the three of them could just speak the truth. "I suppose it is true; at one time—because of our emperors and their plans—we were enemies, especially you and I, Valsin," he said, looking at her. "But then, getting to know you both so well, it's changed things. In my heart. This time we've been together, I'll treasure it."

She removed her bonnet and set it by her side with care, using the motion to disguise a searching glance at his face. "It's been like nothing else, Alexi Davidych," she said, casting her eyes away.

It pleased him, her use of his proper name. Marianne had caught it right off—although she'd soon dropped it in favor of Alyosha—but after months of trying, he'd given up on explaining the etiquette of names to Anne-Marie or to Valsin, who insisted on addressing him in the most personal terms, as a lover or brother would—and at the wrong times.

"I think the two of you, being men," Anne-Marie continued in a low voice, "are surprised by such things—that people can change. Women expect it. Maybe it's because we have to try to be pretty and pleasing all the time; we're more aware of the difference between how we wish to appear and who we really are."

"But the thing that doesn't change is love," Valsin said. "Love is eternal, like freedom."

"A fine maxim," Ruzhensky said. "But—"

"I can say my wish is to love generously, not to grasp at experiences that I want above all to be freely given. But because of who I am, I can't transfer my affections easily. Love binds me, and if it ends, time must pass to heal the rupture. I'm not free."

How has she managed to do that—to speak some things without revealing others? Valsin is smiling; he thinks she's agreeing with him. But she's talking about us; she's made sense of it all. Our afternoon trysts were only free within the time they occurred—the hour of parade. We were free just then, because at all other times, chains linked with cares enclosed us both, binding us to others.

"Ah, the sun is glorious," she said, closing her eyes and leaning her face back into the warmth, smiling as if in acknowledgment of his understanding.

He looked down and saw her ankle—if only he could roll down the stocking, remove her shoes—how wonderful for her to feel unfettered. What if she were to let her hair free of its fastenings? Free to fall behind her in a grand mane. It would all be improper—only, they were such good friends, that's what Valsin said—what he wanted. Her throat strained forward, and he imagined a sigh.

"Do you want to walk some more?" she asked them both.

He had not made love to his friend's lover; he'd made love to Julie, who was portrayed as wise. Somehow she'd stepped out of the book. It was known that characters in works of fiction could represent many real people; Julie represented all the women he'd loved, and she'd inhabited this woman, a lovely vessel containing many. A beautiful illusion.

They began to retrace their steps, and this time, when Valsin took her left arm in his, without speaking or meeting his eyes, she offered Ruzhensky her right.

✳ ✳ ✳

Anne-Marie fell behind, and he and Valsin walked together, forming a wedge to part the throng.

"So you'll return to Russia?" Valsin said.

"Yes, in fact I wanted to ask if you knew what I might expect on the roads."

"The army will move quickly. They'll be few stragglers from the first advance, so I think behind us, the roads will be quiet and safe. Once you're in Prussia, it might be different. I'll see what I can find out and get word to you. I hope something besides responsibility awaits you there."

It suddenly occurred to him that, this time, Valsin did know about Marianne—Merseult had finally told him. He studied the younger man's face for signs of awareness—a knowing grin. Gentle mockery. Thoughts of her, being aware of Marianne, bestowed the curious sense that she'd joined them—not that that was possible, of course. It was more an intuition, as if their party of three had a phantom member who walked apart in a blur. He glanced back at Anne-Marie.

Marianne was behind her, moving quickly forward. He blinked and re-focused, but she really was there, now no more than a horse's length away. Through the heads and shoulders of strangers, her eyes held his, and they burned like two small suns in a time of drought.

She lifted her hands, showing the dagger, the dagger he'd bought and given to Yevgeny. Like a candle in a church procession, she held it upright in front of her breast, and the bare blade glinted darkly. Anne-Marie looked at him in concern; she began to speak and then, following his horrified gaze, turned her head. As Marianne lunged, she gave a cry and twisted away to the side.

He threw himself between them, making a grab for Marianne's shoulder, intending to turn her around, but she swung the dagger toward him, and he stopped. "Where did you get that?" he said, staring at the point. "Where is Yevgeny?" He realized he was whispering, as if she were a phantom who could not hear regular speech.

"I've been following you; it's not the first time either. I've seen you before—with her."

"What's she talking about?" Anne-Marie said. Her voice caught in her throat, and the color drained from her cheeks.

"My God," Valsin said. "You know this woman? Put that down." He came in at an angle, reaching for Marianne's wrist, but she stepped forward, putting Ruzhensky between herself and Valsin.

He felt the butt of the dagger hard against his leg. "This man, this Valsin," Marianne said. "You were supposed to kill him. To settle a score."

Valsin's expression began to lose its shape; a frown pushed between his eyes. Beyond him, a crowd of people had formed, their faces stamped with equal parts curiosity and concern.

Like him, she'd spoken in a low, insistent tone, an intimate voice in his ear, but now she raised it. "This man killed your brother—yes? Then you must kill him; it's simple. It doesn't matter what your father thinks, do this for your own sake. For honor."

He was able to seize her wrist, twisting her arm up so that the dagger was again upright, but—sure he'd be cut—he hesitated to grasp it with his other hand. "Let go; give it to me."

"What's this about?" Valsin said. "She said your brother—that I killed your brother."

"You did," Marianne said, speaking across him to Valsin. "And he tried to kill you—at the battle."

He looked from the dagger to Anne-Marie. For a moment, all he could see was the bouquet of pale blue flowers against her breast. Then she seemed to shrink from them, pulling away inside, as if her skin were tightening, her bones collapsing inward. Her eyes shifted from Marianne back to him, and her mouth twisted. "No," she said. "No, it can't be."

Valsin had stepped away, the way a swordsman would, judging the distance between them. His hand covered the hilt of his saber. "This is crazy. Who is this woman?"

Marianne was struggling, trying to pry his fingers off her wrist, and he pulled her all the way behind him. "Valsin," he said. "I wish you no harm.

It's true; my brother was the cadet you fought in single combat at Wischau. They said you'd murdered him, and I...I didn't know you. Now, everything's changed, she"— he brought Marianne's arm out, clutching the dagger, and waved it like a flag of truce—"doesn't understand. Please—think about all I've said. I've told you everything else. You know me." He tried to catch Anne-Marie's eye. "Please," he said, but she wouldn't look at him. "You know me. We can all go on now."

"At Austerlitz," Valsin said. "It was you?"

"Yes."

"But why? Why have you befriended me this way?"

At that moment, a pair of bicorne hats appeared behind Valsin—gendarmes attracted by the crowd's silence. "Marianne, give me the dagger; the police are coming." He turned halfway around and gestured toward the approaching men. "Give it to me quickly," he said, and ignoring the risk, reached for the naked blade.

"No!" With a sharp twist of her shoulders, she broke his hold on her wrist. The dagger flew up at the end of her hand. Loose like a heavy, fatal bird, it hung in the air, and he made a desperate grab, latching onto her free hand.

Valsin stepped forward, extending his own hand. "Go on, give it to him."

He stepped back, pulling hard to get her away from Valsin, and the force of the pull again broke his grip. Marianne spun free. The dagger hovered, a beat behind the motion she made, and then, just out of his grasp, it turned and plunged into the center of Valsin's chest.

Anne-Marie screamed. Valsin looked at him, and he could see the shock there in his brother's face, the way he began to fade. "No!" he cried, reaching for him. "A mistake—you must understand. I beg you."

But Valsin's legs gave way; he fell, his eyes closed. Had he heard? Ruzhensky sank to his knees and pulled the dagger free. A great gout of blood followed its release; any military man would recognize it was a mortal wound.

21.

Let's talk about what I am. The first thing I did was to love you.

The next day was cold. From the window, she could see people walking on the street with the wind sharp at their backs, glowering at the sky, as if the weather had brought betrayal. The porter delivered a bundle of twigs and two large birch logs. Once the man had gone, she locked the door, split the logs, and started a fire in the stove. Amid the sharp cracks and flares, she took the muslin bag Valsin had given her and emptied the gold onto the table.

Many of the coins were old and had been worn by many hands, some grasping—she imagined—others overgenerous. She arrayed them in lines like the towers of a strong castle and considered how long they might offer protection.

The door to the street slammed, and she scooped the gold away out of sight. Boots thundered up the stairs. For a moment the pain in her throat eased; her face opened in expectation. Then she heard Dalhousie's voice and remembered.

He's dead.

She unlatched and opened the door, and it was Merseult who entered first. "Poor girl."

He'd appeared yesterday, alerted by the gendarmes who recognized Valsin's uniform. A doctor had also been summoned, a doctor who merely looked and shook his head. More soldiers came, and then Merseult issued a series of commands. The gendarmes began interrogating a crowd of witnesses; Ruzhensky's mistress was bound with rope.

Anne-Marie had been left alone, sitting on the ground beside Valsin, already a still form hidden beneath Merseult's greatcoat, already smaller. Ruzhensky had sat twenty paces away at a table with a gendarme at his shoulder; whenever she'd looked up, he'd gazed at her, his face strained as if it were he who was bound.

"*Ma petite*," Dalhousie said, embracing her as he followed Merseult through the door. Witkowski followed him and offered a single white flower.

Both Merseult and Dalhousie regarded her with solemn expressions; Witkowski stared into a corner, and she realized why they'd come. "You're leaving. When?"

"Early tomorrow," Merseult said.

"Where will you go?" she said.

"North through Bohemia, then either into Saxony or Prussia, depending on—" He turned away, as if embarrassed by the subject of war.

"Depending on the Prussian queen," Dalhousie said. "Did you know that, Anne? They say she's the one who's in charge. Go to war, she says to the King, or stay out of my bed. What do you think of that?"

She managed a smile and returned to her seat by the fire. "How long will it take to get there, to Saxony or Prussia?"

"Two weeks, maybe," Dalhousie answered. "The generals will push us hard. I'm sure we'll have the honor of fighting before everyone else." Some, he explained, thought it would be a hard campaign. Prussia had a formidable army, the legacy of Frederick the Great, and the French would be heading once more into winter to fight as they'd done a year before, at

Austerlitz. Others predicted one or two battles—demonstrations, really, of Napoleon's power. Then—a new year in Berlin. As long as they'd be so close, Dalhousie said, "We might as well deal with the Russians again for good measure."

"Dalhousie, be quiet," Merseult said. "How are you today?" he said to her.

Her stomach gave a sudden lurch. *My God—I won't let them see me sick.* Her head spun, as if she were high above the room, an acrobat all alone in a circus.

"I'm all right."

Although she remembered the sound of all the hours in the night, she must have slept some, because—in the morning—she'd awoken burning hot from a dream. Ruzhensky was riding along a highway and had stopped at a post station to change horses. She could see him from above, through an upstairs window within the station, inside a bare room where the sun made a square shape against the dusty floor. Valsin appeared from below, as if he too had been waiting inside, and the two men laughed and joked together until a groom announced that he'd saddled the gentleman's horse—a mare with fine, strong flanks, he said in French. The three of them went inside out of sight, and she wondered what they were doing. Then Ruzhensky walked outside. With an impatient set to his shoulders, he'd looked directly at her and beckoned with a crooked finger.

"The burial will be at a churchyard not far from here," Merseult said. "Tomorrow, at one o'clock. I wrote the directions down for you." He put a folded piece of paper on the table. "I wish we could attend, but..."

Dalhousie shook his head. "What's happened—it's unbelievable; I always thought he'd bury me. All the battles and now this. A woman." He slapped his thigh hard with his gloves. "I told the Capitaine he should have the Russian arrested too, make him sweat, I said—"

"And I told you no," Merseult said. "There's no time for that." He turned to Anne-Marie and shrugged. "The girl was turned over to the

Bavarians; Ruzhensky is free. Would you want him arrested as well? Even though we're leaving, it could be arranged."

"Or he could just turn up dead," Dalhousie said. "That could be arranged too."

Merseult held her eyes, and she wondered what he knew about all of them. "No, leave him alone," she said. "Valsin considered him a friend."

"À merde! How can you say that?" Dalhousie shouted. "He's not who he said he was; he's a liar, and his schemes got the Lieutenant killed. I wouldn't be surprised if he put his woman up to it."

Through the open door to the bedchamber, she could see Valsin's trunk; it had been ready for days. Deeper in the shadows, he was there too, sitting at the foot of the bed with his chin resting on his hands, looking back at her.

Merseult cleared his throat. "I was suspicious of Ruzhensky from the start and made inquiries. I wish I'd done more—perhaps this could have been prevented. I'm sorry."

"It wasn't the way you think," she said. "I was there—it all happened so quickly. I saw him—Alexi; he did try to stop the woman. Valsin did too. She was frightened and struck out at them both."

Yesterday, she'd realized right away the woman was his lover; it was obvious from the way they'd looked at one another, stood close together, even while arguing. It had been her hair on his coat and on the brush in his bedchamber. She'd been frightened that the woman knew about what had happened between them, and that she'd come to accuse her in front of Valsin.

And then her words had begun to register. Kill Valsin; kill him for honor. You tried before, at the battle. And the way the woman looked at her—maybe she had known the truth.

"The police will want to talk to you, I'm sure," Merseult said. He sighed and stood up. "And we must go. Witkowski—go get the horses. Here." He took out a purse from his waistcoat and set it on the table "Many contributed for your welfare; it should see you through the winter, at least.

If there's anything else I can do, just ask. We won't be leaving till mid-morning tomorrow."

She went over to where Dalhousie sat and stood behind him, hugging him with her arms. Her lips brushed the crown of his head, and out of the corner of her eye, she could still see Valsin. He turned away, and she saw his solid shape and sharp outline, all rendered in exquisite detail. He was complete.

✧ ✧ ✧

After they left, she set water to boil in the kettle and sat at the table. Valsin's image was there again, across from her. "But I did kill him," she said, and her voice was very faint. "The one who was going to kill you. I saw him fall. How can—"

It's hard to kill a man, he said. *Usually.* Across the level surface of the table, he smiled and reached for her hand.

Everything tilted. Instead of his outstretched fingers, she saw the other man's, large and bone-white, covering hers.

Why did I allow his touch? He gave me no money, did not force me. In fact, the first time, it was I who reached for his buttons; in that secret language men and women make, my fingers had signed—open me, I'm ready. With words, he bewitched me, tricked me into lying like a whore on the place where Valsin and I had eaten and drank.

Valsin spoke again. *That battle's been over, for many months now.*

Months. An affair of months. Her whole body jerked, as if she'd been struck.

He conducted a courtship of me, as if I were a lady of his own creation instead of what I really am—a soldier's lady. Each time we met, he seduced me with his manners, his assurance—even in front of Valsin. So it took only one more ingredient—to be alone—for him to have his way.

He does deserve to die.

She sat down hard, covered her mouth with her hand, and burst into tears.

In a brief string of moments, she and Valsin, Ruzhensky, and even his woman had all swung off course; the gentle veneer that might have been put over their last days together had been ripped apart. Lost like a child, she cried harder.

Valsin would fade like the lettering on an old gravestone before she was ready to let him go.

I can't see him at all; a spell has been broken, and I'm back among the horsemen struggling to kill each other. Bloody ragdolls sprawl below, already trampled beyond recognition by the frantic hooves. My ears ring with gunshots and the screech of steel, and the stench of smoke fills my nostrils. I feel no fear for myself, and then outrage—when I realize what the Russian intends. "No!" I scream and drive the saber into his side.

She mined her memory for every grain of clarity—a horseman in blue. She sketched a more-recent image of his face onto the uniform. Yes, there was no doubt; it was him.

The purse Merseult had left was heavy with gold coins. She set it down on the table—there on the place where they'd lain—and saw the directions to the cemetery.

After combing her hair, she tried to eat a bit of last night's untouched meal, thinking it would give strength. Just after the bells rang noon, she set out with a basket under her arm. She approached the coffeehouse where the three of them had so often met and stepped to the window to study the interior. Satisfied he wasn't there, she turned on her heel and set off in the opposite way, sticking a hand under the cloth covering the basket, her right fingers resting on the cold handle of the clasp knife.

22.

It's too late to hide anything from me.

The day after the killing, he woke early, aware of the stillness beside him in the bed. Through the shuttered window, the city's bells rang, first the cathedral's, then those of all the lesser churches, each occurring an instant later in succession, like a long roll of thunder. The föhn was exhausted; thick, humid air covered the city the way a heavy lid restrains a simmering pot. In the bedchamber, a solitary fly buzzed overhead—a reminder of early autumns long ago when the heat was like a great sodden blanket and sweat lay along the skin like grease.

He'd dreamt about her—Anne-Marie. In a vast forest that he recognized as Russia, she walked beside him, speaking an unfamiliar language. The trees were also unfamiliar, all alike, the same new species, wrapped in silver bark and hung with delicate green leaves. She wanted to climb one, but he warned her they were not strong enough to support her weight. "Others," he kept repeating in Russian, "others have been killed." Like a child, she insisted on rushing at the thick trunks and hoisting herself up into the lower branches so that he had to grasp her ankles and pull her—laughing—to the ground. He was worried they'd become lost, being so far off the path.

A half jug of water remained from the night, and he rose and drank, leaving most of it for shaving. In the other room, silence came from behind the screen, and he stirred the fire himself.

Yevgeny had confessed to taunting Marianne about being left behind and to showing her the dagger. Just for a moment he turned away—that's what he'd said—and then, the door had slammed shut, and her feet went clattering down the stairs. The dagger was also gone. He'd followed, catching sight of her on the street but losing her in the crowd.

Last night, he accepted some money and went out, returning in the early hours of the morning, very drunk.

Ruzhensky checked the time and began to dress. The wings of the toiletry box fanned open on their small hinges, and he leaned close so his reflection appeared in the mirror. His mustache needed trimming; he withdrew a pair of scissors and began turning his head from one side to the other, snipping away protruding ends.

For many months, his temple locks had been hidden in the rest of his hair; now, on an impulse, he drew them out, separating the long strands and letting them hang free. He would need Yevgeny's help to braid them properly—for now, he pulled them back behind each ear. The middle drawer on the right, the drawer that contained Natasha's ring, yielded to his hand, and the ring lay there, surrounded by heaps of silver chain.

Deep in the marshes south of Brest-Litovsk, she'd stopped him at a place she knew, an old hut made by trappers, a place they'd joked about, referring to it as Julie's Chalet. There, they'd drawn out a farewell, lingering in each other's arms. In memory, he was present and not—a subtle vapor—forced to observe and remember.

"I wish we could stay here forever, never go back," Natasha had said.

"I wish we could keep our souls here," he'd replied in French because Russian was too straightforward to convey the curve of his sentiments. "Even though we must return to live our lives, our souls could remain here. Do you understand?"

"Your soul with mine?" She'd twisted toward him, and the flecks of gold in her eyes had danced.

When they'd mounted their horses to leave, he'd pictured a hut like the trapper's hut, but different—its walls of rough-cut logs lined with shelves where they could store their conjoined lives. A place for their souls to keep house.

In the mirror, my eyes narrow, my lips compress. In these two rooms, Marianne is everywhere, her sewing hoop, the multicolored threads she used to embroider, the sound of her clogs, and all the things I bought her—to please her, to keep her.

I built the trapper's hut but not well enough; and now the shelves are broken.

At the gate of the fortress, the sentry took his name and then called through the iron bars. Soon a young lieutenant emerged from the gatehouse, stiff and straight, his cocked hat jammed low over his brow. He stopped at the inside of the gate and put his hands on his hips. "Yes," he said, "what do you want?"

He seemed surprised that a gentleman would want to see a prisoner and told him to come back the next day.

Ruzhensky held the young man's eyes and shook his head. "Go and get your superior. At once!"

After being admitted, he was led to a guardhouse where he was offered a chair and asked to wait. A series of curious faces appeared around corners; in an adjacent room, there was a whispered conversation and finally, muffled by distance, shouts and then the running of booted feet. The Lieutenant, quite red-faced, appeared with his hat under his arm, bowed, and motioned Ruzhensky to follow. They passed down a long corridor lit by torches, climbed a flight of stairs, turned down another corridor, and halted in front of a large, wooden door. The Lieutenant knocked, and a voice called from within to enter.

A stout man wearing a captain's epaulet sat writing at a desk. "Yes?" he said, not looking up. Strong cigar smoke filled the room; a cloud of it had been trapped near the ceiling, untouched by drafts in the windowless space.

"I'm Monsieur Ruzhensky."

Without moving his head, the officer raised his eyes. His cheeks were pockmarked with tiny scars. "Ah, yes, the Russian gentleman—I was told to expect you; a Herr Montag sent word. I am Captain Studt. You've come about the woman—the one who murdered the French officer. Please, sit." He indicated a plain, wooden chair in front of the desk.

"She didn't murder him; it was an accident."

The officer suspended his pen over the paper and raised his eyebrows. "Of course." He glanced at a different paper to his right side. "I under-stand you were there—when the incident occurred," he said, switching to French. "Can you tell me what happened?"

"I'd prefer to see her now. I told the French what I knew—yesterday."

"Yes, I have a report here, signed by a...Capitaine Merseult. But it would be a great help to hear in your own words; please, it shouldn't take long. The girl isn't going anywhere. I understand you're Russian?"

"She's not been abused?"

"Of course not." Captain Studt smiled and leaned back in his chair. "We're not barbarians, monsieur." He took up the burning cigar from a small ceramic dish and began speaking around it. "Would you care for a cigar? No? I enjoy them; they perfume the air. Tell me, you knew the offi-cer who was killed?"

"Yes, Lieutenant Valsin—he was my friend."

"And the girl—she's known to you as well?"

He began slapping his gloves on his knee. "She lives with me."

"I see." Studt leaned forward and wrote something. "Go on."

"As I told you, it was an accident. The young lady—Marianne—she misunderstood some things I'd said, and thought that Valsin wished me harm. That's why she followed me to the market."

"With a dagger."

"Yes. When she appeared and I realized how upset she was, I tried to take the weapon away, we both did—Valsin and I. In the struggle, I pulled her arm, and she struck out for balance and stabbed him, quite by accident. And that's what happened." The gloves were twisted together, and he straightened them out on his thigh.

"I see. Yes, a tragedy. And there was a Frenchwoman present, a Mademoiselle Fröelich. Did you know her as well?" He squinted through the cloud of aromatic smoke.

"Yes."

"Did Mademoiselle—forgive me, what did you call her?—Marianne—did she know the Frenchwoman?"

"No."

"I was under the impression she did or at least that she knew of her."

"They'd never met."

Studt put down both the cigar and his pen and looked up. "It's an odd situation, monsieur, you must admit. An angry confrontation in public, one involving two gentlemen and two young women, and then one of the women killing one of the men. It has all the signs of a crime of passion. Jealousy. Is that possible, do you think?"

"Jealousy—no. It was as I said; she feared for my safety."

"Of course, a misunderstanding, you said. But forgive me for asking, would the girl also have had any reason to be jealous? It might make a difference to the magistrate. There are different sorts of murder, you see."

"No. It was not murder; as I told you, it was an accident, a stupid mistake." His voice cracked a little. The Captain's eyes were on him, glittering, his chin nodding in encouragement.

"Tell me what you know; it will help her."

"Look, yes, it's possible she may have…she may have been jealous." He rose and walked toward the door. "I was…I had been…intimate with them both," he said, turning around. "The two women. A secret—so I believed. Neither one knew about the other. But Marianne—she may have guessed."

"But then why kill the French officer—if it was jealousy? Why not kill you?"

He shook his head. "I don't believe she meant to. She was upset, angry. We were all struggling together." He felt a wave of nausea, a wave of blood, Valsin's blood, erupting from his chest when the dagger came free, the desperate moment of wanting to put the blood back, of wishing time could reverse. He covered his eyes with his hand. "My friend, he was my friend. I blame myself."

The Captain nodded and took up the pen, writing for several minutes. "Very well, I won't keep you any longer. I must tell you that the girl—well, it's not the first time we've seen her. She's been arrested before for prostitution—twice—and once for theft; with the addition of this latest crime, the magistrate has lost patience. She's to be deported—to Siberia. A convoy is—"

"What?" He shot forward in the chair. "Siberia—but she'll never survive! How can you send her to Russia?"

"Undesirables are accepted for a fee. It's all quite legitimate. The King has an agreement with your Tsar."

"You just said that jealousy would make a difference. I told you; yes, she was jealous—she had reason to be. It was my fault, all of it. She's just a girl."

Studt shrugged. "At least she won't be hanged. What do you expect? After all, she killed a French officer." He threw up his hands. "By the way," he said, glancing at a paper on his desk. "Her name. What name do you know her by?"

"What name? Her name is Marianne. Marianne—" He paused, embarrassed that he'd never asked her family name. Of course, she'd never offered it.

"Her name is Lotte Tag—at least that's what she's called herself before. I think we're done here, monsieur. I'll have someone take you down to the cells." He stepped around his desk to the door and called outside. "As I was saying, the convoy will leave in three days. Because of the war, it will take a more southerly route than usual, toward Prague, and then east through Galicia. It won't be an easy journey."

A guard led him down two flights of stone stairs and then along a corridor lit by torches; he barely registered the dank walls, the strong odor of mildew.

It's a death sentence; even if she survives the long march, she'll perish in the labor camps. I must find a way to free her. She's being sent in the exact direction of Brest-Litovsk.

Another flight down, and he realized he was in one of the casements of the fortress. A line of black cannon extended away into the shadows. The guard stopped halfway down the corridor at one of the small doors set into the wall away from the guns. "Here," he said, selecting a key from a heavy clutch at his belt and inserting it into the lock.

"Just a moment. I wish her taken care of—given food and blankets. Not abused. Here." He handed the man a purse full of coins. "For her care—you understand?"

The guard hefted the purse, looked inside, and then put it into his pocket. "Take all the time you want with her," he said. "You've paid for it. Just call when you're done."

✳ ✳ ✳

She was on her feet just inside the door. "Alyosha!" she cried, throwing her arms around his neck. "Ah God, you're here."

He held her at arm's length, her cheeks between his palms, and searched her face, turning it toward the light that shone through a barred window high up on one wall. There were no bruises, only a smudge of dirt on her forehead. Bits of straw stuck to her hair. "Have they beaten you? Or—"

"No, I'm just hungry. And frightened. The guards said they would hang me."

"They won't mistreat you now; they've been paid to bring food and blankets."

"Will they hang me?" She raised her hands, palms facing him, fingers stretched and trembling. Her wrists were marked in red by the rope they'd bound her with, and on her right sleeve, there was a rust-colored stain.

"No." Tears overflowed her eyes, and she sagged against him, clasping his waist and digging her face into his chest. "Listen," he whispered, smoothing the hair at the back of her head. "We must talk."

"But what's going to happen to me?"

"They plan to send you to Russia."

"Russia? But—"

"Shh, keep your voice low. To Siberia, exile. I'll find some way to rescue you."

"And then we'll go to your home—the way you said?"

"I'll make sure you're safe."

She turned away, taking a handkerchief from her sleeve and blowing her nose. "I've been afraid of going, journeying such a long way from here, from the place I was born." She looked at him. "I've been afraid I'd never return, never see my sisters again, the people who know me. But I hid it from you. All the stories you've told me, about the wolves and the Cossacks; I was afraid I'd disappear."

"But those were just stories, to entertain you."

"I know, I was foolish; I'll go anywhere with you. Especially now—after what's happened."

There was a single chair in the cell, and he turned and went to sit, his knees creaking like the hinges on an old gate. She remained standing, her hands clasped in front; the fine dress he'd bought for her was now creased and bedraggled. "Marianne, why?"

She shrugged. "For you—to protect you. The man told lies; he tricked you, the woman too."

He shook his head. "No."

"It's true. I could see it in her face right away. I killed him for you."

"Stop talking like that—especially to the guards or anyone who asks you what happened. It was an accident, you must remember. An accident—I was trying to take the dagger away, and you stumbled and struck out for balance. If you keep saying just that, it will make a difference."

"What difference will it make? The guards don't care what I say."

He wondered what her name really was. "Don't you understand? It matters to me. The man you killed—he was my friend. I told you that."

"She seduced you. I saw you with her—weeks ago. You were sitting in a coffeehouse. I could tell you'd been together."

"You followed me? More than once?"

"Of course. It was simple to lose him—Yevgeny. A few turns down several alleys, and he'd give up. And you—you were easy to find; you always walked in the same direction, down the same streets. Like the day I met you. I told you I'd find out all your secrets."

"But why kill him?"

"You were going from me to her and back. How could you do that? Was I not enough?"

"You followed me and saw us together—once. Did you imagine I was going to her each time I went out? I wasn't."

"You didn't sleep with her?"

"Only twice. We were intimate twice."

She walked to the iron bed stand and sat on the thin mattress, nodding as if she were agreeing with herself and hugging her ribs with her arms. What was her real name? He didn't want to ask her and then have to wonder if she were telling the truth. Lotte—the Bavarian Captain had said. She wasn't Lotte anymore.

"Marianne, you were jealous; you killed him—to hurt me. Is that the real reason?"

The blueness of her eyes was like a sea sky, empty, reflecting things lying far below. He was one of the things, he knew, his image lay on those pretty mirrors, but their mistress had retreated somewhere deep inside, and her silence was his answer. At that moment, he wanted to strike her. He looked up to the right corner of the cell. "The scar I have—here," he said, tracing his finger across the right side of his abdomen. "She made it. At the battle, she stopped me from killing Valsin. She was dressed as a soldier. I never saw her until it was too late." Marianne was frowning at him, and he looked down at the floor.

"Alyosha, you knew—that she was the one—and you slept with her? My God, how could you?" She rose from the bed, and a fire ship sailed across the sea. Her face mottled red, she began pacing the cell and finally stopped before him, pointing a trembling finger. "You don't know the German word for what you did. *Intimate* isn't right. A new word—fucked, you fucked her—you understand?" She was shouting. "You fucked her to get back at both of them; it was your revenge. You couldn't bring yourself to kill him, so you fucked her to—"

"Enough." He got to his feet.

"No. Now it's clear—even for a simple girl like me. You didn't need to kill him because you fucked her."

"Stop!" He grabbed her by the shoulders, shaking her so that her head snapped back, her hair whipping across half her face. He raised his right palm.

"What?" she cried, turning her cheek. "You'll beat me? It won't change anything—what you've done, what I've done. I've been a whore; I understand whores."

Accompanied by a fleck of spittle, her last, hard consonant leapt at him; her chin trembled, and her lips drew back as if she might spit again. He released her and walked to the other side of the cell. "What I've done," he said, speaking into the wall. "I caused this to happen—all of it."

"Maybe that's true."

"But," he said in a soft voice, "there are no other secrets."

"Not from me, but he didn't know, did he. Your revenge isn't complete."

23.

Each proof of an engraving has particular flaws that make up its character, and if a single perfect one comes along, even though it seems good at first glance, it's necessary to study it for a long time to recognize its perfection.

The door of the fortress thudded shut behind him, and he indicated the sentry should open the gate. The iron latch rattled, the hinges squealed, and he passed through and set off toward the narrow and twisting streets around the market square.

Everything was changing, the sensuous palette of autumn passing to winter's desolate watch. Even the gutters were being swept clean by a sulfurous wind. From dark alleys, soft voices of beggars called out, but he strode on, keeping to the center of the sunlit sidewalk. He turned a corner and saw a column of horsemen across the next intersection. By the time he reached it, all that remained were humming weights of bees settling on fresh piles of dung.

Several blocks along, he stopped in a small square where sere rivulets of red and gold leaves rustled around a stone fountain. The spray of water looked refreshing, and he sat on the stone lip and washed his hands, sure that they reeked from the jail. He cupped them and drank.

On the other side of the square, two boys and a little girl played a game with a ball, passing it between themselves with much giggling and chattering of feet. The boys threw the ball over the girl's head until she surprised them both by jumping high and knocking it to the ground. Holding it close to her chest, she refused to release it as the boys danced around her in circles.

These beings will not last; no one stays the same.

Time beat a heart's rhythm through the small space. Fate's trajectory was complete, Valsin dead, Marianne in prison, and Anne-Marie abandoned; the dagger had destroyed each precious relation.

Valsin. Never again would the two of them have long conversations, conversations that were also confrontations with himself. The river they had paced along, one to each side, had broadened; already it was hard to make him out.

And Marianne—did she also walk with him in her bloodstained dress, matted with dirty prison straw? He passed his hands through the water again and then rose, drying them with a handkerchief.

He'd leave Munich as planned—behind the French but ahead of the convoy of prisoners. After consulting his maps to find the best location, he'd cross their path in the countryside north of Brünn. There, either the guards would respond to a bribe or he'd carry her off by force. He owed her that much.

There was one more thing to do.

✠ ✠ ✠

He struck the door with his stick, but the sound produced nothing more than a boy who peered out from far down the corridor and said that all the soldiers were gone; there was no lady.

On the street, he retraced his path, hoping to see her, hoping he might encounter her the way he often had Valsin. But no.

At the noon hour, the coffeehouse was crowded, but the owner found him a small table. Perhaps it was best to have a little time to sit and compose his thoughts. He ordered coffee, surprised at his craving for it. It arrived scalding hot, and he blew small waves across the surface of the saucer.

Across the light from the windows, a shadow moved. He looked up to see a tall woman, her dress touched with dust, a basket in her hands. "I saw you," she said. "From outside."

He stood and cleared away his hat and gloves, pulling out the other chair. "I looked for you at your rooms. You weren't there."

She remained standing. "I was walking—by myself," she said. "I have to remember to keep my head up so no one bothers me. If I act like a brave person, people treat me as if I am. Isn't that interesting?" A loud burst of laughter from another table made her startle like a nervous horse.

"I thought you were at the burial, that it was today. I'm sorry."

"It's tomorrow. Will you walk with me?"

An edge set into her voice made him look more carefully; he noticed how her bonnet was askew, how her eyes moved restlessly around the room. "Very well," he said. "There are things I wish to speak to you about."

As they left the coffeehouse and began walking along the street, he studied her. Pretty—she always looked pretty—but her eyes continued a tireless search of the street. She was not as he'd seen her at other times, the glittering center of attention at his dinner party, the coquette, the lover unclothed. The woman crouched beside his murdered friend.

After walking for three blocks, their silence had become too awkward. "Mademoiselle Fröelich, I think we—"

"I hate that name. I don't want to be called that anymore; it's never been mine. How can you call me that?"

"What should I call you?" he asked with no expectation of a response. "I was going to say perhaps we could find a public garden so we can sit awhile. We must do something; if we keep walking this way, we'll be in the river." The words fell flat and gray.

She stopped to look with narrowed eyes back down the street. "Could we take a chaise?"

He almost shouted in astonishment. What a thing to propose—a ride in a chaise. That was something whores did—whores and lovers, or husbands and wives. "If you wish," he said. "It would be good to sit—that's why I suggested a garden—but yes, a chaise. I believe there's a stable back this way."

A gentleman and a young woman wanting a midday ride was nothing unusual to the stable master; he grinned with big yellow teeth and named a fee. Within five minutes, a small, closed chaise had been harnessed to a team of two horses, and the postilion helped them both inside. She spoke to the man, and they started off.

Now that they were fully contained by the vehicle's intimate space, she seemed to press herself hard against the door, leaving an arm's length between them. "I asked him to take us around the Gardens," she said, with the basket held stiffly on her lap.

He began to tell her that he'd learned the German language. "The Public Gardens, yes," he said instead. "By all means."

It hardly mattered where they went; the curtains were pulled down for privacy, allowing narrow chinks of brilliant sunshine to illuminate parts and not the whole. Within the fabric of her dress, he saw the shape of her thighs, the double lines of limb ending in a protrusion of knee, and closed his eyes. He couldn't look at her in such a way now, after all that had happened. "There's not much room in here, is there?" he said, shifting his weight until he was leaning against the opposite door, with his feet pushed against the floor to absorb any shocks.

"Valsin said," she whispered out of the gloom where she was a graceful curve, "that you cared for me."

The chaise had turned a corner, and light entered at a new angle, striking the line of her nose but leaving her eyes in darkness.

"I know he wanted me to rely on you once he'd gone to war, rely on your friendship," she continued. Her voice dropped even lower on the last word, and he inclined his head to hear. "Friendship, I said." The basket creaked as if she'd squeezed it. "And I was willing because of...the things we did. But it was all based on a lie; I thought you were someone else."

The shorter hairs at the back of his neck prickled under his hatband. For the two of them—too intimate with both steel and flesh—to be together in this way was dangerous. "Listen, forgive me for misleading you," he said, trying not to make his voice gruff. "You must understand—it's been so long since I meant any harm. Everything else I told you was true."

He looked to the side, to catch her eye and was surprised to find that she'd turned and leaned toward him; in the shadows, her eyes were harder points of dark brown, almost black. He thought she would look away, look down, turn her head, but she did not; she held his gaze. How unusual to see into a woman's eyes—anyone's eyes—for that long. She seemed to be trying to peer inside him, to cut through whatever artifice she thought he still possessed. No longer did she press herself against the far door. She leaned even closer toward him, and he sensed a wildness in her that made him silent and watchful.

"I think if he were alive right now, he'd forgive you. For all of it—even for what you and I did. But you see, it's harder for me," she said in a soft voice. "To be able to kill you that day—and I wanted to, believe me—I had to hate you. Do you understand? You soldiers seem able to let it go; I'm not a soldier."

"A soldier—no," he said. "I dreamt about you; you were laughing." His jaw thickened and pushed against his collar. "All the things I said were true, that I admired you for what you did. Marianne, the woman—my mistress—I had no idea that she'd followed us. No idea what she'd do. But it wasn't an accident; she did it to hurt me. Do you understand? She was jealous of you; I just found out."

"You told her?"

"No, of course not. She knew somehow; she followed me."

"But how could you?" she said, shaking her head. "How could you lie with me? You knew who I was. How could you do it?" She fell back against the cushions. Then she sat up and pulled at the window curtain, letting in a thicker bar of light. "My God, that's better. It's so dark all the time."

From the far side of the basket, her arm made an arc, going up and then out toward him, as if she were shaking her fist, gesturing to make a dramatic point with more than words. His eye caught a thing in her hand, a metal edge, and at the last moment, he blocked her forearm with his own. She pushed back with surprising strength; they strained, and their bones ground together. Then the angle changed, and the knife slipped down, slicing through his coat and shirt and into his skin. A warm ooze of blood started along his arm, and for a moment, it made him weaken. He grabbed her wrist with his other hand and tried to twist her arm down, but the blade cut the other way, making a thin, scarlet line against the white flesh around her wrist. Still they struggled, and their blood flowed together and smeared across their sleeves, their skin. Finally, her arm began shaking, and the knife fell at his feet.

With his other palm, he clasped his wounded forearm, and she did the same with hers. The rhythm of their breathing slowed; she began to cry softly. He realized how slowly she'd moved to strike him, as if it were a struggle through thick currents of water. She'd not struck as a man would have. Her desire to kill him, he understood, had melted long before these tears had begun, melted like snow on a hearth-warmed roof.

"You thought about destroying me? Again?" he said, pulling her wounded wrist up hard so her eyes widened. "But you couldn't do it. Why not?"

She tried to pull away. "You're hurting me. Let go, let me out. I don't want to talk about all this, to feel this way again," she said. "We're bleeding."

The dream was there with him; he'd been half in and half out of it since Valsin's death. And then, for the first time, he stepped back and away from a frozen Pyerits, and the dream disappeared. Sounds began to resurface from outside the carriage—the clip-clop of the horses' hooves, the rhythmic banging of steel against steel as they passed a blacksmith's forge. "Answer me," he said. "What stopped you?"

"Because he's gone—Valsin. You can't hurt him again, and—because you wouldn't have hurt him; I know that now. Neither of us are murderers. Laughing—you dreamt about me laughing," she whispered. "How could I kill you after that?"

He nearly asked her to repeat herself; was she trying to make a joke? The chaise turned again, and the sun came in through the window behind her, making her torso opaque. "Did he know about us?"

He felt her search his face again, her eyes flickering back and forth, as if she thought he already knew the answer. "I never told him. I said you'd come by once; that's all I ever said."

"Yes." Each word was an effort, and it was strange they couldn't speak of it, even to others. Even now, it was so awkward, as if they couldn't acknowledge that, on two occasions that had lasted less than an hour, they'd been only lovers, anonymous in their immersion in one another and—since then—lesser entities possessing other names and faces, other lives.

"You were going to tell me that day you found me on the street. I think you were going to tell me who you were. The day we…made love."

"I wanted to. I wanted to tell Valsin as well—who I was. I'm sorry. I hoped that, if enough time passed, it wouldn't matter. What is it?" he asked, noticing how she'd pressed her hand against her stomach. "You're cut, and—"

The postilion called out that their time was almost up.

"You need my help," he said.

"That's funny, isn't it—let me out here," she called to the driver.

"Wait, there's something…"

The carriage came to a rocking halt that lengthened and settled like the pendulum of an unwound clock. She opened the door. "No, nothing. There's nothing. Good-bye," she said without looking back. The door slammed shut, and the postilion started the horse, shouting out to the pedestrians to watch the lash.

He opened the curtains on both sides. His boot kicked the clasp knife, and he leaned forward and picked it up, closing and opening the blade and then closing it and putting it in his waistcoat pocket.

It was as if he were seeing her—in his memory—for the first time; as if layers and layers of pretty ribbon and paper had been cut away from something of great value, leaving it bare and unadorned so that one must see its true nature.

She is not the Julie of the book—the book is packed in a trunk, prepared to cross borders. She is not Julie; Julie is a character in a book.

Is she a different Julie, perhaps, stored in a different place—in my memory? It could be that Anne-Marie is my Julie, at last, no longer a stranger, as if I'd written her into my own book, a book whose pages were cut open with my own hands. Others are in it, other lovers and friends. The last chapter is to be about her.

He remembered her as she'd been that day in the market, before Marianne had appeared with the dagger. She'd walked between them, laughing. From beneath the edge of her bonnet, her hair had hung halfway down to her waist.

The bells began ringing, and in his memory, she receded, as if she too were crossing a river, crossing to a far bank, becoming indistinct. Drowning. Like Munich, like Austerlitz.

24.

Here's the faithful tableau of my life and the simple story of all that took place in my heart. I will love you always, don't doubt it.

Within the crowded public coach, it was close and hot, and she loosened the straps of her bonnet and fanned herself with her hand. The woman at her side had fallen asleep with her head on Anne-Marie's shoulder. On the other seat, facing her, a young man smiled and addressed her in French, but she pretended not to understand.

The journey to the frontier would take days, then many more to reach Paris. Once again, she reached into her bag and took out the letter Merseult had given her—an introduction to a woman he knew in Paris, someone who would assist her in finding work. When she had revealed her plan, Merseult had claimed to be quite surprised, but—after insisting on bandaging her arm himself—had written out two fair copies.

She pressed her hip, feeling the hard outline of the purse sewn to her shift. It held gold, not a soiled paper currency that might become worthless overnight. Alexi had more than doubled the amount she already had, sending his mute servant over early in the morning to deliver it, along with a sapphire ring set in silver—an acknowledgment that he himself would not see her again. Relief had filled her, regret too, and she'd wondered if that was how it felt to take money for love. If so, it hadn't demeaned it. In return, she'd given the man the directions to the burial. "Tell him it's at noon, you understand? Noon."

He'd sent her the book by the Frenchman, Rousseau, too. *Julie.* But in the dark, jolting coach, it was impossible to read.

Her stomach twitched, and she pressed her hand below her heart. It was too soon to feel life but not too early to begin a sketch of a small boy— dark and handsome. His features must be captured by a careful blending of respect and pity, covered with a wash of kisses—many times over.

She smiled and closed her eyes.

Soon, I'll name him.

Author's Notes

FRENCH DIALECTS

At the time of the novel, there was considerable regional variation in the major European languages, no attempts being made to standardize things till later in the nineteenth century. Marianne and Ruzhensky speak French to each other but in different dialects. Valsin makes fun of Anne-Marie's accent being under a German influence.

TIME

In the beginning years of the nineteenth century in Europe, no uniform standard for time and date existed. Imperial Russia used the Justinian calendar, most of Europe the Gregorian. France was moving away from the calendar system of the Revolution toward the Gregorian. Thus, for Ruzhensky the battle of Austerlitz occurred on November 20, for Anne-Marie and Valsin, December 2. The letters from Ruzhensky's father were offset by twelve days. Time of day was also relative; three o'clock in one community might be celebrated three minutes later in another.

WARFARE

On December 2, 1805, Napoleon Bonaparte's French and Italian army defeated the combined armies of Russia and Austria near the town of Austerlitz in what is now the Czech Republic. Austerlitz was the culmination of a campaign begun in the autumn, and the victory made Napoleon the ruler of most of continental Europe.

The goal of warfare in the early 1800s was to seize and hold territory by destroying the opposing army's morale and driving it from the field. Large masses of infantry attempted to maneuver close enough to deliver point-blank volleys of musket fire into the enemy's ranks. Cavalry units would be ordered to charge an already demoralized infantry formation to force its retreat or surrender. Reconnaissance was an equally important role for the cavalry, as commanders had no recourse to modern communication and had to rely on small parties of horsemen to serve as scouts.

The kind of single combat that takes place between Mischa Ruzhensky and Louis Valsin was officially discouraged but remained important to a culture of masculinity that emphasized personal bravery and honor.

RANK

Alexi Ruzhensky's father is described as objecting to his son's love for Natasha because her family is of lower rank. Since the time of Peter the Great, the Russian nobility had been organized into castes, each with its own uniform and forms of etiquette. It was a dream of many nobles to achieve higher rank by service to the tsar. Ruzhensky belonged to the second rank and was thus entitled to be addressed as "Your Honor." It was considered scandalous, even treasonous, to marry below one's rank.

JULIE

In 1761, Jean-Jacques Rousseau published *Julie, or the New Héloise*. It enjoyed immediate success and became one of the most popular books of the latter part of the eighteenth century. In the first decade of the nineteenth, it was still being read and discussed in many of the major European languages. An edition in Russian was produced during the 1790s.

Julie—told in the form of letters that the characters write one another—is the story of the love affair between Julie, an aristocratic young woman, and her tutor, who is never directly named but is referred to as St. Preux (gallant knight). Their romance must remain a secret because they are from different social classes. After their first kiss in a bower, Julie sends St. Preux away, but neither can bear the separation, and he returns. Julie becomes pregnant but suffers a miscarriage. Her furious father discharges her tutor from his position, and the young man embarks on a round-the-world journey.

Eventually Julie marries a Monsieur de Wolmar, and after many years of traveling, St. Preux visits them at their estate in what is now Switzerland. St. Preux discovers that de Wolmar is an admirable man who accepts all that has occurred between his houseguest and his wife.

At the end, Julie becomes ill after jumping into a lake to save her child from drowning. Before she dies, she writes to St. Preux, requesting that he marry her best friend and care for her children.

The translations from *Julie* are my own. I recommend Philip Stewart and Jean Vaché's English translation of *Julie, or the New Héloise*, published by the University Press of New England (1997).

RUSSIAN NAMES

In naming Russian characters, I relied on the guidance of Leo Tolstoy and Vladimir Nabokov. The manner in which the Russian language of the nineteenth century named people communicated information about social status and relationship. When Russians of the same rank addressed one another formally, they used the person's first name and patronymic. Thus, Alexi Ruzhensky was called Alexi Davidovich—Alexi the son of David. In everyday parlance, this might be shortened to Alexi Davidych. Family members and lovers called each other by diminutives: Ruzhensky would be Alyosha; Mikhail, Mischa; and Natalya, Natasha. Serfs or servants, such as Yevgeny, were called by their first names only.

MILITARY ORGANIZATION

A Russian Hussar regiment of the Napoleonic era was comprised of ten field squadrons, each to number 150 officers and men at full strength. There were two companies per squadron and three squads per company.

The entire regiment was commanded by a general with practical command given to a colonel. Each squadron was commanded by a senior officer, each company by a lieutenant. Cadets were the most-junior rank of officer.

The French Hussar regiments contained four field squadrons, each with 112 officers and men. Each squadron had two companies; each company, two troops.

EXPLANATION OF FRENCH RANKS

Colonel—regimental commander
Chef D'Escadron—squadron commander
Capitaine—company commander
Lieutenant—troop commander

The battles alluded to and described—Amstetten, Durenstein, Wischau, and of course Austerlitz—were all real events. Although I took care to portray them accurately, there is some dramatization. General Bagration, Prince Murat, Marshall Lannes, and Chef D'Escadron Crèpin were real people, all the rest fictional.

Given the amount of time that has passed, the nature of human memory, and the confusion of battle, contemporary historians are presented with conflicting reports of what occurred during the Napoleonic wars. For reference, I relied on Scott Bowden's book, *The Glory Years: Napoleon and Austerlitz* and Leo Tolstoy's *War and Peace*.

Glossary

Brest-Litovsk: a city in present-day Belarus.

Cadanettes: locks of braided hair at the temples.

Föhn: a dry, Alpine wind that can occur in Munich at any time of year. It's blamed for headaches and bad moods.

Pelisse: the Hussars' ornate, braided jacket, lined with fur, worn slung over the left shoulder in full dress.

Mentik: Russian for pelisse.

Post chaise: a closed carriage with four wheels.

Postilion: the driver of a post chaise.

Pounce: powder used to blot ink.

River Bug: pronounced "Boog," a long river that forms the border between present-day Belarus and Poland.

Made in the USA
Charleston, SC
29 November 2016